Baby, I'm Wintertime Cold

**Lock Down Publications and Ca$h
Presents**
Baby, I'm Wintertime Cold
A Novel by *Meesha*

Lock Down Publications
Po Box 944
Stockbridge, Ga 30281

Visit our website @
www.lockdownpublications.com

Copyright 2022 by Meesha
Baby, I'm Wintertime Cold

This is a work of fiction. Names, characters, places, and incidents either are products of the author's imagination or are used fictitiously. Any similarity to actual events or locales or persons, living or dead, is entirely coincidental.

Lock Down Publications
Like our page on Facebook: Lock Down Publications @
www.facebook.com/lockdownpublications.ldp
Book interior design by: **Shawn Walker**
Edited by: **Jill Alicea**

Stay Connected with Us!

Text **LOCKDOWN** to 22828 to stay up-to-date with new releases, sneak peaks, contests and more…
Thank you.

Submission Guideline.

Submit the first three chapters of your completed manuscript to ldpsubmissions@gmail.com, subject line: Your book's title. The manuscript must be in a .doc file and sent as an attachment. Document should be in Times New Roman, double spaced and in size 12 font. Also, provide your synopsis and full contact information. If sending multiple submissions, they must each be in a separate email.

Have a story but no way to send it electronically? You can still submit to LDP/Ca$h Presents. Send in the first three chapters, written or typed, of your completed manuscript to:

LDP: Submissions Dept
Po Box 944
Stockbridge, Ga 30281

DO NOT send original manuscript. Must be a duplicate.

Provide your synopsis and a cover letter containing your full contact information.

Thanks for considering LDP and Ca$h Presents.

Meesha

Prologue

"Introducing, Mr. and Mrs. Leonard Miller!"

Leo and Icy danced into the hall as "Whole Lotta Money" blared through the speakers. The song fit like a muthafucka because the entire entourage looked and smelled like nothing but money. And don't get it twisted; they had the blue faces to back that shit up. Icy was all smiles, holding hands with Leo as he danced around her in his all-white suit with a teal tie and vest.

Ain't gon' keep me 'round no broke shit
That broke shit get old
And don't keep me 'round no ho shit,
These hoes get too bold
I'm allergic to that no shit, my wrist game cold
I might paint my coupe white just to match my toes

The long white and teal dress hugged Icy's curves and the crystals sparkled with every hit of the lights and flashes from cameras. Leo went all out for their wedding and Icy felt like the Queen, but felt like the devil's daughter on the inside. She had been pretending to be blissfully in love with Leo when in fact, she became sick to her stomach at the slightest touch of his hands. To everyone in the room, love was definitely in the air. Little did they know, Icy didn't want to be there. She hadn't heard from Akoni and wondered why since he was the one who suggested she went back to Leo.

"I love you, Mrs. Miller. You just made me the happiest man on earth, and I can't wait to get yo' sexy ass out of that dress," Leo said, breaking Icy from her thoughts.

"Now, you know I'm down for whatever when it comes to you, baby," Icy lied with a smile. There was a time her words rendered true. The shit tasted like manure on her tongue at that precise moment though. "All these folks are here to celebrate our union. We can't bail on them just yet."

"Fuck these muthafuckas! Half of them only here for the open bar and all you can eat food. My hittas already know what it is," he retorted.

Icy laughed nervously as she glanced around the room. All of a sudden, an eerie feeling passed through her body. Surveying the room, nothing seemed out of ordinary. Kia and Julz walked in her direction as Leo whispered in her ear with concern.

"What's wrong, Icy?" he asked, grabbing both of her hands.

"I don't know. Something is off. I really can't tell you what it may be. All I know is, it doesn't feel right."

Leo looked deep into Icy's eyes and saw the fear in them. Thinking back to his revelation of something happening on their wedding day, he frowned, but switched it up so he wouldn't alarm Icy more than she already was. Hugging her to his chest, Leo looked over Icy's head and his orbs landed directly on Desiree. After the night they'd had, Leo was sure she wouldn't be a problem, but the way she stood with her hand in her purse, he wasn't too sure.

"Everything's gon' be aight. We just got married. It's up from here, baby. Let's enjoy our moment and put all the other shit out of your mind. I have my bitch on my hip, so we good."

Icy nodded her head as her cousin stood waiting for Leo to unhand her. Pulling back out of his arms, Icy mustered up a smile as she gestured toward Kia and Julz to come over. Leo took that as his cue to leave them to talk. He bent down, kissing Icy's cheek.

"Holla at ya girls. I'm about to work the room and make sure everything is straight. I want you to have a good time, and you can't do that if you're uneasy around this muthafucka."

Leo walked across the room, facing Desiree. Kia followed his every move, laughing lowly. "That nigga on some snake type shit. Why did you say I do again, cuz? Leo don't deserve you, and he's never going to change."

"What do you mean?" Icy asked.

"Nah, don't answer a question with a question. I knew my theorization about him and Desiree was on point. The entire time Leo held you in your arms, that bitch was muggin'. Not to mention, she wore the same sour-ass expression during the ceremony too. Now

8

he's over there whispering in her fuckin' face like it's nothing. You better than me because I'd be fuckin' both of 'em up."

Icy zoned in on Leo and Desiree, seeing exactly what her cousin saw. A blind man could see there was something going on between them. At that moment, Icy didn't care because she had little to no respect for her new husband. Julz's voice brought her back to the conversation.

"I'm with Kia on this one. They fuckin', and Desiree is making it very obvious. Look at her face. They're in a heated argument. You can tell by the way she's all in his face waving her hands like a banshee. Go over there and regulate that shit before I do it myself."

"Icy, what the fuck is going on over there? Why the fuck is your man all in the next bitch's face?" Sean walked over like he was the main model in a fashion show. "Do we gotta smack a bitch up in here?"

"Y'all, let them have their moment. Whatever they have going on has nothing to do with me and it will continue after today. Believe me, I'm no longer green to the mess that Leo does. All of his skeletons are falling out the closet one bone at a time. There's a reason I went forward with this marriage; I just don't know why," Icy said, biting her bottom lip.

Kia opened her mouth to speak, but Zan's presence prevented her from talking ill about his shit poor excuse of a brother. His wife Cherelle was walking slowly behind him as she peeped Leo across the room with Desiree. She was the first to address Icy once they were in earshot.

"You are so beautiful, sis!" Cherelle said, hugging Icy then stepping back. "Too muthafuckin' beautiful for that sucka to be playing in your face. Y'all ain't been married a good hour and he's over there like he's single."

"That's not your business, babe," Zan said, shaking his head. "That's between Leo and Icy. Stay out of it."

"Mind my business? Yeah, okay. Leo been on hoe shit their entire relationship and you downplaying it. After everything he has done to you, I don't know why you supporting this nonsense. Go over there and talk to your brother before he gets his ass whooped for disrespecting."

Zan knew his wife was correct on all she'd said. He was there because he was the best man and he did his due diligence and stood next to his brother. When everything came to a close, Leo could kiss his ass. Zan had no plans of fucking with him another day. Brother or not, he had shown Zan what he really thought of him.

"Icy, I came over to see how you were doing. I'm sorry my brother refuses to do right by you," Zan said sincerely.

"Why the fuck you apologizing? You ain't did shit to Icy." Cherelle was pissed at Zan for what he was doing at that point. "Leo should be over here apologizing for making her his wife under false pretenses."

"It's cool, Cherelle. Don't raise your blood pressure for this shit. I already know Leo don't give a fuck about me. I'll fill you in at a later date. For now, let's have a ball on his dime and make the best of it."

Icy hugged Zan. "I'm okay, bro. I promise. Leo is just being Leo," she said, glancing back at her husband shaking her head.

She walked to the bar with Kia, Julz, Cherelle, and Sean in tow. They stood waiting for the bartender to finish helping people at the far end of the bar so they could place their orders. It didn't take long for them to be serviced and once they all had drinks in hand, Icy led them to the wedding party table where her mother sat. Concern was etched on her face as she watched her daughter and the rest of her friends gather around the table.

"Icy, is everything okay?" Staci asked, searching Icy's face for any type of discomfort.

"Nothing to worry about, Ma." Icy kissed her mother and hugged her while trying her best not to spill her drink on her dress.

"Alright now. I'm going to leave it alone. Congratulations, baby. You are so beautiful," she whispered before standing up to kiss Icy's cheek.

Leo approached the table, grinning from ear to ear. Kia smacked her lips and sat on the other side of the table, but her eyes never left

Leo. He grabbed Icy around the waist and she shrugged him off, taking a sip from her cup.

"Leo, thank you for making my baby happy. She deserves this and more. I'm so glad y'all settled whatever was going on and the wedding was still able to happen. Protect Icy with everything in you."

"Staci, I got baby girl 'til I take my last breath; that's a promise."

"I don't doubt that one bit. I've always seen the love you possess for my daughter," Staci said to Leo.

The roll of Icy's eyes went unnoticed by her mother, but Julz and Cherelle caught it in real time. Sean opened his mouth, and Icy knew nothing good was going to fall from his lips. She closed her eyes and shook her head slightly at him and he got the hint, sitting down and crossing his leg like a true diva.

"Your dad is looking down from heaven smiling from ear to ear. I wish he was here to experience this with us."

Tears welled in Staci's eyes, and Icy embraced her mother tightly. There wasn't a moment Icy didn't think about her father, who was murdered right in front of her at the age of eighteen. The day her father was taken from her life still gave her nightmares years later. Staci was broken, and it took months to get her life back on track.

Julz walked over and grabbed Staci by the arm as she nodded her head back. Icy looked over her shoulder to see what had her friend's attention. The sight of Akoni stalking across the room had her eyes bulging out of the sockets. Icy didn't want her mother to witness anything up close, and Julz knew the drill without being told. Julz guided Staci to the bar as Icy turned to see Leo's reaction to seeing Duke's son in attendance.

"Congratulations, Leo. I had to come congratulate you on behave of my father since he's no longer here to pay homage on his own." Akoni's gaze softened when he focused on Icy. Licking his lips, he admired her from head to toe, soaking in her beauty. "Damn, beautiful, this nigga got a baddie to carry his last name.

Congratulations," he said, reaching for Icy's hand, planting a light kiss on the back of it.

Leo's jaw clenched as he pushed Icy behind him. It was pretty obvious the man standing before him was someone he didn't care for. Looking around, Icy noticed Zan walking across the room to see what was going on.

"How the fuck you know to show up here, Blaze?" Leo snarled. "I know for a fact you didn't receive an invite because I don't fuck with you, nigga!"

"Baby, is everything okay?" Icy asked, stepping next to Leo, playing her role. No one other than Julz and Kia knew her affiliation to Akoni, and she needed to keep it that way unless she was ready to die. Leo addressed him as Blaze and Icy was confused because she never heard him refer to himself as such.

"Yes, Miss Lady, everything is fine. Can you give me and your *husband* a minute?" he asked.

Icy backpedaled slowly, not knowing what was going to happen between the two men. She knew there wasn't going to be any gunplay because there were too many people around for that. She remembered Leo had his gun on his hip and she became nervous. Icy didn't know if she should've stayed to play referee or not. She was pulled away by her arm by Kia before she could go back to stand between them.

"Bitch! I thought that man's name was Akoni. Who the fuck is Blaze? He looks like he's ready to beat the fuck out of Leo's punk ass. How do they know each other?"

In the middle of the venue was not the place to discuss what Icy knew about the situation. Kia was going to have to wait until she had time to break everything down to her because at that time, she needed to make sure there was no bloodshed in these people's establishment. Blaze led Leo to an empty corner and they were engaged in a heated discussion. Both of their body language told a story of restraint in both of them.

"I'll tell you later. This shit is not good at all. I don't know him as Blaze. I guess there's two sides to his ass because I've never seen him in this light before," Icy said nervously.

12

Zan was standing close enough to Blaze and Leo just in case some shit popped off. The rest of Leo's team was waiting in the cut, watching everything unfold, and they were ready to put in work if need be. They were clueless as to who Blaze was too because Leo never let them in on what he had done. His whole entourage was in the dark, so they were set on go if Leo needed them. They were ready to light the nigga up at the first sight of danger. Little did they know, Leo was already knee deep in some shit he couldn't get out of.

"I came to this muthafucka so you can see that I can find yo' ass wherever you are, nigga. You will pay for the shit you did to my family. I'm gon' let you make it since you have one last thing to celebrate before I take yo' fuckin' life."

"Nigga, I can have yo' ass filled with holes in two point five seconds flat. How dare you come in here threatening me like I'm gon' bow down to your ass?" Leo laughed.

"I'm not worried about that shit, pussy. See, I'm an up close and personal killa. I'm not gon' shoot yo' ass while you not looking. I want you to see everything I have in store for yo' punk ass when I make my shit clap. The only thing that's saving you now is the roomful of witnesses. You gon' walk around looking over yo' shoulders until I take yo' ass out. And when I do, get ready to get that ass killed again when you meet my father on the other side. Enjoy your last day on earth, bitch."

Blaze stared at Zan, then looked around the room, noticing all the men in close proximity of him and Leo. He chuckled as he saw Leo reach for his waist. "Don't do it. You'd be dead before you pull that muthafucka completely, and yo' whole team gon' go out with you. I hope you got eyes in the back of your head, because you will be joining Maven real soon. The only difference, yo' death will far worse than his ever was."

Icy ran over and hugged Leo around his waist as she put a halt to him pulling his gun. She could feel the heat coming from his body and she knew he was itching to start shooting at Akoni. Stepping out of Icy's grasp, Leo moved forward, but Icy grabbed the back of his vest.

"Leave it alone, Leo," she said, looking up at him. "Please just leave. You have caused enough of a scene and I don't want things to get any uglier than they already are," Icy pled with Blaze.

"I'm gon' give you that, beautiful." Leo's jaw clenched while he watched Blaze lust over his wife. "Stay up, Leo. I'll see you around," Blaze smirked.

All eyes were on him as he made his way to the exit. Without another thought, Blaze walked out as casually as he had walked in.

Zan approached Leo with a lot of questions he needed his brother to answer. When he tapped Leo on the shoulder, he looked over at Zan with a look of disgust.

"Why the fuck you didn't come over while that nigga was still in the building, Zan? Get the fuck away from me with yo' scary ass," Leo hissed. "This is an invitation-only event. How did he make it through the door?"

Zan didn't even reply to his brother's bullshit and walked away. He'd already made his mind up about their relationship and he was standing on it for sure.

"The nigga said he was the son of Duke and I figured he was cool. What was that about? Is it something we need to be worried about?" Boom asked.

"Nah, fuck that nigga. I will see his ass another day. Today is about me and Icy, and we're about to party. Make sure nobody else comes through this bitch. Guard the door with yo' life."

Desiree was walking toward Leo and he shook his head no to her, diverting her steps. Icy noticed what happened, but didn't speak on it. Being a lady in the streets was what Icy did every day. She knew the time to beat the fuck out of Desiree would present itself very soon, and Icy was going to love every minute of it.

"Fix your face, Icy. Don't worry; I'm going to handle that. This will be a day to remember, and nothing is going to spoil that shit for you." Leo went to kiss Icy on the lips, but she turned her head, giving him her jaw. He didn't pay it any mind because he knew she was upset about what had taken place and she had every right to be. What Leo didn't know was the fact that Icy knew he was harboring yet another secret with Desiree.

"What the fuck was that about?" Julz asked as Leo and Icy walked onto the dance floor.

"Disrespect, sis. Disrespect. The shit is over, and I'm quite sure Icy will fill you in on it. Not tonight though, because we're about to turn up."

Leo shut down all questions Julz wanted to ask and she wanted to press the issue, but decided to just let it go. She also didn't like the fact of Leo calling her sis because once she found out he wasn't loving Icy properly, she would never call him bro again.

Leo and Icy danced, ate, and danced some more. Time flew when you were having fun, and that's exactly what happened with everyone in the building. The incident with Blaze was a thing of the past and well-forgotten as the party continued. Icy was standing talking to Julz when out of her peripheral she saw Leo heading to the DJ table and a mic was handed to him.

"Can I have y'all attention for a minute?" Leo asked into the mic. The room quieted down and all eyes were on him. "Today was the best day of my life. I married the woman I love, and we will actually get the opportunity to start our forever as husband and wife."

The applause and whistling were deafening, but Icy smiled for the love she was being shown as her name echoed off the walls. Leo was up to something and whatever it was, he owed her for all the shit he had done behind her back. Once again, Icy's eyes landed on Desiree and the expression she wore was unpleasant. In fact, the anger stood out to anyone paying attention.

"Icy Shanté Miller, for years you have held me down in any and every way imaginable. There are many ways for me to profess my love for you, and I have every intention of showing you for the rest of my life. You are the Queen of my castle, and that muthafucka would be cold as hell without you warming it up with your presence. Thank you for loving me the way you do. You were just what the doctor ordered, and I'm holding on for dear life and never letting you go."

Leo walked over and lined her lips with his tongue. Icy pulled back and hugged him instead.

"Back to what I was saying. I love you with every breath I take. You fucked up when you agreed to be Mrs. Miller, because ain't no breaking up. Thank you for giving me another chance to prove my love to you." Leo's words went into one ear and out the other. Icy wasn't trying to hear the lies he told. "I want y'all to meet me outside. We got thirty minutes before we ring in the New Year, and I want to give my baby her first of many gifts as a Miller."

The entire room of people were up on their feet, scrambling to get their coats. Zan brought Icy's floor-length white mink along with the matching hat. Leo slipped his arm in his matching waist-length mink and grabbed her hand.

"I have to drain the weasel, baby. Give me a minute and I'll meet you outside."

Icy looked around, trying to see what Leo could possibly have waiting for her outside in the dead of winter. Instead of following the crowd, Icy waited for Leo to return. When he emerged from the hall about five minutes later, he waltzed over to Icy and led the way out of the venue.

"There's nothing out here, bae," Icy said, pulling the coat tighter around her neck."

"Be patient," he said, shifting his feet.

Leo looked around at the crowd of people and nodded his head. A big truck made its way down the street and Icy was curious as it got closer to where they stood. The driver got out and went to the back of the truck with his partner. Leo placed his hands over her eyes, preventing Icy from seeing anything until he was ready for her to do so. Icy could hear the whispers and she wanted to see too. The sound of something being lowered had her excited.

"Baby, you know I love you and will give you anything your heart desires. Today is the day I present you with this." Leo's voice was a tad bit higher than usual, but the excitement she felt had her canceling it out.

Leo lowered his hands and Icy screamed as she jumped up and down. Leo had bought her the Porsche Cayenne coupe that she had her eye on for the longest time. Icy even had a name picked out for it. Midnight, because the car was midnight black from the exterior to the interior. He'd given her a brand-new home as an engagement present and Icy loved that house even though there wasn't any genuine love within the walls.

"Thank you, baby!" Icy screamed, more so about the car than Leo presenting it to her.

Leo pulled her towards the car and handed over the keys. Icy opened the door and that baby was fully loaded! She loved every aspect of the vehicle and all she could think about was cruising the streets of Chicago in her new whip. Sitting in the driver seat, Leo leaned down and kissed Icy tenderly and stood tall with his chest out then hit the pavement with a thud.

"Leo!" Icy cried.

Jumping out of the car, Icy got down on her knees as she cradled his head in her lap. Leo's blood was soaking through her coat as his brain matter oozed into the palm of Icy's hand.

Meesha

Chapter 1

"Come on, Leo. Let me explain!" Rico cried out the minute his boss walked into the warehouse.

When Leo didn't respond right away, Rico's thoughts went back to the night he was stripped of his entire shipment. Rico had one job and he fucked up royally when he allowed the lil bitch to ride with him on a run. The decision turned out to be the biggest mistake of his life. The number one rule was, never bring anyone outside of the organization along when making a drop. Rico had nothing other than pussy on the brain and wanted to kill two birds with one stone. The slim thick baddie didn't hesitate riding along with him. The inevitable happened and his pussy thirsty ass didn't see it coming until it was too late. Eva, the name she had given when she and Rico met months prior, set him up in the worst way.

Rico decided to hit the highway in the middle of the night because the traffic would be light. They were barely out of Chicago, heading to Iowa, when they were ambushed on I-80W. Niggas dressed in black jumped out of several cars with guns drawn. Rico reached for his heat and Eva pulled her tool, placing it to his temple.

"I wouldn't do that shit if I was you," Eva said roughly. "Get yo' ass out now!"

Rico was outnumbered and knew better than to attempt defending himself on the deserted highway. There was no way he would live to see another day, so he complied with the order and did what he was told. Opening the door, Rico was snatched out by a big, burly nigga and another popped the trunk from the inside of the car.

"Bingo! We got twenty birds!" somebody yelled.

Rico had never seen any of the niggas before and he was taking in their features. The images were embedded in his head. The only way they knew about the shit in his ride was if Eva told 'em. That's why it didn't pay to pillow talk with random-ass females. It would lead a muthafucka straight up the highway to hell.

19

Adorned in a tailor-made Givenchy suit with matching loafers, Leo Miller glided across the floor with precision and grace. The diamonds glistened around his neck and cufflinks like a ray of sun as the light bounced off of them. Leo's Rayban sunglasses hid the demonic look in his eyes, but Rico knew he had nothing other than murder on his mind.

"I don't need you to explain a muthafuckin' thang to me, nigga," Leo growled, taking off his glasses. "All I know is, my shit got snatched and you lived to see that shit happen. How, muthafucka? That's what I want to know."

"I don't know why they didn't kill me. They—"

"Who the fuck is *they*, Rico?" Leo's voice echoed through the empty warehouse.

"I don't know!" Rico screamed jumping to his feet.

"Well, if you don't know shit, what the fuck I need you in this bitch fo'? Ain't shit you can tell me, so sayonara, muthafucka."

Leo pulled his Glock from his back and sent a single shot between Rico's eyes. His body fell back, hitting the floor with a loud thud with blood instantly spreading around his head. Rico's eyes stared blankly upward as Leo placed his glasses over his eyes and turned to leave.

"Clean this shit up! Take notes, because this is lesson 101 on not fucking with my money!" Leo barked, turning back around to address his team. "If some shit goes down, I want to know ASAP! Don't hide, stall, nor walk around contemplating. That shit lets me know the shit is shady and a nigga tryin' to get over. Protect my shit like it's your own, because if you don't, I won't be nice with the next muthafucka that tries me."

Leo walked out of the warehouse and climbed into his Audi SQ7, heading home to his woman. Firing up the wood he rolled before going into the warehouse, Leo took a long pull, holding the smoke in his lungs until it burned. He blew the smoke out through his nose, filling his ride with that good shit that relaxed him instantly. One thing Leo never did was take the shit he had to deal with in the streets home to his lady.

There were two sides to him, The streets knew one and only Icy knew the other. Leo was determined to keep his business and personal life separate at all times. He learned the concept of differentiating between the two with lots of practice. His worlds collided at every turn because he didn't have a woman in his life that he gave a fuck about. Everything changed when he met Icy Winters.

It was a cold, blistering night in Chicago and Leo was out making pick-ups from his traps. There was a bad winter storm that basically shut the city down, but that didn't stop the fiends from coming out to get the medicine that would warm the blood in their bodies. Business was booming and money was flowing like water. As Leo was walking to his whip, he heard a commotion coming from one of the houses across the street. Usually, when shit went down Leo would mind his business without intervening. That night was different because a woman was being dragged out into the cold.

"Let me go, Daron!"

"Bitch, fuck you!" the weak nigga yelled as he continued dragging her by her long hair. "I told yo' ass not to question me about the shit I do! All you had to do was sit in the room while I fucked, but nawl, you had to get in yo' muthafuckin' feelings."

Baby girl wiggled until Daron released her hair. Standing toe to toe with the nigga, her chest heaved up and down as she caught her breath from struggling to free herself. With a finger in his face, she told his ass how she really felt about the bullshit he'd thrown at her.

"You got the game fucked up! How the fuck you thought for one minute I was going to be okay with you bringing a dusty-ass bitch in my shit to fuck? Do I look that gullible to yo' stupid ass? I pay all the bills and you think yo' ass Magic Don Juan or somebody when you wouldn't have a pot to piss in if it wasn't for me! Nickle and diming-ass nigga, get yo' weight up before trying to call shots! As a matter of fact, how the fuck you trying to put me out of my own shit?"

Leo laughed lowly as he walked around to the driver's side of his car. Lil mama was putting all Daron's business in the street and she held valid points too. There was no way Leo would disrespect a female that resided in a home with him in that manner. Dude was dead-ass wrong. Opening the door and lifting his foot, Leo looked behind him to make sure ol' girl was cool because the two of them were going back and forth with each other. Dude drew his hand back and punched her like she was a man. That type of shit is what Leo didn't like.

Once she hit the pavement, Daron hovered over her body, punching her repeatedly in the face. Without thought, Leo snatched his tool from his waist and stormed across the street. With no words spoken, he sent a single bullet to the top of his dome. Leo kicked Daron's body off the woman and pulled her up. Icy has been Leo's most prized possession ever since.

Leo pulled into the gate after entering the code and drove up the driveway toward the three-story home he shared with Icy. Thinking about how she became a part of his life brought a sense of sadness to him, but knowing how far she'd come in the past five years brightened his mood. Icy was a tough woman. After the incident with the pussy-ass nigga, Leo flew her out to a plastic surgeon because Daron fucked Icy's face up. Leo wanted to make sure the scars weren't permanent and her self-esteem wasn't tarnished. The shit worked because Icy walked around with her head held high.

As he killed the engine, Leo's phone rang and Duke's name appeared on the screen. Duke was his connect and there had to be a problem if he was hittin' Leo up before it was time to re-up. He let out a low sigh before hitting the icon to connect the call.

"What up, Duke?" The line was silent, so Leo spoke again. "Duke, you there?" he asked with a hint of concern.

"I'm here. Um, I need you to come to Jamaica pronto. We need to sit down and talk business face to face. Don't tell me it's not possible. The wife will understand."

"How long do I have?" Leo asked, getting out of his whip.

"Two, three hours tops," Duke replied in his heavy accent. "The plane is already gassed up and waiting. All you gotta do is get on."

"Say less," Leo said, ending the call.

Duke had been Leo's connect for the past ten years. Their relationship had progressed from business to brotherhood early on. Leo learned a lot from the old head and he sucked that shit up like a sponge. Duke's knowledge helped him rise in the streets of Chicago. Leo's money was always on point and there was never any drama brought back to the head nigga in charge. Leo didn't have plans of telling Duke about the hit he took behind Rico's carelessness. He would just have to dig deep in his own pockets and pay up when the time came. The last thing Leo needed was Duke believing he wasn't running a tight ship. What happened on his turf was Leo's problem. No one else's.

Leo made his way into the house to break the news of his abrupt departure to Icy. The house was eerily quiet when he entered. Leo crept slowly through the living room and eased the same tool he used to lay down Rico from his hip. Icy left at least one light on downstairs or at least a television. In his gut, Leo felt something was wrong because it was pitch black in that muthafucka.

With his tool locked and loaded, Leo crept up the steps, praying he didn't find anything wrong with Icy. The closer he got to the bedroom, the faster his heart hammered in his chest. When he reached out to push the door open, he could hear the sound of Icy's favorite toy humming throughout the room along with her soft moans.

"Mmmmm, suck that pussy, Leo."

Leo shook his head and laughed lowly. It was good to know Icy included him in her solo sexual endeavors, even in his absence. He gathered himself before going in to give Icy the business. When he opened the door, the sight before him stilled his steps. Icy was laid back on the California King bed with her legs spread wide. The light from the TV hit her moist center with just enough light and the shit had his dick pushing the front of his slacks with a vengeance. Icy's back arched upward while she rubbed the vibrator vigorously over her engorged clit.

"Fuck! Babbbbbyyyy!" she cried out as her flood gates opened and she squirted her juices to the foot of the bed.

Icy dropped the gadget while trying to catch her breath the assault on herself caused. Leo eased out of his suit jacket and placed his tool on the dresser quietly. Icy's eyes were closed as her chest rose and fell slowly.

"Want company?" he asked, unbuttoning his shirt.

Icy smirked, realizing the man she was fantasizing about was indeed in the building. "I'm always down for your deep stroke. You're right on time to join the party. It's always better with daddy in the mix," Icy said sensually as she rubbed her fingers over her wet center.

"I love when you boost my ego, baby. Seeing you cum did something to me. Don't hold back. Be free with me just as you did with that damn toy lying beside you."

Leo came out the rest of his clothes and squeezed the head of his dick. The pressure he felt in his muscle had him fighting the urge to moan out loud. Icy loved the way Leo tried to hide his anxiousness. His manhood was always on the line when he came in contact with her. Leo and Icy had no qualms when it came to their sex life.

Climbing on the bed, lying flat on his stomach, Leo watched as Icy played in her snatch while licking his lips. "Put yo' hands over your head and keep 'em there."

Icy did as she was told as Leo gripped her thighs. The cool air of the air conditioner grazed her pearl, sending a shiver up her spine. The tip of his tongue connected with the flesh of her lower lips and the electronic device had nothing on the mouth of Leo Miller. He made love to her pussy, causing Icy to bring her hands to the back of his head.

"Where the fuck did I tell you I wanted yo' hands? If I have to tie yo' ass up, Icy, there will be no mercy once I get in that pussy."

Putting her hands back over her head, Icy rocked her mound against Leo's tongue and fought the urge to hold his head between her legs. If he couldn't do nothing else, Leo knew how to devour her cat. Icy's orgasm was rising and for the second time that night, she was about erupt down his throat and Leo was ready to swallow every drop. Icy's warm liquid quenched Leo's thirst and he loved every bit of it. Wiping his hand down his face, he rose and positioned himself between her legs.

Leo rocked Icy into a coma with the strokes he delivered. They rode the wave for over an hour and the thought of telling Icy about going to Jamaica never entered his mind. Her inner folds had his mind occupied, and nothing would be able to take him away from that. Icy would find out about his trip before he made his way to the airport.

***

Icy was curled up like a newborn baby after the sex session she and Leo had. Her soft snores made Leo feel as if he accomplished what he set out to do when he came home. Getting his clothes packed up quietly for his trip, Leo stepped out of the closet with his luggage in hand. Icy rolled over, stretching like a feline kitten. Her caramel breasts with darkened areolas stood perkily on her chest. Her abs were sculpted beautifully as Leo's gaze trailed down her entire body. Licking his lips, he shook his head as the thought of crawling back in bed with her crossed his mind.

"Where are you off to?" Icy asked, propping up on her elbow.

"I have to head out to Jamaica. Duke hit me up before I came into the house. I was coming in to tell you about it, but you distracted a nigga from the gate."

"What time are you supposed to be at the airstrip?"

Glancing at the time on the clock, Leo chuckled just as his phone rang for the fifth time. "I'm supposed to be there in the next thirty minutes. That's probably Zan blowing my line down now," he said, gesturing toward his phone. "I have to jump in the shower, then I'm heading out."

Icy really didn't complain when Leo had to go on the impromptu trips. She never questioned him, and that was one of the things he loved about her. Icy was his peace in so many ways. Leo had never had a relationship that was so calming. All of his past relationships were filled with nothing but problems which stemmed from Leo being in the streets all the time. Not because the females were assuming, but because their assumptions were dead on for the most part. However, Leo always wiggled his way out of every situation. He got lucky with Icy because as long as she didn't see anything, nothing was going on in her eyes. Leo loved Icy and they were planning their dream wedding. They were set to recite their vows to become husband and wife before the clock struck twelve on December thirty-first.

While Leo was in the shower, his phone rang nonstop. Icy didn't move from the position she was in as she tuned out the constant noise. She had never answered his phone and wasn't going to start in that moment. Instead, she got up and left the room to go downstairs for a bottled water.

There were many things Icy had to do the next morning and she had to get some type of rest. Knowing she would be home alone for a few days made her a little sad, but that was part of the game. Icy knew what type of business Leo was into after the day he came to the rescue when Daron was beating her. Never wanting Icy to be too deep into his business affairs, Leo kept her on the back end of the business and just wanted Icy to be a stay-at-home wife. That wasn't what Icy was about because she could never just sit around doing nothing while a man took care of her.

Growing up, Icy was around her father Jerome "Birdman" Winters all the time. Her mother didn't like when her husband allowed a young Icy to sit with him while he counted money, cooked dope, and sometimes made his drops. In that time frame, Icy learned a lot about the drug game and retained every detail. She idolized her father. not because of what he did for a living, but how he handled his business while doing it.

The day her father was killed would forever be etched in Icy's mind. It took years to get her life together because she just shut down from the trauma it had caused. She remembered dancing, and having a good time in the park with her friends while eating barbeque.

Every summer Birdman hosted a back-to-school bash for the kids in Washington Park. Icy and her girls were dancing, having a good time, when four masked men came out of nowhere, guns blazing. Icy was a few feet away from her father when he was struck in the head. He died two days later from the gunshot wound because his brain swelled and eventually stopped working in his favor. The gunmen where never apprehended, and that left a hole in Icy's heart. She was never the same from that day forward. Icy went off to college, maintained her degree in business management, and came back to the mean streets of Chicago to be with her mother.

Landing a job as a Human Resource Assistant, Icy spent one year in the position until she decided to open a salon. She didn't know how to do hair personally, but Icy knew there was money to be made in the business. At the age of twenty-three, Icy opened her first salon. Five years later at the age of twenty-nine, she had a total of three, one on the southside of the city, another on the northside, and the newest one in the western suburbs.

"Why are you sitting down here like you got a lot on your mind?" Leo asked, walking into the kitchen, snapping Icy from her thoughts.

"I was just thinking about all the things I have to do in the morning," she said, taking a sip from the bottle. "You heading out?" she asked.

"Yeah, I'll be back in a couple days," Leo said, pulling Icy into a kiss. "Don't overthink this wedding shit, babe. Whatever you want, you shall have. It should be easy for you to make decisions."

"I know. Just be careful. I love you," Icy said, releasing the hold she had on his shirt.

Leo picked up his luggage and walked out of the house. Icy worried about him every time he left, and that night was no different. She was afraid he wouldn't return, just like her father didn't years before.

Meesha

Chapter 2

Leo made it to Duke's jet late as hell and didn't give two fucks. When he boarded the aircraft, his brother Zan was sitting with a glass of brown in hand. When he noticed Leo, his face scrunched up in a frown.

"Nigga, you gon' be late to yo' own funeral," Zan scoffed. "I called you many times and I know Duke did too."

"Save that shit, brah. You know damn well this shit was last minute and I'm on my time, not some other muthafucka's. I needed to make sure Icy was good on all levels before up and leaving that muthafucka. Plus, I had to release some stress after murkin' that nigga Rico. The shit had me lava hot. Speaking of, where the fuck were you?"

"I had to go over to Cherelle's because Zymia wasn't feeling well. You know my damn daughter comes before any of this shit. I should've called to let you know what was going on, but it slipped my mind. I knew you could handle that shit solo anyway."

Zander Miller was Leo's younger brother by six years. At twenty-nine, he was established in life and had a wife and a five-month-old daughter. Leo didn't want his brother in the game, but Zan's pride wouldn't allow him to accept the money Leo offered him years ago while he worked an honest nine-to-five. Zan wanted to get his hands dirty and earn his keep in the business, and who was Leo to tell him no?

"What's wrong with Z baby?" Leo asked as he sat across from his brother. The stewardess came down the aisle and approached him with a glass of his own. "What's this?" he asked, looking at the golden liquid.

"It's Remy Martin, Sir."

"Thank you, but take this back and bring me tequila, please." The stewardess took the glass and turned to walk away.

"Hold up," Zan called out. "I'll take that."

When they were alone again, Zan took a sip out of one of his two glasses and faced his brother. "She has an ear infection and was running a fever of a hunnid and three. We went to the emergency room and they diagnosed her with an ear infection. They prescribed her ear drops and Tylenol for the fever. She was sleeping when I got the call from Duke. What the hell he want anyway? It's not even time to re-up."

"I don't know. We'll find out once we get there."

Leo's drink was placed in his hand and once again he thanked the stewardess. The entire time he drove to the airstrip, Leo thought about why Duke wanted to see him on such short notice. Nothing came to mind because there was no way he knew about the shipment he lost by the hands of Rico's stupid ass.

Zan sat back in his seat and closed his eyes while Leo did the same. They had five hours to be in the air and Leo was tired as hell from the work he'd done in the sheets and in the streets. The pilot announced they were ready for takeoff and Leo put his Airpods in his ear and let the sounds of Nas put him to sleep.

Two hours into the flight, Leo was jolted awake by the ringing of the phone in his ear. Looking down at the device, he thought about not answering, but knew the person on the other end would keep blowing his shit up. Soon as the call connected, Leo regretted it the minute the voice filled his eardrum.

"Where the hell are you, Leo?"

"Last time I checked, yo' muthafuckin' name wasn't Icy. Play yo' role, shawty. Don't call my shit questioning me like you got it like that."

"Why you always gotta bring that bitch up every time I say something?"

Leo ended the call because he wasn't going there with her while Zan was sitting so close. One thing about his brother, he hated the fact that Leo planned to marry, but refused to let the other women in his life go. According to Zan, Icy was the one for Leo and he should do right by her. Leo knew he was right, but at the same time, there was something about having a variety of pussy to fall into whenever he wanted. Every female Leo fucked with knew their position. His number one was definitely Icy hands down. A text came through and Leo groaned lowly as he read it.

You must be with that bitch! Don't make promises you can't keep, nigga. Today supposed to be my time! It's bad enough you put a ring on that bitch finger and made plans to marry her gullible ass. You need to think twice about that shit because it's obvious her pussy trash if you still holding on to me.

Leo laughed because the hoe sounded bitter and mad at the same muthafuckin' time. She always got worked up about the time he spent with her and the fact that he wouldn't leave Icy. That wasn't part of the plan when they started doing their thing. Leo knew she only tried to get under his skin because the sex was better whenever he went over to choke her ass out. He didn't put his hands on women, but he would yoke a bitch up quickly when they got out of line.

What I tell yo' ass about disrespecting her like that? Watch what comes out yo' mouth, Shawty. I don't have to run my plans by you because you ain't my woman. But just to appease yo' spoiled ass, I'm on a flight to Jamaica because I have business to attend to. When I get back, you will be the first to see me. Stop with all the bullshit, it's not necessary.

Closing his eyes to get more rest, Leo thought about all the things he had going on outside of his relationship with Icy. At times, it was hard keeping things out of her eyesight. If Icy knew about half the shit Leo had done, she would not walk down the aisle to be his wife. Leo knew he was wrong, but there was no chance in hell he was going to stop.

Feeling the wheels of the plane touch the pavement hours later, Leo stretched his limbs as he prepared to get off the plane. Zan was gathering his things so he could be ready to exit as well. Once the door was opened the two brothers wasted no time stepping off the plane. There was a black SUV waiting to take them to the home of Duke Ottey.

Zan watched the scenery as they drove through the streets of Kingston, he was grateful for the things he had back home in the States. The conditions of the villages weren't the best, but the smiles on the faces of the people were what warmed his heart. It made him realize, it's not what you have, but how you make the best of what you have. As they got closer to the estate Duke owned, the atmosphere seemed to get a lot brighter. There was definitely a change of scenery and you could tell that money was behind the reasoning.

Duke had a mansion in the middle of nowhere and the structure could probably fit ten of the families they had passed on the ride. Zan didn't know what type of community service Duke provided for the less fortunate, but he hoped he did something instead of nothing at all. Riding through the iron gates of the estate, Leo and Zan saw Duke standing out front with his right-hand Maven by his side waiting for them.

"Leo, Zan, good to see you," Duke said in his thick Jamaican accent as they stepped out of the truck. "Follow me inside. I know you two are hungry. We'll talk over lunch."

Trailing Duke into his home, Leo noticed some changes Duke had made on the inside of his home. He had installed an elevator, crystal chandeliers, and huge bay windows throughout the estate. Duke had even brightened the paint in the place, and it was more welcoming than before. Kenise, Duke's wife, was sitting at the head of the table with a glass filled with mimosa in hand.

Kenise didn't look a day over thirty, but Leo knew she was in her late fifties. Duke's wife had never sat in on any of their business meetings until that day, and it only made Leo wonder what was really up. The chef and his cooks were placing food on the table as Duke gestured for them to have a seat. Leo watched as Duke lowered himself into the chair at the head of the table slowly, bringing a hint of concern to Duke's protégé.

"Aye, Duke. You good over there?" Leo asked, rising up to give him a hand.

Holding his hand up to halt Leo's approach, Duke sat with a loud grunt as he breathed heavily. "I'm fine, Leo. It's just the things old folks go through in their walk through life."

The food on the table looked delicious and smelled even better. There was more than enough food and Leo's mouth was watering with anticipation. Kenise cleared her throat as the last dish was placed in the center of the table.

"I would like to introduce you to the lovely dishes of Jamaica." She smiled, showing her beautiful white teeth. "You will have the pleasure of enjoying ackee and codfish, jerk chicken and fish, fish escovitch, rice and peas, fried plantains, callaloo, bammy, and curry goat. For dessert, we will have banana bread, toto, and coconut drops."

"What is this one?" Zan asked, pointing to one of the dishes. "It looks damn good."

"That is fish escovitch. Its fried Red Snapper topped with pickled vegetables - carrots, onions, peppers, pimentos, and chayote. You can pair it with bammy and get an explosive taste of greatness inside of your mouth."

"Sounds good. I'll try a little of everything because I truly can't decide." Zan smiled, rubbing his hands together. "Thanks for giving me the rundown. I appreciate that."

Leo, on the other hand, filled his plate with jerk chicken, rice and peas, and plantains. He waited patiently for everyone to settle in with their food. He wanted to get to the point of why they were in Jamaica. Akiel, Duke's nephew, walked into the dining room with a huge smile on his face as he sat to the right of Leo.

"Waah gwaan, Uncle Duke? Mi get yuh message an mi deh yah just inna time tuh nyam."

"Speak English, Akiel, we have guests. Give us a moment to enjoy the meal that was prepared for us."

Leo swallowed the food he had chewed before speaking. "I'm with him on this one, Duke. There's no time like the present to speak on why we are all here today. I'm quite sure we can talk while eating. We do it all the time in the States. The shit won't sound any different if we wait until after."

Duke wiped his mouth with a napkin and adjusted himself in his chair. Looking around the table, his eyes landed on each person sitting around him. The only one missing was his son, Akoni. Duke had called him several times without getting him on the line. The meeting was an important one and he wanted his son in attendance more than anything, but there was no way Duke could force his son to do anything. Akoni was the only person that didn't bow down to his father's commands.

"The reason I've called this meeting in such a short time frame is because time waits on no one. I've been running this operation for over forty years and my health isn't what it used to be. I've been diagnosed with stage four cancer and I don't know how much longer I will be around."

"Damn, Duke. Why didn't you tell me this before now?" Leo asked, dropping his fork into his plate.

"There was no need to announce my illness. This is part of life, and there's nothing more the doctors can do. Enough about that though. Business must go on with or without me. I've given all of you the tools to be great in this world and I have faith in every one of you. Stepping into my shoes is a great responsibility and I want the one that's capable of running a tight ship to take over my empire. That's what this meeting is all about." Duke took a drink from his goblet and pushed his plate away.

"My initial plan was to give my son, Akoni, the throne, but he wants no parts of my business. I don't blame him at all because he went to America, got an education, and is thriving on his own. So, that led me back to you all. Leo, Akiel, and Maven. The three of you have been by my side through thick and thin, and I am proud of everything you guys have done. This was a hard decision for me to make. Before I reveal my decision, I want you all to understand, I thought long and hard about this."

Sitting back in his chair, Leo's heart swelled in his chest. He knew for a fact Duke would make the right decision and hand the keys to the operation over to him. There hadn't been one time he'd been short with money, and he re-upped on product twice, sometimes three times a month. Business was good between the two of them, and that proved a lot to the plug. Leo was next in line, and all he wanted to do was hear the words come out of Duke's mouth before he started celebrating what he knew was victory for him and his brother. Zan looked over at Leo with a smirk and nodded his head as they tuned back in on Duke.

"Maven, you have been with me for twenty years and I love you like a blood brother. You already know I got you, even in death." Duke moved his attention to Akiel, and his nephew glared at Leo with menace in his eyes. "Akiel, you have soaked in everything I've taught you throughout the years. I never wanted you in this line of work, but you have conquered every obstacle I've presented to you. There haven't been any mishaps on your part and I'm here to tell you, I'm so proud."

Leo's demeanor changed with the praises Duke was throwing at his nephew, and the shit didn't sit well with him. At that point, he didn't know which way Duke was going with his speech. At first, he was for sure he would take over the throne, but at that moment, Leo didn't know.

Zan saw the change in his brother and knew for a fact if Duke said the wrong shit, Leo was going to snap. Zan didn't think Leo was ready to take over an entire empire and in all honesty, he was ready to walk away from the game. He had already put some moves in motion to invest in many businesses to go legit. Hell, he had a family to look after and running the streets, watching his back, wasn't something Zan wanted to do for the rest of his life.

"Leo." Duke shifted in his seat without giving Leo any eye contact. That was red flag number one for Leo. "You have been down with me for the past ten years and there have been no issues with us until a few weeks ago. There has never been a time you haven't come to me about an issue you were having in the States. I was pretty disappointed to learn that you kept something so important from me."

"I didn't keep shit from you!" Leo barked. "What happened in my territory was taken care of, and I took that loss like a real nigga! Yeah, I planned to pay you outta pocket, but that shit shouldn't matter because you gon' get yo' bread regardless. I've earned this spot, Duke!"

One thing Duke didn't like was a man who thought he was entitled to something that didn't rightfully belong to them. The one hiccup Leo had was a major one in Duke's eyes. It made him think about all the other things he had hidden from him. Deception is one of the quickest ways to gain little things and lose big.

"You thought you earned it. But my decision is final. I'm turning the throne over to Akiel. He has given me no reason to doubt his loyalty to me, and that's all there is to it."

"Thank yuh, Duke. Mi a guh mak yuh proud. Di operation needs tuh stay inna di fambly anyway."

"Nigga, speak English so I can understand what the fuck you just said. If I heard yo' ass correctly, you said the operation needs to stay in the family anyway. Don't sit over there and gloat, nigga, because you ain't done shit that I know of. Yo' ass been hangin' off Duke's dick since you came on the scene. Get the fuck outta here with that bullshit."

Leo pushed his seat back and stood. He was heated and couldn't sit in the presence of Duke and his minion a minute longer. Heading for the door, Leo went straight to the SUV and into his luggage. Grabbing a blunt from the side pocket, he flamed up and took a long pull. Duke had really set him off, and Leo didn't appreciate being brought all the way to Jamaica to be made a fool of.

The door of the house opened and Maven stepped out.

"Come on, Leo. You can't let Duke's decision work you up like this."

"Man, fuck that! Akiel's muthafuckin' ass ain't nowhere near ready to run this shit if Duke croaks tomorrow. You can't stand there and tell me he is either," Leo huffed.

"You're not lying, but we don't have a say so over the matter. Duke made his decision, and that's what we have to go along with. We're still in the game to make money and that's all that matters, right?"

"Hell nawl, that's not what matters. The fuck you talking about! You've been riding Duke's coattail for twenty years and all he can say is he got you dead or alive. I would've been cool if he handed the shit over to you, Mav, you deserve that shit more than Akiel's lame ass. All he knows how to do is spend money. Muthafuckas gon' roll on his soft ass every chance they get."

"Had you stayed back and listened, you would've found out that Duke is giving Akiel a trial period. If he doesn't work out, you are next in line."

"Maven, do I look like a second option-ass nigga? I'm not about to wait for this nigga to fuck up. I already know he's either gon' fuck up or get bumped off. Duke probably got a few crumbs lined up for yo' ass when he dies when he's worth billions. How do you feel about that shit?"

Maven stood thinking shit over without responding. He always felt he should be next in line to take over for Duke and was just as salty as Leo. Maven would never undermine anything Duke had in place about his business, but he knew better than to express his feelings openly. Maven had plans of his own, and he would definitely need Leo's help with making it come together. Leo had to have a level head and calm the fuck down before he brought anything to his attention though.

"When you calm down, I want to run some shit by you. It will benefit both of us in the end. When you get back home, I need you to buy a burner for communication purposes."

"What do you got cooking, Mav?" Leo asked with an evil grin.

"I'll let you know soon enough. For now, I need you to go back inside and let the boss know everything is cool."

"Nah, I'm straight on all that. I won't fake the funk for nobody."

"Bring yo' bullheaded ass on, Leo. This shit gotta get smoothed over on our end. Trust me."

Leo finished his blunt and snubbed it out with his foot before following Maven back into the estate. He didn't like to apologize to anyone, especially when he knew he wasn't wrong. Biting his tongue was something he had never done, but it was necessary in that instance. If Maven was up to something that would benefit both of them in the end, Leo was all for it, especially if it meant he would get a piece of the pie he rightfully deserved.

Meesha

Chapter 3

"This cake is delicious," Icy said, licking her lips. "I think this buttercream frosting and yellow cake is the one I'm going with. It's too damn good to pass up."

"With all the cake you've tested, I can't believe your tastebuds can distinguish which is better. I stopped a long time ago." Julz frowned, watching Icy stuff another forkful of cake in her mouth.

Julz, Icy, and Desiree were seated in Fantastic Cakes, sampling cakes for the wedding. Icy had already went to the bridal shop earlier and found the perfect dress and that was the last stop before she called it a day. Desiree looked as if she was mad at the world and wasn't too enthused about being dragged from place to place along with Icy.

"Desiree, you have been in a funk since we picked you up. What's going on?" Icy asked.

"I don't want to talk about it. Don't worry about me. Today is all about you, Icy."

Desiree turned her head and looked out of the window. She fumbled around in her bag and retrieved her phone, frowning even more. Icy knew whoever was on the other end of the message was getting cursed out by the rapid strokes of her fingers. Julz smirked as she looked on, waiting for Desiree to finish.

"Okay, Des. What's really going on? Some ninja got you heated."

"You knew better than to say nigga!" Desiree snapped.

"Girl, fuck you." Julz chuckled. "I may be a white girl, but there's no punk in my blood. Whoever you're mad at, take that shit out on them. While you're at it, tell that motherfucker to stick his dick in your mouth."

"Whoa, it's time to go," Icy said, gathering her purse. "We're not about to show out in these people's place of business."

Icy hated when Julz and Desiree were in the same room because they always ended up causing a scene. It was mainly Desiree, but Julz didn't make things any better. After Julz opened her mouth, Icy had to intervene every time. As they walked out to Icy's truck, Desiree stood back tapping away vigorously on her phone.

"Are you coming?" Icy asked, pulling the door of her vehicle open.

"Nah, I'm going to catch a Lyft. Go ahead without me."

"Desiree, you know if we come together, we leave together."

"I'm good. Enjoy the rest of your day. Your dress is beautiful, by the way," she said dryly.

Julz got in the truck and sat in the passenger seat. Icy glanced at Desiree one more time before joining her best friend. "Call me when you get home, okay?"

Desiree nodded her head without looking up from her phone. Icy started the engine, backed up, and sped out of the parking lot. Julz kept her eye on Desiree until she was out of sight, turning around in her seat, popping her lips.

"Something is wrong with that bitch. She's giving off bad vibes, and I can't put my finger on the shit."

"Just ignore Desiree and her mood swings, Julz. I've told you time again not to allow her to get underneath your skin. Constantly going back and forth with her only causes more problems between the two of y'all. Honestly, I'm getting tired of the shit."

"One of these days, I'm going to beat that ass."

Icy laughed, turning the music up. She didn't want to go into any of the violent shit with her best friend. She had left the arguing and fighting for no reason back in high school. The only time she popped off was if she was provoked. Icy was too grown for the childish shit Julz and Desiree had going on.

Icy and Julz had been friends since their freshman year at Fenger High School. They met by chance when a group of girls surrounded Julz in the hall. One thing Icy couldn't stand early on was bitches that thought jumping someone was cool. Julz was scared shitless, but Icy and her cousin Kia stepped in and cleared that shit right out. Julz had no chance of scratching a bitch because once they handled the ringleader and her big mouth clown, the rest was history.

Julz was from Hartville, Wyoming. The population of her town was just a tad bit larger than one of the classrooms at the school, according to her. Convincing her parents to allow her to move with her aunt in Chicago to get away from the farm life, Julz was living in pure hell and was bullied for not having the things other kids had. That was, until Icy came along and saved the day. The two of them were basically joined at the hip from that day forward.

"Seriously, Icy, I know Desiree is basically Leo's friend, but to me, it seems she's envious of you. I've brought it to your attention plenty of times and you downplay it."

"I don't downplay anything. Getting in other people's business is something I don't do. You know that," Icy said, glancing at Julz.

"You're always in my shit!" Julz exclaimed.

"That's different. I'm going to know everything you have going on. If you keep anything from me, we gon' fight like dogs in the street."

Julz laughed because she knew Icy was serious about what she'd said. From high school to the present day, the two had been by each other's side. Julz appreciated Icy for never judging her and being a true friend turned sister. Icy was the one who taught Julz to be the woman she had become. With the help of her parents, Julz was wearing the latest fashions, getting her hair and nails done, and even getting a weekly allowance, just as Icy was given. When Bird-man passed away, there was money set aside for Julz as if she was his daughter. She had basically moved in with the Winters her sophomore year of high school.

Julz found out her aunt was using drugs, and that was the reason she was never home to properly care for her niece. One day, a local drug dealer came by the house to collect a debt, and had his way with Julz as repayment; at least, that's what he said. In the end, he caught up with Paula and shot her in the head. Julz's parents didn't want her back at the house, so Julz had nowhere to go. Once again, Icy made a way, and she was forever grateful.

Going off to college alongside Icy, Julz got her degree in Graphic Design and her online business, "Julz Creations", was booming. She did a lot of work for many authors, providing any and everything they might need for their promotional needs. It didn't stop there though. Julz designed websites, T-shirts, and many other things. The woman was a jack of all trades. In other words, her money was flowing nicely.

"You know not to play with me," Icy went on. "Desiree, on the other hand, doesn't owe me anything. She's only in my space because of Leo. If she wasn't his assistant, she wouldn't be tagging along for this wedding."

"What exactly do she assist though?" Julz asked, rolling her eyes. "The bitch is his property manager at the condos. It seems to me, his ass has her watching you while he's out of town. I've told you this before."

"There's no reason for Leo to have anyone clockin' my moves. You're overexaggerating, Julz."

"If you want me to be truthful, I believe there's more to their relationship than business. Desiree is managing more than Leo's condos."

"Shut the fuck up!" Icy screamed, laughing. "Leonard Miller knows not to play in my face like that. He's not ready to meet his muthafuckin' maker. If some shit *is* going down, Desiree and that nigga better keep that shit under wraps and I bet' not find out. You of all people know I've toned shit down since getting with Leo. I am my daddy's child, and I will plan that nigga's funeral while smiling with every tear that falls from my eyes."

"When shit hits the fan, I'll be front and center watching everything unfold." Julz smirked.

Pulling up to the entrance of Julz's building, Icy hugged her before she got out of the truck.

"You're going to wear the shit out of that dress, sis. Let's just hope you get to walk down the aisle without anything getting in the way."

"The wedding is taking place on New Year's Eve no matter what transpires," Icy said, blowing off what Julz said. "Thanks for going through the motions with me today. I would've been so indecisive had I gone alone."

"Icy, that's what the Maid of Honor is for. Just wait until your bachelorette party. We gon' be lit!"

Julz started twerking her ass with her tongue hanging out of her mouth. Icy couldn't do anything except laugh because Julz was stacked to be a white girl. Standing at 5'7" a good 170 pounds, and a big ole ass, she was for sure cornbread fed living in the house with black folks. Her auburn hair with blond highlights blew in the cool wind as she popped her ass. Julz waltzed in the building after blowing a kiss in her friend's direction.

Icy loved the humor Julz possessed. The fact that she had been saying there was something going on between Leo and Desiree for quite some time ran through her mind the entire way home. For some reason, that day, Julz's words had Icy wondering if it was possible. Getting to her home, the ride was a blur because Icy was deep in the thought. Opening the door, her phone rang and she shuffled to get it out of her purse. The name on the screen brought a smile to her face instantly.

"Cousin! I wish you could've been with me today! That damn job has to go because it's keeping you away from my me time," Icy said in one breath.

Kia laughed on the other end because she loved the excitement in her cousin's voice. "Girl, I know, and I'm sorry. I'm getting off soon so I can go in for my fitting. My dress better not be ugly, bitch!"

"Ain't shit gon' be ugly around these parts. All the dresses are bomb, and you're going to love them. How's work going?"

"Man, it's work. There's nothing exciting about this shit. My damn head hurts sitting here going over all these damn numbers all day. But hey, it pays the bills, so I won't complain too much. Where's my favorite cousin?"

"He left last night on a business trip to Jamaica. I'm home alone for the next couple of days."

Icy walked up the steps to her bedroom and removed her jacket along the way. The September breeze allowed her to dress cute for the day with a pair of black jeans, a mustard-colored long-sleeved tee, and thigh high boots to match. She hung the waist length black leather jacket in the closet and sat on the side of the bed to remove her boots.

"His ass always on the go," Kia said as she snacked on something that had her sounding as if she was eating steak. "Icy, let me tell you about this nigga Troy."

"Oh, lord. What the hell he do now?" Icy asked, laughing.

"This muthafucka had the nerve to invite me to his muthafuckin' house and he had another bitch there. He must've forgot who the fuck I was, because I beat the fuck outta both of their asses. He will think twice about playing with me from this day forward."

Kia was crazy as hell. She was always beating on somebody. Kia didn't give a damn if it was a man, woman, or child, if she was rubbed the wrong way, it was on sight. Don't let her have a bottle of brown and some good weed; it's over from that point on. The government fucked up giving her a conceal and carry license because she stayed strapped. Busting out windows, slicing tires, and walking up to a muthafucka's front door just to kick ass was her specialties. The woman was an accountant by day and hell by night. Icy didn't know where she got the energy to do all that she did and still get up to punch a clock.

"Kia, you need to just leave these men alone. They always got you in the middle of some type of bullshit. Aren't you tired of fighting all the time?" Icy asked seriously.

"Leave men alone? You gotta be out your mind. In a way, I think you're suggesting I go out and fuck with bitches instead. Nah, that's not my cup of tea. See, all niggas got that test a bitch button they like to push at some point, so it's gonna be the same shit with a different nigga too. And guess what? I will have an ass whoopin' waiting for his ass too."

Icy fell back on the bed laughing while holding her stomach. There was never a dull moment when she talked to her cousin. She needed that laugh because her mind was traveling in unforbidden territory from what Julz said earlier.

"As far as leaving Troy alone, that shit ain't gon' happen. The dick too good, and as long as he come out of his pockets and keep eating my ass, the nigga straight right where he at. I don't give a damn who he fuckin' around with long as he don't push that shit in my face. I know one thing, there won't be no kissing involved because if he's doing me right, he's doing the same thing with the next bitch. I provide all the condoms to protect me."

Icy had tears rolling down her face listening to her cousin's rant. Rushing to the bathroom, she muted the phone because she had to pee badly. Icy was glad to be home because had she been in the car when Kia called, she would've for sure pissed on herself.

"Icy, this nigga calling now. Let me see how much he willing to pay to make this shit go away. I'll call you after I come from the fitting. I may spend the night with you."

"Okay, cuz. Talk to you later."

Kia and Icy were close as kids and the two of them made sure their relationship stayed that way throughout the years. Kia's father Kenny was in and out of her life, and Birdman picked up the slack and acted as her father. Kia and her mother Brenda lived in the city, but Kia spent a lot of time with Icy at her house. The relationship between her and her father was strained, and that was because he never spent any quality time with her. When Icy's father was murdered, it was as if Kia lost her father as well because Kenny left without even saying goodbye after the funeral.

Icy shook her head as she threw the phone on the bed. Gathering clothes to get comfortable, she jumped in the shower and prepared to relax before she cooked something quick for dinner. The moment her head hit the pillow, she was out like a light. It never crossed her mind that she hadn't heard from Leo since he left to go to the airport.

Meesha

Chapter 4

Zan sat in his hotel room, thinking about what transpired at Duke's estate the day before. Leo decided staying at the estate was out of the question once Duke called him out on the missing shipment and passing over him with the empire. In Zan's opinion, Leo couldn't get mad because Duke decided to keep his business in the family. Hell, if the shoe was on the other foot, Leo would've done the same shit.

Zan had to do damage control when his brother stormed out. Basically telling Duke to kiss his ass, Leo was on the verge of losing his life behind that shit. If Zan hadn't smoothed things over, Leo would've been shit out of luck when it was time to re-up. Duke was ready to sever all ties with him. Leo's actions pushed Zan closer to his decision of walking away from the entire operation.

With millions in the bank, pushing drugs was something Zan was tired of doing. He had a wife and five-month-old daughter to protect. Being out in the streets watching his back, wondering what type of target was aimed in his direction, just wasn't hitting it anymore. There was more to life than hustling. Zan was twenty-nine years old and he knew there was more to life than the shit he and his brother was doing in the streets. It was time to go one hundred percent legit.

On top of that, Leo was getting more reckless as the days went by. Zan stood behind him when he murked Rico; he had that shit coming to him. But the senseless killings he had been doing to take over territories were uncalled for. To Zan, that was pure greed, and he didn't want any parts of it. The shit wasn't going to work in Leo's favor. Now, with the shit going on with Duke, there was no telling what his brother had up his sleeve. There was no way Leo was going to take direct orders or cop anything from Akiel.

It was easy for Zan to run his business plan down to Duke. That was how he obtained the businesses he had opened behind his brother's back. If Duke hadn't given Zan the start-up funds, he wouldn't be in the position to walk away from the shit his brother was letting crumble. Leo, on the other hand, would be a totally different outcome because he wouldn't be understanding at all.

Zan went to Leo's room after a brief nap and knocked repeatedly with no answer. No matter how many times he called his brother, the calls went unanswered. There was only one place Leo could be, and Zan hoped like hell his assumption was wrong.

Picking his phone up, Zan pressed the button and waited for the call to connect. He was hungry as hell and figured he would order room service after his conversation. Cherelle's face appeared on the screen, and Zan smiled. His wife was lying in the bed in all her glory. She stretched her arms over her head, causing her breasts to perk up at him.

"Did I wake you?" Zan asked, lying back on the bed.

"Yeah, but it's alright. Zymia had me up all night. Baby, you're gonna have to stop putting her to sleep on your chest. She has become accustomed to that, and I'm not doing it. She screamed for what felt like forever until I put her on my chest. She's lucky I hate seeing her cry for long periods because I would've let her little ass exercise those lungs."

"Cherelle, you bet' not ever let my baby cry like that. If she's crying for two minutes, her little face turns red as hell."

"Well, I guess she will be a human tomato until you get ya ass back here to cater to her privileged tail. You have her spoiled rotten, and she's not even six months yet. Anyway, how's things going in Jamaica?"

Zan rubbed his hand over his waves and licked his lips. Cherelle's kitty jumped as she watched her husband. His caramel skin tone along with his bushy eyebrows did something to her every time. His pink lips gave off James Todd Smith vibes. Zan seemed to have zoned out in deep thought.

"Is everything okay, babe?" Cherelle asked with concern.

"I want out. Leo is about to do something stupid; I can feel it in my soul. Usually when I have that gut feeling, it's never wrong."

"What happened? Talk to me, Zan."

Zan ran everything down to Cherelle and she sat listening without interruption. It was music to her ears hearing that her husband wanted to get out of the game for the sake of her and their daughter. Cherelle wanted Zan to leave the streets alone when they were in the dating stages of their relationship. He always said the timing wasn't right. The fear of getting a call saying he was shot or dead always forced Cherelle to be up practically all-night waiting for Zan to come home.

"I don't know how Leo is going to handle my decision."

"Leo has to honor that shit! The fuck you mean? He has his life and you have yours. You've made money hand over fist, bought us a home, and have plenty of money in the bank to live comfortably. You have money coming in while you're sleeping, Zan. The only reason you're still running around in the streets is because of Leo's ass!"

"You're not wrong. That's why I love you, baby. You may not like me being in the streets, but you didn't stress me the fuck out every day reminding me about the shit."

"Nah, I don't have time for that. You wanted to be in the streets, and that was your choice. All I did was make sure the insurance was paid every month. You're a grown-ass man and I'm not your mother. The only thing I could ever do is make suggestions to you. It's up to you to take heed. I loved you in the streets, and I will love you even more once you get out."

The sound of Zymia's soft cries filled Zan's ears and he started smiling again. Cherelle propped the phone against the pillow and got up to get the baby out of the bassinet on the side of the bed. Zan's wife was butterball naked, and the view caused his member to brick up. He had plans to wax that ass soon as he stepped foot back in that house. Watching her from afar was nothing short of torture.

Cherelle climbed back on the bed and plopped her left titty in Zamia's mouth. Zan's mouth watered just observing the natural task.

"Back to what I was saying," Cherelle said as she got comfortable. "Don't hesitate to tell Leo your plans. It's either he accepts it or he won't. What is he gon' do, say you can't get out?"

"I'm gon' tell him when I believe he is up and about. Tend to my baby, and I love you. I need to get some food in my system before my stomach growls again."

"I love you too, Zander Miller." Cherelle smirked because she knew Zan hated when she called him by his full name.

"I see you got jokes. Get off my phone. I'll talk to you later on tonight."

Zan ended the call and immediately ordered food while scrolling to find something to watch on television. While waiting for his food to arrive, he called Leo again and got the same result. No answer. Not being able to contact his brother was truly bothering Zan. Leo had never gone so long without answering his phone, especially when they were so far away from home.

***

"Damn, Avita! Yo' shit tight as fuck," Leo groaned as he bit the side of her neck. "Throw that pussy back on me."

Leo had been deep in Avita's guts since he walked through the door of her home. She jumped in his arms, kissing him passionately, and he carried her straight to the bedroom. The two of them were attached like Siamese twins from sun up to sundown. Leo knew just where to go when he hit the Jamaican streets to relieve stress, and he wasn't disappointed.

"I'm about to cum, baby!"

"Wet me up then!" Leo growled as he stroked deeper.

"Aaaaaahhhh!" Avita squirted on Leo's dick and did just what he demanded.

The flow seemed to be everlasting. Leo let his load loose in her love cave, causing his spine to stiffen as he collapsed on her back. Rolling to the side, Leo breathed in deeply as he struggled to catch his breath. Avita rose from the bed and walked into the bathroom. The sound of water running could be heard, but Leo couldn't move. With his eyes closed, Leo felt the warmth of wetness as Avita wiped away their sins of lovemaking.

"Thank you, baby. I don't have the strength to get up right now."

"Mommy! Mommy!" The sound of little knocks on the door brought a smile to Leo's face.

He gathered up strength from within as he hopped up from the bed and slipped on a pair of shorts. Avita put on a robe as she walked across the room. Opening the door, she looked down into the pair of hazel-colored eyes of her three-year-old daughter, Amoy. The chocolate beauty was a replica of her mother. Her long black wavy hair flowed over her shoulders as she stood looking up at Avita. A beautiful goddess. Amoy was definitely living up to her name.

"I'm hungry," Amoy said in her little Jamaican accent. "Are you going to cook soon, Mommy?"

Avita nodded her head and stepped aside. Amoy looked deeper into the room and her deep dimples appeared when her eyes landed on Leo. Like a track star, Amoy jetted across the room and jumped into Leo's arms, hugging his neck tightly.

"Daddy! I've missed you! When did you get home? Are you staying this time?"

Amoy's mouth ran a mile a minute, not giving Leo a chance to answer any of her questions. Pulling back and letting his neck go, Amoy palmed his face in her little hands. Leo fell in love all over again. He missed his daughter just as much as she missed him.

"I've missed you too, Munchkin. Have you been good for mommy while I've been away?"

"Yes, Daddy." She smiled. "Are you staying? Mommy is so sad when you're not here with us."

Amoy tried to whisper, but Avita heard every word she said, and it warmed her heart knowing her daughter was looking out for her. Leo glanced over Amoy's shoulder at Avita before giving his daughter his undivided attention.

"I'm here for a couple days, baby girl. You know Daddy has to work."

"But you're always working. The other kids have their daddies all the time. I want mine too." A lone tear rolled down Amoy's face and that tugged at Leo's heart. He kissed her cheek as he wiped the tear away.

"How about I make arrangements to stay for a little while longer? Remember, I still have to leave again for work."

"Yes, stay!" Amoy's face beamed.

Leo laughed as he put his daughter down. "Go get your house slippers so we can go in the kitchen and make chocolate chip pancakes."

"Yayyyyyyy! My favorite. Meet you in the kitchen, Daddy," Amoy screamed as she ran from the room.

Leo glanced in Avita's direction and anger was evident on her face. He knew it broke her heart every time he popped up and had to leave soon after. Leo and Avita had been messing around for the past four years, and Amoy was created without plans. When he came to visit Duke to re-up, Avita hit him with news about the baby. She wanted him to take their relationship to the next level and move to Jamaica. Leo didn't see himself living in the village and refused to move. Avita instantly said she was going to terminate the pregnancy causing him to yoke her up quickly. After a heated argument that led to passionate sex, Avita decided to keep the baby and live with the terms Leo set in place; to be his woman while caring for his child until he returned. Leo sent plenty of money to Avita every month and made sure he called when he could.

"Are you staying longer, or are you playing with my daughter's emotions?" Avita asked crossing her arms.

"I don't lie to *our* child. If I said I was staying, that's what the fuck I meant. Long as I'm taking care of Amoy and she knows I'm her daddy, there shouldn't be any problems," Leo said, walking up on Avita. "You know I love you, right?"

"You don't love nobody but yourself, Leo. Coming through to get the pussy doesn't equate to loving me. That's about all you love besides Amoy."

"The pussy is mine by passage, Avita. That's not the only reason I love you," Leo said, kissing the side of her mouth. "You are the mother of my only child, and that speaks volume."

"Being here for Amoy is far better than sending a fucking check every month! She needs her daddy. Hell, I need you, Leo. Loving you from a distance is getting old. For the past four years, I've dedicated my life to you, and I only see you when it benefits you. I'm tired of living this life that's only good for you. There's someone out there that would be willing to love me the way I deserve to be loved. I don't need this sometime love you are dishing out to me. It's either you're going to love me wholeheartedly, or you're going to leave me the fuck alone."

The only words Leo heard was, there's somebody out there that would be willing to love her the way she needs to be loved. Grabbing her around the neck lightly, Leo pushed Avita against the wall and placed his mouth against her ear. "I will kill yo' ass if I ever find out you got a nigga around my daughter or my pussy. Do you hear me? This is not a game you want to play, Avita. If you ever say some slick shit like that to me again, there will be hell to pay."

"Daddy, I'm ready for pancakes now." Amoy appeared in the doorway with a little apron draped over her body.

Leo stepped away from Avita and slipped his feet in a pair of slides. Leo grabbed his phone then his daughter's hand, then walked out of the bedroom leaving Avita with tears running down her face. For years, she thought about Leo's life in Chicago. There was no way he was going without being with other women. It was months on end before she saw him, and when he was in her presence, his phone never rang. That was a red flag itself, but Avita never questioned him about it. She wasn't stupid by far. Someone was keeping his side of the bed warm when he was in hers getting her back broke in two.

Avita swiped a hand down her face and went into the bathroom to shower. She couldn't be mad because she agreed to the arrangements that were set in place. Having Leo there was better than not having him at all. It hurt to know that he wasn't willing to become a family man, but what could she actually do about it? Avita had what no other woman in the world had, and that was a child by the man she loved with every fiber of her being.

Thirty minutes later, Avita joined Leo and Amoy in the kitchen. The table was set for three and there were pancakes, eggs, bacon, toast, coffee, and orange juice for Amoy ready to be eaten. Taking a seat, Avita started putting food on plates as Leo walked over while helping Amoy carry a platter of fruit to the table.

"Mommy, we did good, right?" Amoy asked, jumping up and down.

"Yes, baby. Everything smells delicious. Sit so we can eat before the food gets cold."

Leo stared at Avita's face and she didn't possess the happiness she had when he first showed up. He knew it was his fault for her mood change, but there was nothing more he could do other than extend his stay. Being with Avita and Amoy full-time was out of the question because he had Icy back at home. Loving two women at once with a slew of other bitches at his beck and call was hard fucking work. Leo managed to make the shit work to his advantage though.

Icy would forever be the woman that won his heart. That was the reason he made plans to make her his wife. Leo had love for Avita as well, but she would never be anything other than the mother of his child. When he was in Jamaica, she was his everything. That shit came to halt when he touched American soul. It went back to his worlds never colliding, and that was the way it would always be.

"Mommy, wi cya guh out inna di village todah? Mi wa fi show daadie di island"

"Amoy, remember I told you when Daddy is around, you have to speak English so he can understand."

"Sorry, Mommy. Can we?"

"You have to ask Daddy," Avita said, looking over at Leo.

"Daddy, can we go to the village? I want to show you the island."

Leo couldn't tell her no because Amoy won him over with the puppy dog eyes she threw at him.

"Anything for you, pretty girl. We can go when I wake up from a nap. Daddy's tired." Leo's phone vibrated on the table. Turning the phone over, he saw Zan calling for the thousandth time since he left him the night before. "I'll be right back. I have to take this," Leo said, standing to his feet. Walking quickly to the patio, Leo answered the phone before it went to voicemail.

"Where the fuck you at?" his brother snapped before Leo could utter hello.

"Don't question my whereabouts, brah. Listen to me and listen to me good. I want you to head back to Chicago. Do not get on Duke's private jet."

"Leo, what the fuck are you about to do?" Zan asked. "You moving funny, nigga, and I don't like that shit. I've been blowing yo' shit up and this is the first time you've answered."

Leo didn't want to tell Zan where he was because he didn't know anything about Avita and Amoy. In fact, nobody knew about his life in Jamaica, and he wanted to keep it that way. Zan loved Icy as if she was his blood sister and he would go in on his brother if he knew Leo had a whole family he failed to mention.

"I'm not up to nothing. The shit Duke pulled didn't sit well with me, and I needed time to clear my fuckin' head of the bullshit. Do I need permission to kick back and enjoy the sun in Jamaica? Last time I checked, I was a nigga that paid his own muthafuckin' bills and is grown as hell."

"We were only supposed to be here a couple days and head back together. Since when do we change plans without consulting each other?"

"Since now, nigga! You know how to hold shit down 'til I return," Leo barked.

"That's what I wanted to talk to you about. Brah, you gon' have to get on the line and call Stack, Smooth, Boom, or Pip to run your shit 'til you get back."

"The fuck you mean?" Leo snapped. "You my muthafuckin' eyes and ears when I'm away. What the fuck has changed now?"

"I've been thinking about this for a while and the time to tell you is now. I'm out, Leo. Zymia made me think about the changes I needed to make in my life. Dealing and being in the streets isn't something I want to do anymore. I have a family to care for, bro.

Being in that line of work would only lead us to jail or in the grave, and my baby girl needs me for the long haul."

The line went quiet. Leo was pacing back and forth as he deciphered what his brother had said to him. Zan was his heavy hitta, and hearing he wanted to bow out was pissing him off. At a time when Duke stabbed him in the back with his position, and now he was losing his right hand. Nah, there was no way he could agree with that shit,

"You think it's that easy to walk away from this operation, Zan? The rules that apply to any other nigga apply to yo' ass too. There's no getting out! You know too much about my shit for me to just let you walk away."

Zan was surprised at the way his brother was coming for him. Leo knew how much he loved his daughter, and jeopardizing his livelihood for the streets was nonnegotiable. His response further let Zan know that he didn't give a damn about anyone but himself.

"You don't have to *let* me do shit! I stand on what the fuck I said. I'm out, nigga! If you want to handle me like the niggas standing behind you, my brother, you got me fucked all the way up. We got the same blood running through our veins, and there's no way you gon' force me to do something I'm against. My word is bond, Leo. I don't give a damn what you do. Nigga, I was there doing the dirt with you. Why the fuck would I rat yo' ass out? Think about that shit the next time you clutter me up with the muthafuckas in yo' camp."

"Muthafucka, I made you!" Leo screamed.

The line was dead silent and prompted Leo to looked at the screen. The call was no longer active, indicating his brother had hung up. Zan's actions had Leo seeing red. There was no way he would leave the conversation hanging the way it was. He was definitely going to bring the shit back to the forefront.

Leo went back inside and finished his breakfast while chopping it up with his daughter. He was going to enjoy the few weeks he decided to spend in Jamaica. He would get in touch with one of his niggas to hold things down until he returned.

Chapter 5

It'd been five days and Leo hadn't returned from his trip in Jamaica. He hadn't returned any of Icy's phone calls and hadn't attempted to pick up the phone to see if she was alright. Never in their entire relationship had Leo ever gone days without communicating. The pit of her stomach churned at the thought of something tragically happening to him. Thinking back on the night Leo was heading to the airport, Icy remembered him saying Zan was blowing his phone up. She raced to the bedroom and grabbed her phone. Dialing Zan's number, she waiting for him to answer while biting on her gel nail.

"What's up, Ice?" he asked when he answered.

"Zan, where's Leo? I haven't heard from him in the past five days."

Zan could hear the nervousness in Icy's voice. Shaking his head, he knew Leo was on some fucked-up shit if he hadn't even called Icy. Not wanting to be the one to tell her what he assumed was going on with Leo, he just told her what he knew as a fact.

"Leo stayed in Jamaica, Ice. He said he would return in a couple weeks."

"What do you mean he will return in a couple weeks? Aren't you with him?"

Zan huffed lowly as he rubbed the top of his head. "No, sis. I'm not with him. I left Jamaica after I told Leo I was done with the streets. He didn't take that shit too well. Look, I don't know what my brother is on. Try calling him. I'm quite sure he will respond for you. Me, not too much. If you need anything, Ice, don't hesitate to call."

"Thank you for answering, Zan. I'll just wait for Leo to call me. I don't want to interrupt whatever he has going on."

"My brother is good. Keep in mind what I said. I'll be in touch."

Icy ended the call with Zan and sat wondering what was going on with her man. Instead of sitting in limbo, she got up to get dressed so she could begin her day. Icy needed to collect booth rent at all three of her salons plus make sure the inventory had arrived. Even though she wasn't in the salons on a regular, she still popped in to make sure her establishments were run accordingly. She had three of the best managers running her businesses and they hadn't failed her as of yet.

She decided on a pair of high-waisted jeans, a lime green shirt, and a pair of lime green Chucks. Icy pulled her hair into a high ponytail and put on a thin coat of lip gloss before gathering everything she needed to put in her purse. Phone in hand, Icy left the house and jumped in her Range Rover, heading to the city. The cool September breeze flowed inside the truck as she jumped on the expressway. With the music keeping her company, Icy's phone rang with an unknown number. Declining the call, she tuned back in to Saweetie's "Best Friend" and Julz entered her mind. Another call from the same unknown number came through, causing the music to stop once again. Icy accepted the call irritably.

"Who the fuck is this?"

There was silence on the other end, and one thing Icy didn't do was play stupid-ass phone games. Over the years, there were plenty of bitches that would call to start shit between her and Leo. At that point, Icy was too grown for the shit and she wasn't about to indulge in the nonsense. Instead of talking to herself, she hung up and automatically called Leo's line. It rang a couple times before he answered.

"What's up, baby?" Leo said smoothly.

"Don't what's up baby me. Why haven't I heard from you?"

"Come on, Icy. You know I'm in Jamaica on business. This shit is taking longer than I expected and I've been tied up so I couldn't call. I told Zan to tell you what was up when he touched back down. He didn't tell you?"

"Yeah, he told me you would be back in a couple weeks, but that wasn't his job to deliver the message to me. You, on the other hand, should've been the one to tell me your plans. Now, what could possibly have you ghosting me for five muthafuckin' days? You have never left our home and not called under any circumstances. What has changed this time?"

Leo hadn't been in a heated confrontation with Icy in nearly a year. He kept his shit tighter than virgin pussy when it came to the women he frequented, but there was no way he could get away to call with Avita on his ass every minute of the day. Just like no one knew about her and Amoy, Avita didn't know anything about Icy. Luck was on Leo's side because he was standing on Duke's property choppin' it up with Maven when he received the call.

"Check my fuckin' location, Icy! What do I have to lie about? I'm still at Duke's crib. You better get the venom out yo' tone because I'm about my money right now."

Icy checked the location and sure enough, Leo was still in Kingston. That didn't make her feel any better because someone was playing on her line, and she knew it had everything to do with the man that claimed he was doing nothing foul.

"If I find out you're fucking around, I will call this wedding off in a heartbeat!"

"Fucking around? Icy, we're not going there. Where is this coming from?"

"One of your minions are on my phone again. When these silent calls start, that's when the bullshit surfaces, Leo. So, whoever you've been ignoring lately, tell them to leave me out of the equation. I'm not dealing with this shit again."

Leo thought about the text he received on the plane and every one thereafter. He knew Icy had every right to be suspicious if someone was calling her phone and not saying anything. Leo was going to nip that shit in the bud soon as he finished his business with Maven. In the meantime, he had to continue lying to the woman on the other end of the line.

There were plenty of times Icy dealt with Leo's drama with other women. On a couple occasions, Icy had to show them hoes not to play with her intelligence. She had to throw hands because she was judged by the way she carried herself instead of where she was actually born and raised. Taking her kindness for weakness, the women were left with a few lumps and some choice words that were delivered personally by Icy. Leo didn't get away scot-free by any means. Icy gave him the silent treatment and made him pay for his indiscretions. She may have forgiven him a couple times, but Leo knew the shit wasn't going to go over so well if she found out he was still stepping out on their relationship.

"I promise, babe, no one should be bothering you because I'm not out here doing nothing. Don't let these hoes narrate a storyline that don't exist. What we have, they want and never will have. So, the only thing they know is to try and destroy us. Nothing can break us, Icy. You're it for me."

The words Leo had spoken sounded good, but Icy was no fool. He had gone through the same song and dance previously. Time would tell what her husband-to-be was doing behind her back.

"Yeah, okay, I'll let you get to what you're doing. I'm pulling up to the salon on the southside."

"I love you, Icy," Leo professed.

"Yup," was Icy's response before ending the call.

Parking in front of Winter's Dreamz, Icy disengaged the engine of her truck and got out. As soon as she walked inside of her establishment, everyone greeted her as if she was a celebrity. Glancing around, she saw there was a full house of clients and stylists, except one person.

"Hey, everyone. I hope everything's going well," Icy said cheerfully. "Um, Cerita, Where's Shonda?"

Icy made her way to the back of the office she shared with Cerita and she knew to follow suit. Once the door was closed, Icy sat in the chair in front of the desk as Cerita dragged her feet to the other side. Icy waited patiently to hear the reason Shonda wasn't at her station perfecting her craft. There was always something going on with her, and it was consistently around the time booth rent was due.

"Shonda called yesterday and said she wouldn't be in today. She sounded as if she had been crying. I believe her dude is putting his hands on her again. Don't quote me on that because I'm not for certain. Last week she came in with a lace front on that covered her left eye. Please give her some slack, Icy. When Shonda shows up, she takes care of her business for sure. If she was slacking, I would be the first to tell you about it."

"Shonda is a damn good stylist. I would never take that from her. But she has to make sure whatever she is going through doesn't interfere with the day I come in to collect my money. Regardless of what she has going on, I need my money," Icy said calmly.

"Speaking of that," Cerita said, opening a drawer. "Shonda paid her rent, Icy."

Cerita slid an envelope across the desk. Icy felt bad for questioning Shonda about payment when she could be going through something more drastic. Taking her phone from her purse, she found Shonda's contact information and pressed the button. The phone rang a couple times and then went into voicemail. She waited for the prompt to leave a message as she looked past Cerita and took in the scene out the window.

"Shonda, this is Icy. Give me a call so that I know you are alright. Thank you for your booth payment, and let me know if you need anything."

Icy ended the call and set back in the chair, thinking about the last encounter Shonda had with her live-in boyfriend Al. He had beaten Shonda so badly that she ended up in the hospital and made a vow to leave him alone. Icy offered to put her up in one of Leo's condos until she was able to save for a place of her own, but Shonda declined after Al promised it would never happen again. Not the one to pry into anyone's affairs, Icy left the situation alone. Until Shonda came to her for help, she wasn't going to force her to leave the toxic relationship she was in.

"What else been going on around here other than the inventory coming in?" Icy asked.

"A woman came by looking for you the other day. She looked as if she came from money. Lots of money," Cerita responded. "When I asked what it was about, she dismissed what I said and told me to tell you to give her a call. I have the card in my purse."

Cerita handed Icy the business card. She stared at the name, Cynthia Scott, and it didn't ring a bell. Icy had never heard of the woman a day in her life, and she was puzzled as to why the woman wanted to speak with her. Putting the card in the small pocket of her purse, Icy stood from her seat and stretched. She hated doing inventory in her salons, but she felt going in to get the job done gave her stylists the opportunity to conduct business up front instead of missing out on business while putting away product. Another reason was to have an accurate count on what she had in stock. There was an issue a while back where product was coming up missing at one point.

"Cerita, your client is waiting in your chair," Yvonne said from the doorway.

"Okay, I'll be right out." Cerita turned to Icy. "Is there anything else you need from me?"

"No, I'm going to go through the inventory and then send your money. After that, I'm out. I have to do this shit two more times, so I won't be too long."

"You know I can do the inventory for you, Icy," Cerita said, stopping at the door.

"I know, and I may take you up on that offer. I appreciate you, boo."

Cerita smiled and walked to take care of her client. Icy got to work, making sure her orders were correct. After an hour of working, she was finally ready to head across town. As she walked through the salon, every stylist handed her an envelope for their booth rent, including Cerita. She thanked each of them and left without looking back.

Sitting in her car, Icy placed an order for lunch for her employees. It was something she did at least twice a week to show her appreciation for the work and upkeep they did at the salon.

Backing out of her designated parking spot, Icy hit her playlist and allowed Lil Kim's "Get Money" to flow from the speakers. As she cruised on the Dan Ryan, traffic was pretty light. Cynthia Scott kept running through her mind, but she couldn't put a face with the name.

Icy's phone rang, interrupting her thoughts as she merged on to I-290 toward Maywood. Hitting the button to connect the call to the sound system, Icy smiled when she heard her mother's voice.

"Icy, baby. It sounds like you're driving."

"I am, Ma. How you doing over there?" Icy asked.

"I'm alright. I was wondering if you wanted to go shopping with me. You know an old lady like myself hates to hit up the stores alone."

Icy laughed because her mother was full of shit. Staci didn't need anyone to help her spend money. "Since when?"

"Since today, dammit!" her mother scoffed.

"If you just want me to come along to keep you company, say that. Stop beating around the bush as if you won't go without me."

"If you don't go, I'll call my other daughter to go with me."

Staci waited for Icy to burst a blood vessel at the mention of another daughter, but Icy didn't fall for her shenanigans that day. Her mother got a kick out of calling Julz her daughter when they were younger, and the reaction from Icy was priceless. As they got older, Julz and Icy really thought they were sisters in real life. The statement didn't get under her skin anymore.

"You probably called her first anyway. What time are you talking? Because I'm heading to Maywood to do inventory and collect rent," Icy said, getting off the expressway at First Avenue.

"What do you pay management for if you have to do the work on your own, Icy? Go collect the money and meet me at the house in two hours. We can head out from there. You have to start trusting the folks that's in your salons every day to do their job accordingly. If they don't handle business, replace their asses."

"Believe it or not, I was just thinking about that after I left Winter's Dreamz on the southside. Hearing you confirm my thoughts, I'm going to give it a shot. I'll meet you at your house in two. I love you, mean old lady."

"I love you too, baby girl. Now, I have to go in here and pay the water bill," Staci said, scrambling around.

"Why can't you pay the bill online like I showed you, Ma?"

"There's only one place I can pay *this* bill Icy, and over the phone ain't it."

"I don't understand why you can't pay the bill from your phone. If you forgot how, just say that."

"Girl, I'm going to piss. Is that better?"

Icy couldn't do anything but laugh. Her mother had a way with words when she wanted to say something discreetly. That phrase took the cake because Icy was laughing hard as hell as she pulled into the parking lot of her salon. Wiping the tears from her eyes, she lowered the visor to check her eyeliner.

"Get off my phone and I'll see you soon."

"Remember what I said, Icy. Collect the money and get out of there. I don't have all day to play with you."

"I heard you loud and clear, woman. I got you."

Icy ended the call and chucked her phone inside her purse as she killed the engine and got out. Entering the salon, she noticed once again business was popping, and all she saw was dollar signs. The sound of R&B was lowly playing, and a few conversations were going on as well. Sean was the first to notice Icy, and he immediately went into his dramatics that she came to love when she first met him.

"Yasssssss, the Queen has arrived! It's time to pay up, bitches, because time is money!" He clapped his hands as he walked around, making sure the stylists were gathering Icy's coins.

"Why you didn't do this shit before Boss Lady entered the building?" Red asked, rolling her eyes as she dug deep into her purse.

"She wasn't here, and now she is. The fuck!"

"Aye, language please," Icy sternly said. "This is still a place of business. I don't care how comfortable you are with your clients. My place will not become the ratchet place that gets talked about in reviews. We will continue to be classy and far from trashy."

One of the clients scoffed before saying, "If you only knew how things are handled when you're not here. It's like a whole club in this place. That's probably why it takes so long for me to get in and out of a chair."

The way Sean's head swiveled in her direction caused Icy to laugh out loud. She knew the woman wasn't lying because there were a few instances she had come in to a bunch of nonsense. Icy had talked to Sean about it because he was in charge when she wasn't around. It seemed as if things hadn't changed because the same thing was still going on.

"You have been sitting there maybe twenty minutes and you're complaining. Stop with the madness, bi—"

"Sean, you bet' not!" Icy scolded him. "No matter what is said or done, always conduct yourself in a professional manner at all times."

"Yes, listen to your shop mama, lil simp," the client said with a smirk.

Icy turned on her feet like a ballerina in the woman's direction. "See, I just got him off your ass and you want to come back with some slick shit. Get yo' ass out of my place of business. All money isn't good money, and if you can't respect my staff, you can go get your hair done someplace else."

"This ain't the only salon in Illinois. I've been to better places than this dump." Storming out of the salon, the woman stomped all the way to her car and peeled out of the parking lot.

"Let me tell y'all something. I want all the bullshit to stop today. We didn't lose a client today because of whatever goes on in here. We lost a client because I had to check myself before I beat the fuck out of her ass. In order for me to keep my professionalism, I'm going to need y'all to act like this is a place of business. If I have to repeat myself again, I will close this bitch down and get a whole new staff. Respect my shit as if I'm in here alongside y'all all day." Icy looked around the salon at her stylists, and she had their undivided attention.

"Sorry for having to express myself publicly, but it needed to be done. Sean, I need to see you in the back. The rest of you, have my money ready when I return."

Icy made her way to the back of the salon because she wasn't finished with her rant. Sean had been warned before about the way he handled her business. She was going to make sure this time was the last. When Sean entered the office, he closed the door and sat on the sofa along the wall, crossing his legs at the ankles.

Flamboyant as they came, Sean was a fashionista. With his short rainbow-colored hair spiked on top his head, his face was beat better than most women Icy had ever seen. The black leather pants fit his thighs like a glove along with a black one-sleeved midriff shirt that showed off his toned abs. The black and pink Balenciaga sneakers took his outfit to another level, and it looked damn good on him.

"Sean, we've had this conversation before about this being a salon and not a nightclub. If you can't conduct business and manage my shit respectfully, let me know now," Icy snarled. "The last thing I want to do is release you of your duties because other than this shit, you are doing your fucking job. How hard is it for you to remain professional?"

"Icy, I'm not going to lie to you. We have fun. Yes, we listen to music. Yup, we dance while still styling hair, but it doesn't interfere with what we do as stylists. The nail techs are even rocking in their seats without missing a beat. That bitch who just complained to you has a problem with me because her man won't stay the fuck out my ass!"

Icy choked on the little bit of saliva that eased down her throat after hearing what Sean said. After getting her breathing under control, Icy looked at Sean with a smirk on her face. Reaching over to the mini refrigerator for a bottled water, she unscrewed the top and took a hefty drink.

"You mean to tell me she wasn't in here to get her hair done?" Icy finally found her voice to ask.

"Hell nawl! That bitch been sitting in here following my every move for the past thirty minutes. I didn't put her on blast because you interrupted me." He laughed. "Her nigga been on the downlow for the past year that I know of. That's how long he's been fuckin' with me and paying all my bills. The bitch is mad and is blaming me for the muthafucka not making his way home."

"Sean, you know that shit is wrong. If you know he has a woman, why keep messing around with him?"

"Ask his ass why he's fuckin' with me! All I wanted was an ounce of weed, and he offered that and dick. How was I supposed to turn that down? Ain't no way. And his ass hung like a horse too." Sean twerked in his seat with his hands in the air. "I don't want him as a man because he's not trustworthy. I'm straight with him coming through dropping dick and cash. I don't need a commitment from his cheating ass. On top of that, I'm not fit to be nobody's step-mama."

Icy was once again in tears because Sean was the realest man she knew. He may have loved the same things Icy did, but he was true to his way of living. Sean and Icy had met one night at a club the year her father was murdered. She and Julz went out to get their minds off what was going on around them and they had the time of their lives with Sean. When she opened her first salon, he wanted to be her first stylist, but refused to work on the southside. Icy didn't think twice about calling him soon as she bought the building in Maywood. Sean became her manager off top, and he was the most sought-out stylist she had at that location.

Once she got herself under control, Icy put her professional face back on. She knew deep down she couldn't control what Sean did outside of the shop on his time, but he was definitely going to have to keep that shit from disturbing the peace inside her establishment. Whatever he had to do, she wanted him to do it by any means necessary.

"All I ask is that you don't bring your affairs here, Sean. That shit is bad for business. I don't need any negativity being posted about my place of business. This is not a place I want *Zeewiththetea* to get any dirt."

"I'll talk to the nigga about his rugrat. There isn't much more I can do than that. It's up to him to control her moves. With me still being a man, Icy, I can only have my lil cousins on standby to whoop her ass. The only promise I can definitely make is the shit won't happen anywhere near here. You have my word on that." Sean sat back, admiring his coffin-shaped nails as if he was seeing them for the first time.

"Well, long as I got my point across, we should be good, right?" Sean nodded his head yes, and that's all the confirmation Icy needed. "Onto other things. With you being manager, I'm handing all inventory duties over to you. We haven't had any problems with product walking out the door. Let's keep it that way."

"Queen Ice, who you think you're talking to, them southside bitches?" Sean asked with his right eyebrow raised. "I've been doing inventory here for the longest. That's why when you come in, you collect yo' money and leave. Carry on, boo. I got you."

"You know I'm with you when you're right." Icy chuckled. "I kind of forgot how lucrative you were with my spot. It's your shenanigans I can do without. Thanks for staying on top of shit for me. I gotta roll out of here though. My mama wanna go shopping, and now I'm on her time."

Icy stood and threw her purse over her shoulder and walked from around the desk. Sean stood as well, and the two embraced and gave air kisses before heading out the door. He looked at Icy's ass before patting her on it as she strutted down the hall.

"Leo putting a hurting on them cheeks, hunty! That ass getting phat!"

"Sean, stop playing with me. Ain't a soul going in that entrance baby! It hurts to shit, let alone allowing a dick to violate my sacred hole. I'm gon' leave that shit to you, because I don't play those type of games."

"Ain't nothing to it, but to do it," Sean sang before laughing. "Girl, you don't know what you missing."

"Long as I don't know, there's no way for me to wonder. Now shut up talking to me." Icy was mad as hell. She walked around the room, snatching money from each stylist before she made her way to the door. Turning around, she pointed her finger at Sean with a scowl on her face. "Remember what we talked about. Hit my line if anything go down in here."

"I'm calling you anyway because we gotta go out and have some fun. It's been a while."

Icy threw her middle finger in the air and left without saying anything verbally to Sean. As she sat in the driver seat of her truck, Icy could see Sean cackling while looking out of the window. She wanted to go back inside and smack the taste out his mouth for saying that bullshit to her. Deciding to skip the trip to the northside, Icy instead called and informed Nycie that she would come collect the rent the next day. She also told her about taking care of the inventory. Once she had conducted her business, Icy headed back to the south suburbs to her mother's house.

Meesha

Chapter 6

Leo sat outside of Avita's home, thinking about everything that was taking place in Kingston, along with the conversation he had with Icy the day before. The last thing he wanted to do was allow Icy's suspiciousness to throw him off the tasks he should've been focusing on. Leo was for sure going to get to the bottom of the harassment as soon as he stepped on US soil because he knew exactly who the culprit was. The chime of the burner phone he purchased after extending his trip brought him out of his thoughts, causing him to open the message immediately.

Maven: Stage one under way. Akiel won't step off his front porch when he emerges from behind the door. Duke won't live through tonight. I think it would be best for you to get out of Dodge before shit hits the fan. Be ready for the call and have a strong alibi. Far as everyone knows, you left when your brother left, so make sure you keep that in mind. Also, remember what I told you.

Leo: Say less.

Standing to his feet, Leo sighed lowly as he prepared himself mentally to tell Avita he was heading out immediately. After he met up with Maven, Leo had booked a flight just in case he had to leave abruptly, and he was glad he followed his first mind. Having Maven on his side for the revenge plot was sweet. Maven didn't like the way Duke overlooked him just the same as Leo.

Maven told Leo what was going on in depth with Duke's condition. He was suffering from a rare form of brain cancer that was breaking his mentor down with each passing day. Duke was given six months to live, and that was the reason he wanted to discuss the changes in his operation. Thinking quick on his feet, Leo asked Maven if he knew anyone that he could discreetly obtain cyanide from, and Maven just nodded his head.

"Don't worry about Duke. There's no way you would be able to get close to him. Leave that part to me. I know his and Kenise's nighttime schedule. Duke takes capsules, so it will be easy to fill his medication with the poison. I wasn't always just the right-hand; I

*was Duke's deadly weapon that is about to be formed against him."
Maven smiled evilly. "This is definitely going to bring Akoni back
to the Motherland. We have to be prepared."*

Leo didn't know a lot about Duke's only son, but what he did
know about Akoni was that he wasn't to be fucked with. Akoni may
not have wanted anything to do with his father's business, but that
didn't mean he didn't care about the man that raised him to be the
man he had become. Duke rarely spoke about his son to anyone. In
fact, he told everyone he had written him off as his son. Leo didn't
know how true that was, so he had to tread lightly after the shit he'd
put in place to bring down Duke.

After all Duke had done for Leo, one would wonder why he
wanted to take the old man out. For starters, with Duke gone, Leo
learned he would benefit more with Duke being dead than alive.
Maven disclosed that Duke had put Leo in his will and he was set
to inherit one hundred million upon Duke's demise. That was more
than Leo had made in the ten years of working under Duke, and he
was all for it. With Akiel out of the picture, an additional two million would go to Leo, and so would the empire. It was a win-win for
the nigga from Chicago, and he could taste the wealth a mile away.

"Leo, you've been quiet today. Is everything alright?" Avita
asked from the opened patio door.

"Yeah, I'm good," he said, walking to the door, encircling his
arms around her waist. "Look, don't be upset. I have to fly back out
today. In the next hour, to be exact."

"Come on, Leo." Avita groaned, twisting out of his grasp. "You
said you would be here for a couple weeks and it's only been what,
one week? I'm tired of dis shit! Yuh cum an guh as yuh please an
tink funds wit tek di place of yuh absence. Amoy needs her fada full
time! Hell, mi need yuh!"

The hurt in Avita's eyes was mixed with a tint of anger as well.
Leo knew she was mad because she refrained from using her native
tongue when addressing him. He understood her frustrations, but
there was nothing he could do to change the plans he had arranged.
Avita would just have to understand and wait for his return. Whenever that may be.

"I'm sorry, babe. Some shit came up that needs my undivided attention—"

"Your daughter needs your attention! What could be more important than that, Leo?"

"Business! How the fuck do you think I'm able to send you damn near ten grand a month? I hope you don't think that shit comes magically out the sky, Avita. A nigga busts his ass to provide for y'all and I have to go handle some shit that's jeopardizing my paper. You act like I'm never coming back!"

Leo didn't have time to deal with Avita's temper tantrum. He had to pack and get the hell out of there before all hell broke loose in Kingston. Once shit hit the fan, Duke's people were going to lock every fuckin' thing down and he would be stuck in that muthafucka. It was something he couldn't risk because Leo wouldn't make it another day in Jamaica if he was to get locked in.

"There's more to your story, and don't think I'm blind to the fact. Every time your phone rings, you head outside out of earshot. I'm not crazy by far, Leo. Whatever you're doing back in the States will eventually come to light. Trust me though, there is something going on that I don't know about, but you won't be able to keep that secret too much longer."

Walking away from Avita and her angry rant, Leo entered the bedroom and started packing. Avita was still talking shit and he had tuned her all the way out. He was going to allow her to think whatever she thought was going on in his life. If she kept it up, she might find out the hurtful truth she was seeking. Leo wasn't trying to go the route Avita was pushing him toward, so he kept packing without saying a word.

Amoy halted her mother's words when she stood in the doorway with tears in her little eyes. "Where you going, Daddy?" she sniffled.

Leo stood to his full height and in a couple of strides, scooped his daughter in his arms, hugging her tightly. "Daddy has to go away for a while. I'll make sure to call you every day, okay?"

"How long will you be gone?"

As Leo and Amoy talked, Avita left the room fuming. She had been watching Leo go from hot to cold in a matter of seconds since the day before. She witnessed him take phone calls outside while giving her the cold shoulder while doing it. Without addressing her thoughts, she kept them to herself because she didn't want Amoy to see her parents going back and forth with each other in an aggressive manner. That wasn't the way she wanted to raise her daughter, but she couldn't hold back any longer.

Avita sacrificed a lot to be with Leo for him not to even try to take them away from Kingston. Her family as a whole disowned her when she refused to marry the man they'd chosen for her to be with. Avita didn't give a damn about the amount of money Kimbo had; she just didn't love him. Kimbo was old enough to be her father and her parents expected her to just devote herself to a man that had been looking at her like prey since she had budding breasts at the age of thirteen. With her refusal, Avita was forced to live by any means necessary until the day she met Leo.

Leo took her away from the village and treated her like royalty, especially when she found out she was pregnant. The smile Leo had on his face was everything to her and he was in Kingston the very next day. The father of her daughter was very attentive throughout her entire pregnancy. Everything seemed very promising, and Avita truly thought she would've been heading back to Chicago with him. Amoy was three, going on four years old, and they were still in Kingston without the man she loved.

"I'm about to get out of here so I can catch this flight," Leo said as he walked into the living room with Amoy in one arm and his luggage in the other.

Avita broke her gaze from the window and stared at him uncaringly.

Placing Amoy on the sofa next to her mother, Leo leaned in to kiss Avita's cheek and she turned her head completely, causing him to catch her ear. Shaking his head, he kissed his daughter and left without another word. Tears flowed down Avita's face as she tried her best to hide her emotions from her daughter.

"Don't cry, Mommy. Daddy will be back in a little bit. He promised," Amoy assured her mother while wiping her small hands down her face.

Avita's heart was hammering in her chest, but she had to gather herself in front of her child. While Amoy thought her mama was sad because her daddy had to leave, Avita's heart was hurting because she knew Leo was going back to the States to appease another woman. Business wasn't his reason for leaving. He had to do damage control. Leo would only be able to lie for so long before all his dishonesty smacked him in the face.

***

Leo slept through the entire flight and was well rested. He had put his phone on do not disturb because Avita was calling non-stop, crying and fussing about why she felt he left Kingston. Leo understood why she was upset, but there was no way he could pack her and Amoy up, move them to the States, and still keep their relationship a secret. He'd brainstormed many scenarios and came up with quite a few that may actually work. But, in reality, they were disasters waiting to happen, and Leo didn't think the risk was worth it.

"We are about to land in the Windy City!" the pilot said over the intercom system. "The temperature is sixty-five degrees, a little bit chilly, so hopefully, all of you have a sweater or jacket to keep you warm. The Chicago wind can be really disrespectful at times. Thank you for flying with us."

Stretching his limbs, Leo couldn't wait for the doors to open so he could be the first to get off. Soon as he was able, he snatched his luggage from the overhead bin and made his way out of the aircraft. Leo turned his phone on as he walked through the tunnel and his notifications starting sounding immediately. Stack had left a message stating he'd left Leo's car in the airport parking lot on the third floor, which he was happy about because he wasn't trying to be sitting around waiting for anyone to pick him up on their time. Avita had sent several messages, but he bypassed all of them because he wasn't trying to hear all the shit she was probably saying. Icy, on the other hand, hadn't reached out to him, which he wasn't necessarily worried about because she had no clue he was back in town. The one that got his attention was from Maven. Stepping out of the way of people trying to get out of the airport, Leo leaned against the wall and opened the text.

Maven: Mission Accomplished. Check number two for details.

Leo searched his bag for his burner to see what awaited from Maven. He knew it was something great, but had to see with his own eyes. Leo clicked the link and noticed it was a video. Opting to wait until he was alone in his car, he walked in search of his vehicle. It took fifteen minutes to find his Audi R8 Coupe. Walking around to the back tire, Leo ran his hand under the frame and retrieved his key fob. After throwing his luggage in the trunk, he walked around his ride to make sure there wasn't a scratch in sight. He let Stack hold his baby down while he was gone and knew the nigga was stunting hard in his shit. Satisfied with the results, Leo got into the driver's seat and pulled his phone out of his pocket. After pushing the button to bring his car to life, he clicked on the link.

A news reporter stood broadcasting in front of a home in Kingston where police officers were on the scene collecting evidence. A small crowd of people could be seen in the distance behind a barricade that prevented them from getting close to the crime scene.

"We are broadcasting live in front of a residence in Orange Grove, where twenty-nine-year-old Akiel Ottey was gunned down in cold blood," the female reporter said in her heavy Jamaican accent. *"The Jamaican Constabulary Force was summoned to the home after receiving several calls for shots fired. Ottey was found face down in a pool of blood on the front lawn. Ottey suffered ten gunshot wounds to his chest, head, and legs, and succumbed to his injuries."*

Leo smiled as if he had won the lottery as he pumped his fist. Focusing back to the video, he listened with raised eyebrows. The end results were the icing on the cake.

"The Ottey family not only endured one tragedy, but two. After hearing about his nephew's murder, Aduke "Duke" Ottey suffered a heart attack and died in his wife's arms. The multi-millionaire was well loved in the villages, and everyone appreciated all the help he provided to families in need. There aren't any suspects in custody for Akiel's murder at this time. Law Enforcement is planning to investigate this crime diligently. If you know anything about this crime, please contact the Kingston Police immediately."

Leo put the gear in drive and drove out of the airport parking lot smiling like a Cheshire cat. "In a Minute" by Lil Baby blasted through the speakers as he flamed up while cruising though the garage. He dialed Maven as he hit the street heading to his destination.

"I guess you got my message," Maven said without saying hello.

"Hell yeah, I did! How's the atmosphere that way?"

"Shit is hectic," Maven responded. "Kenise is distraught. I didn't think about how much Duke's death would impact her."

"Man, fuck that! Both of them niggas had to go. Duke brought this shit on himself and he was the one to cost Akiel his life. The muthafucka was gon' run the business into the ground anyway."

"Have a heart, Leo!"

"My heart is colder than Antarctica, nigga! When it comes to the Ottey family, I have no feelings. The way Duke played me was never going to be the talk of the town," Leo snapped. "I know you not going soft on me now. Your hands are just as dirty as mine. I was the mastermind, but you made that shit happen. Let me know if you about to roll on me, Mav."

"You're right. I'm all the way in this shit just like you are. So, how do you think I can roll on you? My hands are just as bloody as the person that pulled the trigga. Telling on you would be telling on myself. Do I look stupid?"

"You the one over there sounding softer than a marshmallow. This shit better stay under investigation and go unsolved. If anyone becomes suspicious, you better plead the fifth!"

Maven didn't like the way Leo was coming at him. At some point things were going to go in a different direction because of his mouth. While he was acting as if Maven would snitch, Leo was showing his true colors. If shit got hot, he would be the first to run his mouth like diarrhea to get the heat off his ass. Maven was strategizing in case he was put in the spotlight. He knew how the Ottey clan reacted to deception. Death was the sentence for what he and Leo had done.

"Whatever. I'll be in contact with information about the memorial services. They will be in the next couple days, so be ready to hop on the jet. We need things to be normal as possible."

"What about my money, nigga?"

"Duke's body isn't even cold, greedy son of a bitch! There's no way we can jump in and take that money right now. Duke has an estate that has to be read by a lawyer. We are talking about millions of dollars, not a couple thousand. This is not some ghetto shit that can be done without a middle man. You're ready to put yourself in the spotlight. You're pathetic!" Maven was angry and ended the call without allowing Leo to respond.

"I'm gon' end up killin' his ass," Leo mumbled as he accelerated on the highway.

Twenty minutes later, he pulled into the parking lot of his downtown condo. Counting to ten, he got out of his vehicle and made his way inside. Instead of waiting on the elevator, Leo took the stairs to the fourth floor. Entering with his key, he headed to the bedroom after locking the door, Leo didn't bother turning on the light as he walked to the bed.

"Get the fuck up!" he barked.

Desiree scrambled under the covers as Leo's voice jolted her out of the deep sleep she was enjoying. He had scared her shitless. Leo hadn't responded to any of her calls nor texts for over a week. Figuring he was ignoring her purposely caused her messages to become darker by the day. Little did Desiree know, her messages had nothing to do with the anger Leo was about to unleash.

"What, what—" Desiree stammered as she tried to untangle herself from the sheet.

"What, what my ass, Desi! Why yo' childish ass playing on Icy's phone?"

Shocked turned to anger as Desiree realized why Leo had come barging in her place like the police. So what if she called Icy and muted her phone? The bitch thought she was on top of the world because her man wanted to marry her. If Icy only knew, his dick partially belonged to Desiree.

"How you gon' come in here talking shit ova a bitch you really don't give a fuck about?" Desiree hopped out of the bed butt ass naked. "You picked through the litter and chose me because obviously Icy called you about somebody playing on her phone. Why me?"

"Yo' ass is the one that's mad. I saw some of your messages you left thinking I was back in the states and with Icy. If I was, so what? You ain't my bitch, Desi! Stay in yo' fuckin' lane. Icy ain't going nowhere, bitch. You will forever play second fiddle when it comes to her. You are one of many. She is the only one that matters."

Desiree's blood boiled lava hot listening to Leo talk his shit about another bitch, especially Icy. Her face contorted as if she was possessed. Leo kept going without a care of how she felt about the situation. If he thought she was about to beg and cry, Leo had Desiree all the way fucked up.

"You're mad because you will never be Icy. Her place is locked in stone. Desi, you are another pussy that I can fuck whenever I want to do so. Stop calling her muthafuckin' phone!" Leo snarled.

"Yeah, I called her phone, and you better be lucky I didn't give her the rundown about our relationship. Even though she needs to know you ain't all about her, I couldn't bring myself to deliver that news to her." Desiree paused.

"Yo' ass know—"

"I'm not finished!" she yelled. "You pay all the bills around this muthafucka, keep my pockets laced, and fuck me every chance you get, but you got the nerve to tell me this bitch above me! Every day you're disrespecting that woman behind her back and in the same breath, you got her sitting on a pedestal as if she's a delicate masterpiece. What type of nigga tells his *woman* another bitch is his property manager just to keep her close? A sucka-ass nigga, that's what!"

Leo laughed, leaning on the edge of the dresser with his arms folded over his chest. Desiree sounded stupid to him, and the shit was funny as hell. "I told her that for your safety. If you know like I know, the minute you puff yo' chest out to tell Icy you fuckin' on me, be prepared to fall on yo' shit. I'll still be standing because it's yo' word against mine. But you know not to test me like that. You have nobody outside of me, so choose your words wisely." Leo smirked.

He knew Desiree didn't have anyone to help her if she decided to walk away from Leo. He caught her at a time when she didn't have a pot to piss in and he boosted her up from nothing. The bank account she had was in his name. All Leo had to do was cancel that shit and Desiree would be right back where she started; on the streets. He knew it was wrong to manipulate her in that manner, but Leo didn't want to be without her, even if it was on temporary terms. Many would tell Desiree to run if the situation was known. Since it wasn't, Leo stood watching her facial expression soften with every second that ticked away.

"Fuck you, Leo! Just leave. I'm done with this shit." Desiree snatched a shirt from the drawer beside the bed and pushed her arms through the holes. As she moved to put the shirt over her head, Leo grabbed it, halting her movement.

"I don't know why you puttin' that shit on? I need some pussy."

"I wish I would fuck you after the shit you said to me. Get the hell out of my face."

Desiree tried to snatch away, but Leo wasn't having it. He grabbed her by the throat and pushed her body against the wall. Digging her nails into his hand, Desiree fought to get him off her.

"Let me go!" she screamed in his face.

Instead of doing what she demanded, Leo placed his free hand between her legs and massaged her clit. For someone that didn't want to be bothered, Desiree's love box reacted to his touch instantly. She hated that Leo had so much control over her mind, body, and bank account. She knew she had to do anything possible

80

to ensure he wouldn't strip her of everything she had, even if it meant ignoring the fact that he would never leave Icy. Desiree's heart hurt with every thought of Leo leaving to go back home. Her body shook as the orgasm he was searching for fast approached her core.

"Oh shit," Desiree moaned, sinking her teeth into Leo's chest. "I'm not doing this with you."

"You may not want to do *this*, but your pussy is saying otherwise." Leo strummed her pearl faster.

As he applied pressure on her neck, Desiree squealed like a pig as her secretions flooded the palm of his hand. Before she could catch her breath, Leo had his muscle out of his pants and at her opening. Desiree tried to forcibly push him away, but failed miserably. Guiding his member into her love cave, Leo stroked her inner folds like he loved her, but only got lost in her essence.

"Damn, this pussy is way better than the attitude you got," Leo groaned in Desiree's ear. "Where's all that shit you were talking, Desi? Nothing to say now that you got what you really wanted, huh?"

Desiree couldn't utter a word because with her mouth hanging opened, it dried out completely as the warm air filled it. The way Leo had her feeling, he was correct. She was acting out of character because she was dick deprived and didn't like it. Clawing at his back, Desiree hoped like hell she left evidence of their tryst so Icy would leave Leo for stepping out on her. In addition to that, she gripped his member tightly, knowing it would cause him to prematurely release his babies into her womb.

"Stop gripping my shit like that," Leo growled.

As he released the hold he had on her neck, Leo cupped Desiree's ass, stroking deeper. She wrapped her legs around his waist, throwing nothing but pussy back at him. Desiree was meeting Leo stroke for stroke, and both of them worked up a good sweat. The only sound in the room was the skin-to-skin contact between the two. Desiree moaned out seductively as she fought hard not to cum. The swell of Leo's meat let her know he was at the brink of cummin', and she wanted to make sure he coated her uterine wall with his kids.

"I'm about to cum!" she screamed, biting the side of Leo's neck.

That was all it took for Leo to forget he wasn't wearing a condom because he drilled her ass like a jackhammer and released without thought. Desiree smiled as she hugged his neck tightly as his knees buckled. She was ovulating and had stopped taking her pills months before, and in her gut, Desiree knew they had just made a baby. She was going to have a hold on Leo Miller by any means necessary.

Chapter 7

Zan hadn't spoken to his brother since leaving Kingston. His workers were calling him about issues that didn't concern him, and there was no way he was going backwards in his decision. Whatever was going on would have to wait until their boss returned. For the past week, Zan had been looking into buildings for multiple establishments. He was waiting on a long-time friend from college that wanted to talk business.

The waitress brought Zan his appetizer and he tuned in to the national news on the television that rested on the wall in front of him. There was a segment from Kingston, and his antennas went up immediately as thoughts of Leo filled his head. The reporter was standing in front of Duke's estate, and that further pulled Zan into what was being said. He prayed silently in hopes that his brother wasn't the topic of discussion.

"Yesterday was tragic for the Ottey family, and law enforcement isn't any closer to solving the horrific murder of Akiel Ottey. As you can see behind me, there are many cars in the driveway of Aduke Ottey's estate. Family and friends are arriving by the carloads as they come to console the wife of Aduke." The reporter turned toward the gated estate with sadness displayed on her face.

"Aduke Ottey suffered a heart attack after receiving the news of his nephew's murder. Aduke will be missed within the villages as well as with his family. It's a total loss for everyone involved and I send my sincere condolences to the family."

Zan was stunned with what he'd heard about Duke and Akiel. The meeting with Duke replayed in his head and right away, he knew the tragedy had Leo written all over it. He didn't have proof, but the anger his brother displayed the day Duke handed over his empire told him all he needed to know. Reaching for his phone, Zan was about to push Leo's contact when Sam walked up to the table greeting him with a smile.

"Zander Miller! Man, long time no see." Zan placed his phone on the table and stood to his feet.

"Samuel Jackson, what's happenin', bro? It's been a minute," Zan said, pulling Sam in for a brotherly hug. Both of the men sat down as the waitress came over to take their food orders. After she left the table, Zan took a sip of his water and folded his hands in front of him. "I was surprised to see a message from you on social media, man."

"I'd been searching for you for months now. When I finally tracked you down, I was happier than a sissy in a room full of dicks." Zan looked at Sam questionably when he finished his statement. "Don't look at me like that, Zan. It's a figure of speech. I'm still the nigga that gets more pussy than I can handle out here."

"Yeah, aight. Tell me about this business you opened up."

"Man, Zan, I think I bit off more than I can chew with this dispensary. I didn't know how much money it would take to get the ball rolling on actually making a profit. I bought the building, got the repairs done, and didn't have a penny to my name to get any product to open up shop. I've sat around for damn near a year trying to figure out what to do and came up blank every time. Then I thought of you. The valedictorian of our class. The nerd of the bunch. The man that always had a plan. I knew you were the man who could help me get this shit going."

"Sam, all that shit is flattering as fuck. What exactly are you looking for from me?"

"Word is, you have the means to make shit happen. I heard how you and your brother is running the streets, and that shit comes with plenty of dough." Sam laughed.

"I don't know where you getting yo' muthafuckin' information from, but I want you to stop speaking on me like the shit is accurate. I'm not running shit in these streets, nigga. The way it sounds to me, you looking for a muthafucka to come in and save the day for your ass with your business. From the looks of things, you've been sitting on a gold mine for over a year and all you've been able to do is pay taxes that you probably had to take out loans to accomplish. Am I correct?"

Sam's happy demeanor vanished as Zan read him like a book. He was broke as fuck and on the verge of losing everything he worked hard for; including his wife. Without Zan's help, the dispensary along with his home would go into foreclosure and Sam couldn't afford for that to happen.

"You're not wrong. Look, Zan, I need your help."

"That's not telling me what the fuck you need, Sam. So, let me tell you what I'm willing to do. I will pay all the back taxes that you owe, in addition to getting all the inventory for the dispensary. I already have a license, so that won't be a problem. I'm not doing all this shit for you to get all the profit. I'm basically helping you out of a bind, and the ownership is going to change drastically. It's up to you, if you are willing to make those changes."

Sam listened to Zan lay everything on the table and waited patiently for him to get to the end result.

"Before I finalize anything, my name needs to be added to all documentation. We will do a thirty-seventy split with the higher percentage going my way. This will stand until you show me you are capable of running this business alongside me and not behind me. Are we clear?" Zan asked.

"That shit ain't fair—"

"What the fuck you mean it's not fair? Ain't no nigga gon' fatten no frog for a snake! I'm correcting your mistakes out of my pockets, and you're not bringing anything to the table besides the structure of the building. It's either you gon' take this shit, or I'll wait for the shit to go into foreclosure and buy the shit from under yo' ass. I'm trying to give you a piece of the pie and you crying about the shit. What's it gon' be, Sam?"

Zan knew Sam was stuck between a rock and a hard place and only had one choice in the matter. He was prepared to go over Sam's head if it came to it. That's what happened when one revealed their hand when in a bind. Business is just that; business. Money talk and the bullshit Sam thought he was speaking was about to walk if he didn't get his shit together.

Sam didn't think Zan would hustle him out of his business the way he was trying to do, but there was no other way around it. When he heard how Leo and Zan were making money hand over fists in the streets, he knew Zan was the man he needed by his side. Without Zan's finances, Sam didn't have a leg to stand on.

"I'll have my lawyer get the paperwork in order and I will get back to you when everything is ready. I appreciate you, Zan, and I promise to get on my shit. Thanks, man."

"Don't thank me yet. I still want to see the building, and I'm not dropping a dime until my name is legally on the documents. You got my number. Don't have me waiting too long before hearing back from you."

Zan stood from his seat and dropped three hundred dollars on the table. He didn't even want the food he ordered. Tracking down his brother was on the forefront of his mind now that he had squared things away with Sam. Leo had a lot of explaining to do about the situation in Kingston.

***

Zan left the restaurant and hopped in his truck. He'd called Leo's phone back-to-back without his brother answering. Zan hated when Leo did that shit because he didn't know if his brother was dead or alive, and it bothered him. Trying Leo's number once more, Zan was prepared to leave a message, but his brother answered at the last minute.

"Why the fuck you blowing my line down like you my bitch?" Leo snapped. "I know this call ain't about business because you quit, remember?"

"Nigga, have you seen the fuckin' news? If me being worried about yo' hotheaded ass is a problem, sue me, muthafucka! Where you at?"

Zan may have been the calm brother, but he could get boisterous just like his brother. One thing he had never done was allow Leo to throw his weight around without a clapping back. That keeping silent shit was for those punk niggas out on the street, not Zan.

When they were younger, Leo used to beat his ass at every turn. Throughout the years, his brother's bullying ways only made Zan a silent beast. He weaseled his way into the gym every day, and eventually the owner helped him to box properly. It took one time for Leo to step to his brother and he got knocked on his ass. From that day forth, Leo knew how far to take it with Zan.

"Don't worry about where I am. I'm not at home, so don't go there looking for me." Zan could hear a female snicker in the background and knew Leo was up to no good.

"You don't deserve Ice, man. But that's none of my business. What's going on there in Kingston?"

"I'm not in Kingston either, so I don't know what the fuck you talking about," Leo responded nonchalantly. "I got back a couple days ago.

"And you ain't been home? Nigga, are dumb or stupid?"

"Stop worrying about what the fuck I have going on at the crib. What have you heard about Kingston that got you questioning me like you the police?"

"Duke and Akiel is dead. Man, meet me at my crib," Zan said, hanging up.

In Zan's mind, Leo was stupid for stepping out on Icy. The woman did everything imaginable for his brother, and he abused the fact that she wasn't out there acting a damn fool behind him. They were set to get married and Leo hadn't changed one bit. The only thing he had done was gotten better at hiding his infidelities. Leo thought Zan didn't know, but he knew all about his situation with Desiree. That, too, was going to bite him in the ass once Icy caught wind of it. Zan wanted to expose his brother, but that wasn't his place, so he kept his mouth shut. His logic about his brother's treacherous acts was that what happens in the dark, always comes to light.

Pulling into the driveway of his two-story home, Zan killed the engine and got out of his car. All of the tension left his body the closer he got to his front door. It seemed to amaze him how that actually worked whenever he was about to enter his home. There was some type of calming spirit that wouldn't allow any negative energy inside his sacred place. His home along with his family was his sanctuary, causing Zan not to have any worries when he was there.

Zan entered the code to enter the house and the smell of a good ole homecooked meal met him at the door. Locking the door, he made his way to the kitchen and was met by the gummy smile of his baby girl. Zymia was a mixture of Zan and Cherelle. She had Cherelle's China-like eyes, curly hair, and pouty lips, whereas she had Zan's caramel complexion, and his long-ass legs. As the months passed, Zan swore up and down that his daughter looked exactly like her father, but she would only have the height that he possessed.

Standing at 6'4" inches, Zan was tall and muscular in build with tattoos all over his body. The artwork is what attracted Cherelle to him three years prior, but his loving demeanor was what reeled her all the way into his life. Zan was out in the streets just as bad as his brother, but it took the right woman to put all the foolishness to an end. Cherelle was all the woman Zan needed, and that was the reason he didn't hesitate to make her his wife.

"Well, hello, handsome," Cherelle said as she continued stirring in the pot on the stove.

"Hey, babe. It smells good in here," Zan responded, kissing the back of her neck while trying to see what she was cooking. "What ya mixing up over here?"

"Oh, just a little macaroni and cheese, cabbage, and some ox-tails smothered in gravy in the slow cooker."

Zan's stomach growled with the thought of smashing the food his wife had called out. One thing he loved about Cherelle was the fact that she cooked like his late grandmother, and Zan always went back to the good old days every night at dinner time. Never getting the chance to meet his mother because she died right after giving birth to him, Zan missed his grandmother every day, and Cherelle unknowingly brought back very fond memories all the time.

"Waaaa, waaaa."

Zan turned and looked at his daughter having a fit because he wasn't giving her the attention she desired. Washing his hands in the kitchen sink, he dried them with a paper towel and removed his jacket. Zymia drooled while smiling as she kicked her feet wildly.

"How's Daddy's baby?" Zan asked, unhooking the restraints of the bouncer.

Lifting Zymia into his arms, she grabbed his face with both hands, bringing her wet mouth to his cheek. The vibrations from her little hums tickled his face, and Zan couldn't do anything but laugh. He sat down in one of the chairs and bounced his daughter on his knee.

"Be careful with all that bouncing. She just finished eating not long ago," Cherelle warned Zan. It was a little too late because Zymia threw up all over his red shirt and chuckled as she bit her tiny fist. "I tried to tell you."

"It's okay," Zan said, standing to his feet. "I'm going to clean her up and change my clothes. Leo should be on his way over here, so just let him know to get comfortable."

Cherelle glared at her husband because she didn't really care for his brother, mainly because of the way he treated Icy behind her back. There was a time or two when Leo would bring his dip-offs to their home until Cherelle put a stop to the shit. She couldn't allow him to disrespect the woman she had grown to love like a sister in her presence, so whenever Leo was around, she left the room instead of speaking her mind on his actions. Respect for her husband was the only reason she kept her mouth closed.

"Why you couldn't meet him someplace else, Zan? You of all people know Leo is my least favorite person in the world."

"Yeah, I know. Just send him down to the mancave. That's all you need to do; nothing more."

Cherelle went back to tending to the food without responding. If it was up to her, Leo would sit on the front steps until his brother came out to get him. Icy was a good one in Cherelle's mind, and she couldn't fathom how she put up with Leo's bullshit. The last laugh was going to be on his ass once Icy left him for good because the time was coming. Cherelle wanted to be a fly on the wall when the shit played out.

Thirty minutes later, the food was ready, and Cherelle went upstairs to see what was taking Zan so long to come back downstairs. Leo hadn't shown up and she was happy he didn't. When she walked into their bedroom, Cherelle found her two favorite people sleeping like both of them were babies. Zymia was lying on Zan's chest and he was holding her across the back. Using that moment, Cherelle captured the image on her phone before snuggling next to her husband.

"Babe, the food is ready," she whispered in his ear. "Come on so you can eat."

Zan opened his eyes slowly and pulled his wife's head down for a kiss. "Did Leo show up?"

"Nah. You should've known he wouldn't, especially if you were the one that asked him to come through. Word on the street is, Rico's brother Slick is looking all around for him. I don't care to know what happened, but what I do know is you need to be careful. If someone is looking for Leo and can't catch up with him, you're the next best thing to the man himself."

"I'm not worried about a muthafucka coming for me. Just because I decided to leave that part of my life behind me, that doesn't mean I won't blow a nigga's wig back. I stay ready so I won't have to get ready. Remember that, ma."

"I understand all of that, Zan. You are still involved by association. Promise me you will stay on point when you're out of this house. We need you," Cherelle said, running her hand over his fade.

"Indeed, baby. Enough about that shit. I'll be sure to ask Leo about that shit as well. In the meantime, let's go eat while fat-fat is sleeping. Maybe I can get a taste of your sweetness for dessert."

"We can make that happen, daddy." Cherelle kissed Zan deeply and got up.

Following suit, he put Zymia in her bassinet and covered her with a blanket. Zan grabbed his phone and called Leo as he made his way to the kitchen. When his brother didn't answer, he knew for a fact Leo was dodging him because he didn't want to discuss what happened to Duke and Akiel in Kingston.

Chapter 8

Icy had been spending time at her salon in Maywood to ensure Sean was on his best behavior. She actually wanted to make sure the female that was in there at the beginning of the month didn't show her face again. Leo being out of town and the bullshit she'd bet her life he was on, kind of had Icy in a bad head space. She hadn't heard from Leo in almost two weeks and didn't pick up the phone once to call his ass. He must've felt the same way because he hadn't attempted to call her either, and Icy was cool with that.

"Girl, what the hell you over there thinking about?" Kia asked. "I know you not carrying around the long face over Leo."

"Kia, not today. I'm just thinking. That's all."

"Yeah, okay," she said, scrolling through her phone.

Kia and Julz had persuaded Icy to come out with them to do a little bit of shopping on Michigan Avenue. Their goal was to really get Icy out of the house to enjoy the last of the nice days before the cold front hit the Windy City. On top of that, Icy had been down since Leo hadn't returned back to the States from the business trip he had in Jamaica. They'd walked store to store and laughed at some of the folks that were more frightened than shopping, walking around clutching their handbags.

"Man, did y'all hear about this shit? A nigga got knocked and his uncle died finding out about his murder?"

"Nawl! Where that shit happen at, the westside?" Julz asked while searching a rack full of shirts.

"In Kingston, Jamaica. That's wild to lose two family members in one day."

Icy paused as she let what her cousin said marinate in her mind. Leo was in Kingston, and now she was worried that something went wrong and that's why she hadn't heard from him. Taking her phone out of her purse, she called Leo and his phone rang until it finally went to voicemail. While sending a text, Icy's hands shook with every letter she typed.

My Baby, are you okay over there? I haven't heard from you. Call me when you get this message.

"The dude Akiel got shot up outside his crib and his uncle Duke had a massive heart attack," Kia said reading from wherever she was getting the information.

"Did you say Duke? Is his last name Ottey?" Icy asked nervously.

Kia skimmed the page and found the name of the family and paused. "Yeah, that's their name. How the hell you know about these folks, Icy?"

"I'll talk to y'all about it once I hear back from Leo. Let's go get something to eat. I'm hungry."

"We can go to Ronnie's Steakhouse once I find a shirt to go with these pants," Julz said, continuing her search.

"I'm going outside to call Leo. I'll be right back."

Icy walked through the store with her head in her phone. She smacked into what felt like a brick wall and her phone fell face down on the floor. Shaking her head from being stunned, she looked up slowly, coming face to face with the most gorgeous man she'd ever seen.

With his milk chocolate skin tone, muscles ripping through the long-sleeved blue dress shirt he wore, with a thick silver Cuban link chain hanging from his neck, Icy had to start over from the bottom of his blue and white Jordans, up to his light blue jeans. When she made it to his face, her breath caught in her throat. The long thick beard hung almost to his chest and the mustache connecting perfectly around his full set of lips had her kitty humming a tune Icy had never felt before. She wanted to run her fingertips across his eyebrows and ease his turban off his head just to see what his hair looked like underneath.

"Did you hear what I said, beautiful?" His Jamaican accent snapped her out of the trance she was under by the sight of him alone.

In honesty, Icy hadn't heard a word the man said until that moment. "No. No, I didn't hear you. Would you mind repeating yourself, please?" Icy stammered.

The mystery man laughed showing his perfectly white teeth and Icy swooned all over again. "I'm sorry for bumping into you," he said, bending over, picking up her phone. The screen was shattered and he felt bad for the damage he'd caused. Handing her the device, he reached in his pocket and pulled out a wad of cash that was secured by a silver money clip and handed it over to Icy. "This is for the damage to your phone. My apologies again."

"It's okay. You don't need to pay for it. I'll just get it fixed before I get home. I should've been watching where I was going anyway."

Icy refused to take the money and bypassed the handsome man to exit the building. She was trying to get as far away from the man that had her heart hammering in her chest. Icy had to remember she was set to get married at the end of December, and the way her body was reacting at that time, Icy would be too tempted to see how hard her yoni could cry all over his beard.

"Slow down, beautiful," he said, following Icy onto the busy street. "Please take this money. I need to make sure I'll be able to contact you after today."

Icy stopped in her tracks and turned to face the man she was highly smitten with. "There's no chance in hell I would be able to communicate with you after today. I'm engaged to be married, and there's no room in my life for another man. I'm not equipped for an entanglement and on top of that, you don't look like the type of guy that would knowingly share any woman."

"You are absolutely correct, I wouldn't. But when I want something, I tend to make a way to get it, and I've come to the conclusion that I want you," he smirked. "We will meet again, beautiful. Until then, keep it wet for me."

The mystery man slid the bills in the front of Icy's low cut shirt as his fingers grazed the top of her right breast. Leaning in, he kissed her cheek and walked back into the store Icy had vacated. Forgetting why she came outside, Icy spotted a T-Mobile store and headed in that direction as the Jamaican accent played on repeat in her head. It took less than ten minutes for her to get a new phone and all of her data transferred. Soon as she was about to walk out of the store, her phone rang with a call from Kia.

"Where the hell did you go, Icy? We've been looking all over for you." Kia asked as she looked around like a lost puppy as she searched for her cousin.

"I'm down the street, about to walk out of T-Mobile. I dropped my phone and broke it and had to come purchase a new one. I'm on my way back to y'all."

"Hurry up so I can tell you about this fine-ass nigga we just saw. The nigga had the nerve to say he's saving himself for his future wife. Whoever the fuck the bitch is gon' be happy than a mutha-fucka waking up to his ass every night. His beard alone had my pussy drippin' with delight."

Icy laughed because the same nigga had her thinking about his ass too. She wouldn't let her cousin know about their encounter be-cause she would tell her to ditch Leo and get with the sexy Jamai-can. As she got closer to the store, she saw Kia and Julz walking in her direction. They stopped and allowed Icy to catch up before they turned to walk in the opposite direction.

"Girl, there his fine ass go!"

Kia damn near screamed drawing the attention of a couple pass-ersby and the man in question. When he laid eyes on Icy, his face lit up with the sunlight. He stood rubbing his hands together while licking the succulent lips that Icy became fascinated with during their brief encounter. The duo had a long stare down as Icy walked past him. She didn't get too far away before he reached out and grabbed her hand.

"So, we meet again," he smiled. "I'm not going to let you leave a second time without properly introducing myself. My name is Akoni, and you are?" he asked, holding her hand tighter.

Icy blushed harder than she ever had in life as she diverted her eyes toward the sky. "I'm engaged," she replied sheepishly.

"Aht, aht, her name is Icy. And she is pleased to meet you, Akoni. What is the meaning behind your name?" Julz asked.

Without taking his eyes off Icy, he smiled, showing a deep dimple she didn't notice before. "It means someone who is a brave warrior, and has excellent leadership qualities."

"He's the one, Icy! This man can lead you all the way around a bedroom and protect you from anything that comes to harm you. Including the man you won't be marrying after tahday!" Kia's overly exaggerated ass was doing the most, and Icy couldn't even be mad at her for her outburst.

Icy laughed nervously as she gently removed her hand from his. She stepped back and cleared her throat as she continued to undress Akoni with her eyes. There was definitely chemistry between the two, but like Icy said before, she didn't need any added situations in her life at the time.

"Please don't listen to my cousin. She's always on some funny shit. I'm definitely getting married, so it was a pleasure meeting you, Akoni. Enjoy the rest of your day." Icy walked away with Julz on her heels. Kia, of course, stayed behind for a few seconds to do what she did best; start some shit.

"That nigga don't really love her and she hasn't figured it out yet. I hope your memory is sharp, because I'm only gonna say this once, then I have to go. Her number is (555) *WINTERS*," Kia said, walking away.

Akoni stood puzzled as he watched the women round the corner. He thought about the number Icy's cousin recited and thought it was a joke, but it didn't prevent him from repeating it in his head all the way to his rented Infinite Q50. Sitting in the car, Akoni took his phone out and went to the keypad. He entered "555" then thought about "winters" for a few minutes. Looking at the letters under the numbers, a smile spread across his face as he entered "946-8377" and saved the number under My Icy.

***

"Icy, you're crazy as hell for not giving that man your number. He could've been on standby whenever that nigga Leo fucked up," Kia said as they sat waiting for their food at the steakhouse.

"Kia, I'm nothing like you. I don't need a man on reserve because Leo isn't going anywhere. He may have been a cheater before, but he hasn't been on that shit as of late," Icy stated irritably. "Sometimes I hate that I told y'all about Leo stepping out on me. Both of y'all find any reason to say he's still up to no good when I know he's not even on that anymore."

"I'm not trying to get under your skin, Icy, but do you know that for sure?" Julz asked, sipping from her Long Island iced tea. "I mean, Leo's been gone for what, damn near two weeks, and you haven't heard from him? That shit ain't never happened. Then, his lil flunky was all on yo' ass when he first left and now, she is nowhere to be found. Sounds a little fishy to me."

"I'm with Julz's white ass on this one. She's actually on to something, if you ask me," Kia chimed in. "Whenever Leo goes out of town, there's never a time that he don't come back at the same time as Zan. If Leo is still out of town, how is it that I saw Cherelle and Zan at the grocery store just the other day?"

Icy didn't like the way Julz and her cousin were coming at her. She knew they meant well, but they didn't know what the fuck they were talking about when it came to her man's business. If she didn't know the reason Zan came back beforehand, what Kia said would've hit a nerve. It didn't make her feel any type of way because she knew the truth.

"For your information, Kia, Zan came back from Jamaica early because he no longer works with Leo. That's how you saw him and his wife together. What else you got? So I can set yo' ass straight."

"Save the anger for that nigga. I may have been wrong about Zan, but I know for a fact I'm not wrong about Leo's ass. He is out playing in your face behind yo' back and the truth will be revealed. That bitch Desiree is part of the problem. I don't know if she's the only one, but she fits right in. Mark my words. I will leave the shit alone for now, Icy. Just know, I'll be there with my brass knuckles in hand with Vaseline all over my face when you need me."

Kia sat back looking at her cousin as if she wanted to wring her neck for being so naïve when it came to Leo. Icy was in deep thought, and that's how Kia wanted her to be; thinking about all the shit she'd been through with Leo's ass. Icy had men approaching her all the time and she turned them down because of him. To see Akoni swooning over her and Icy looked right through him, pissed Kia off because she could tell he was a different type of man. A man that was on his shit, and Icy couldn't see anything outside of Leo.

"If it comes to that, I know you will have my back. I'm not even about to think about things in a negative light. When it's brought to my attention, then that's when I'll address it. Until then, leave it alone, Kia."

Nodding her head, Kia left the subject lingering in the air, but that didn't mean it left the forefront of her mind. After ordering their food when the waitress came to their table, the trio found it hard to talk to one another because Kia wanted to bash the fuck out of Leo and Julz just wanted to keep the peace because she knew how the cousins could get if they got angry enough. There would be a whole massacre in the steakhouse if they came to blows.

Back in the day, Kia and Icy used to fight each other like cats and dogs, but Icy mellowed out a lot and Kia acted as if she didn't remember how Icy's hands were in real life. Julz had a feeling Leo was back to his old tricks. She was just going to sit back and watch until everything unfolds.

"So, word on the street is, Slick is looking for Leo and Zan. I think you need to put him up on game whenever you talk to his snake ass," Kia blurted out as she sipped her drink.

"What do you mean he is looking for them?"

"Slick is Rico's older brother and he hasn't been seen in weeks. Everybody knows Rico works for Leo. For him to come up missing and nobody is even questioning where he is has the rumors swarming like flies in the streets," Kia said low enough for only the occupants at their table could hear. "A couple of weeks ago, Rico was hit for a shipment; a huge shipment."

Icy was green to what Kia was referring to because Leo didn't come home talking about what he did outside of their home. But she knew the consequences that came behind fuckin' up money if there wasn't a good enough reason behind it. Kia knew anything and everything that went on around Chicago, plus she had somewhat of an inside connect to Leo's operation because Stack was forever pillow talking whenever he and Kia hooked up. So, she knew there was a lot of truth behind what she had said. Thinking about the article Kia read from earlier, Icy hoped Leo wasn't being messy and leaving bodies lying out to rot with his name attached. That was the last thing she needed in her life at the time.

"Rico deserved that shit because I think he was in on that hit. According to Stack—"

"Nope, I don't want to hear it. It has nothing to do with me, and the less I know the better," Icy said, cutting Kia off. "If you knew what was good for you, you would tell Stack the same shit. Stay out of their street business, Kia."

"Girl, boo. One of us needs to know what the fuck going on. Your *I don't want to know ass* should stay up on what's happening. Just in case you have to pack the fuck up because a muthafucka out to get you because they can't get to Leo's reckless ass. I'm the best you got as far as keeping you in the loop. Don't think I didn't notice you brushed off the fact that you still haven't told me how you know the niggas that got dropped in Kingston. I bet Leo's name is written all over that shit too."

Icy looked at her phone and realized Leo still hadn't responded to the text she'd sent over thirty minutes prior. The more she thought about it, she became scared because he would've responded or called by that time. Knowing that Leo was affiliated with Duke had her on pins and needles because she didn't know what was really going on. She decided to text Zan to see if he had heard anything about Leo.

Ice: Zan, have you heard from Leo? I'm worried about him.

Zan was playing with his daughter when he was alerted to the text. He was hoping it was Leo since he hadn't heard back from him since the day he was supposed to come over to holla at him and didn't show. When he saw it was a message from Ice, he sighed deeply because he didn't want to be the one to tell the woman he loved like a sister that her man was back in the States. It was obvious Leo still hadn't been home and the shit pissed him off just thinking about it.

Zan: Hey, Ice. I heard from him the other day. He's good. When I talk to him, I'll tell hm to give you a call. You good over there?
Icy: Yeah.

Knowing that Leo answered for his brother and not her was a red flag in itself. The nigga was alive and well, but hadn't had the decency to pick up the phone to tell her that. In her mind, she wondered what Zan wasn't telling her. There was something going on for sure. Zan never told Icy anything Leo was doing and she respected it. After all, Leo was his brother. But Zan said a lot without saying much at all. That's why she responded with one word. Icy sighed as she placed her phone face down on the table.

"This shit stays here. Kia, that means don't slip up and tell Stack I'm even discussing this with y'all." Icy took a deep swig of her drink and wiped her hands on her pants as she thought about telling the two people, she was closest to what she was about to. "Duke is Leo's connect. He went to Kingston to meet him and I don't know the details, but something didn't go well. If something happened to Duke while Leo was there, he would've called to tell me about it. I met Duke several times, and he was like a father to me from afar. Akiel was his nephew, and he adored that man because it was the closest he had to a son since Duke's son left Kingston when he turned eighteen. I don't know much about Duke's biological son, but one thing I did know was that Duke missed him every day."

"So, in other words, you think Leo had a hand in what happened to them?" Julz asked.

"It is possible. The thing is, I don't know why Leo would do anything to Duke. That man would give Leo the shirt off his back if he needed it. There are so many unanswered questions flowing through my head right now. Leo isn't accepting my calls or texts, and I don't know what to make of it."

"His ass deep in some pussy that don't belong to yo' ass," Kia mumbled. Icy heard what Kia said and opted not to reply.

When the waitress came with their food, Icy no longer had an appetite and asked for her food to be packed to go. From the text Zan responded to, down to Leo's lack of concern for how Icy felt, she just wanted to go home to figure shit out on her own.

The image of the sexy stranger named Akoni came to mind and Icy closed her eyes to bring the image to life behind her eye lids. She sat quietly as Kia and Julz ate, then they left the same way they came in after Icy gave the waitress a hefty tip. The trio piled into Kia's truck in total silence.

Icy thought about the wine she was going to enjoy to ease her mind the minute she was home. The reflection on her life was running rapidly as she relaxed tuning out the reality of everything she was silently battling.

Chapter 9

Akoni thought about hitting up Icy since her girl lowkey shot him her digits, but he didn't want to overstep his boundaries knowing she had a nigga. He saw beautiful women everywhere he went, but there was something about that one. What it was, he didn't know. Akoni did know something though, and it was the fact he would have Icy in his grasp one day.

He was sitting in his hotel room sipping on a glass of apple Crown after returning from the site to make sure his workers were on their shit. Being the owner of Blazin' Builders was a great accomplishment for Akoni. He was proud of himself for following his dreams and getting from under his father's tutelage when he did.

Akoni had made millions in a matter of years; the right way. When he left Kingston, Jamaica at the age of eighteen, he didn't know exactly what he wanted to do with his life. With the money he'd save since he was a youngin, he packed up and moved to the place the cursor landed when he entered U.S. cities on an electronic wheel on his phone. New York was the place and he resided there 'til present day. He just traveled a lot because he was hands-on with his company.

Arriving in the Big Apple was scary at first because Akoni didn't know anything outside of Kingston. He found a small apartment in the heart of Brooklyn and couldn't believe how much the rent was for the little-ass space he occupied. Just the thought of being cramped in a box was a problem for him. Coming from living in a big house with more than enough space to house three families, Akoni didn't want to be cramped too long. He had no choice in the matter then because he had to make the money he had stretch.

Doing his research, Akoni enrolled in school at NYU on a grant and became a temporary citizen on a visa. He took advantage of the perks he had at his fingertips and rolled with it. Going to school for Construction Management was challenging and in his spare time, he became bored as hell. Akoni became Blaze during the night while excelling in his classes during the day. The streets of

Brooklyn gave him a rush he never thought he had within and he loved that; until he didn't. Akoni still had ties in the street, but he had an entire team to work for him while he kept his hands clean while profiting in the background.

Many would think, why would he move away from the life his father lived to do the same from afar? Akoni could've stayed in Kingston, but he was his own man. One thing he wasn't willing to do was marry just anybody. His father was trying to force an arrangement on him that he wasn't going for. Akoni wanted to marry the woman he chose, not one that was chosen for him. In order to do that, he had to separate himself from the generational curse his father tried to force upon him. After damn near fifteen years, Akoni still hadn't found the one he wanted to settle down with. That is, until his eyes fell upon Icy Winters.

Akoni was brought out of his thoughts by the ringing of his phone. He looked over and saw his mother calling and silenced the noise. Akoni wasn't in the mood to talk to his parents. He'd just taken both of them off the block list because they never called to see how he was doing or congratulate him on his accomplishments. Now, he was probably back at square one with them asking when he would come back home. The phone rang again two more times without Akoni answering. He wanted to go to the contacts and block them again before the harassment started back up. His antennas rose when his mother's name appeared for the fourth time in less than five minutes. Kenise wouldn't call like that unless something was wrong, so Akoni answered the call placing it on speaker.

"What's wrong, Ma?" Akoni asked, sitting up on the sofa.

"Akoni, yuh fada and Akiel dead!" she cried into his ear. The words didn't register right away until, his mother continued to cry hysterically. "Dem shot mi sista's baby ten times! Who wud duh such a ting tuh fi wi fambly?"

Akoni morphed into his alter ego Blaze in the blink of an eye after hearing what his mother said. His ears burned and the tears were stinging his eyes as he tried his best not to let emotions get the best of him. The word "dead" kept repeatedly playing in his head and he couldn't shake it away, no matter how hard he tried.

"I've been calling fi days an couldn't get through tuh yuh. Please cum home cuz mi refuse tuh put yuh fada an cousin inna dirt without yuh being here, Akoni. Mi need yuh."

The sorrow in his mother's voice moved Akoni to tears. He muted the phone so she wouldn't hear his cries. Losing his father was a stab to his heart because he didn't get the chance to tell him how much he loved him. Regardless of the strain in their relationship, Akoni loved his mother and father the long way. Now, he regretted staying away from his family so long.

"I'm on my way. Stay strong until I get there. I'm sorry, Ma, and I love you."

"I luh yuh too, Akoni."

His mother hung up and Akoni could still hear her crying in his head. The pain hit him like a ton of bricks once he was off the phone with his mother. His father's voice echoed in the room as tears streamed down his face. Akoni raised to his feet, went into the bedroom of the hotel, and did something he had tried to stay away from for many years; rolled a blunt. He brought some weed for one of his workers because he couldn't get the cannabis on his flight to Chicago. Akoni, on the other hand, didn't have to worry about that type of shit on the private plane his father had gifted him for his twenty-first birthday.

Akoni sat as the weed cleared his mind with every pull he took. In the midst of it all, Akoni felt himself transforming into who the niggas in the streets of Brooklyn called Blaze. Somebody better answer all his questions when he got to Jamaica because plenty of bodies were going to hit the pavement for taking the man that birthed a beast away from his family.

After taking two blunts to the head, Blaze waited patiently for his driver to pick him up to take him to the hangar at the airport. There would be no problem with him getting through the FBO terminal. When he received the text message he was looking for, he picked up his luggage and left the room. Blaze allowed the likes of Nas to blast through his Airpods to disconnect from everything that was going on in his world. "N.Y. State of Mind" was filling his head with all the negativity he tried to keep out of his everyday life since becoming a businessman. That shit went out the window when he got the call that his father was no longer breathing on the same side of earth as he.

Once he was comfortably on the plane, Blaze didn't say a word to anyone and they knew to stay the fuck away from him for the entire flight. The weed Blaze smoked made him sleepy as hell. Before the plane took off good, he was sleeping like a baby, dreaming about all the memories he had with his father before things took a drastic turn.

***

Sitting in the blacked-out Mercedes truck outside of his parent's house, Blaze couldn't even attempt to get out to go inside. Knowing his father wasn't on the other side of the door conducting business in his office only made Blaze madder than when he heard the news of his demise. The front door opened, getting his attention. When he saw Maven make his exit, Blaze jumped out of the truck, leaving the door wide open.

"What the fuck happened to my father?" Blaze snapped. "You were supposed to protect him by any muthafuckin' means necessary!"

"I would've laid my body down to protect Dukes. You know that shit," Maven lied through his teeth. "There was no way for me to save him from the heart attack that took his life. Duke died after he found out what happened to Akiel. I was in my room when he received the call and I ran out upon hearing Kenise screaming for help. I did all I could to keep him alive, but he died in the process and I'm sorry, nephew."

"What about Akiel? How the hell did he get shot so many times? Where the fuck was his security?" Blaze was shooting questions left and right and Maven didn't have the answers to any of them.

"Akoni, the only thing I can say about Akiel is, he was coming out of his home. That's about all I know."

"The shit don't make sense. Why would anyone want Akiel dead? If anything, the muthafuckas would've gone after the big fish. He didn't even carry big weight when he was out and about."

"That's where you're wrong. Akiel *was* the big fish. Duke handed the empire to him almost two weeks ago. You know how he is. Maybe he was out letting it be known that he was the king in the streets of Kingston and someone didn't like how cocky he may have been. I don't know for sure. That's just my take on the matter."

Blaze noticed how Maven's eyes were focused everywhere except on him. As much as he didn't want to believe his gut feeling, he had to keep the shit in mind that Maven had a hand in the shit that happened with his cousin. Maven had been in line to call the shots for the longest and he wouldn't put it past him if he was jealous of the position Akiel possessed.

Keeping his eyes and ears open was a must for Blaze. He already had one suspect on his radar. It was time to figure out the rest of the muthafuckas. Without saying another word, he walked away from his father's long-time friend and finally walked through the doors of the home his father worked hard to build.

Walking through the home looking for his mother, Blaze was approached by different family members, but he pushed right past in search for the woman that needed him as if he was oxygen at the moment. Checking the kitchen, he saw everyone but his mother. Same thing when he checked the family room. Blaze ran to the stairs without paying attention to what was being said to him. The man had tunnel vision and clogged ears when it came to the irrelevant folks who were parading around his father's home as if they came to check on him regularly. Not being able to find his mother caused Blaze to become nervous because she wasn't in her bedroom. Making his way back down the stairs, he stopped the first person he laid eyes on to inquire about his mother's whereabouts.

"She's outside by di pool," his uncle said, throwing his hands out in front of him.

Shaking his head, Blaze left out one of the many doors in the house and found his mother crying into the chest of his aunt Delyse. Kenise was broken far more than her son imagined. He understood her losing the only man she'd ever loved was taking a total toll on her being. Blaze couldn't stand back and watch his mother suffer another minute. He walked forward slowly, causing his aunt to look up at him in surprise as he moved closer to her and his mother. Placing his hand on his mother's shoulder, she immediately looked up through tear-soaked eyes and screamed out.

"Akoni! Akoni! Akoni, yuh cum! Mi baby cum tuh mi!"

Kenise jumped into her only son's arms and wept like a baby. Blaze had to hold her around her waist tightly because she collapsed after a couple minutes of crying her heart out. Lifting her body in his arms, he carried her into the house and up to her room with tears falling from his eyes into her hair. Blaze laid his mother gently in the California King bed, taking her shoes off in the process before crawling in right behind her. He was never too old to make sure his favorite girl was okay. Even though he had slept the entire way to Jamaica, Blaze didn't have any trouble falling asleep alongside his mother.

Waking up with the sun shining in his face, Blaze reached over to hug his mother, but her side of the bed was empty. He stretched his arms over his head, then reality set in, reminding him why he was lying in his parents' bed. The smell of his father's musky oil filled his nostrils and the anger returned from the night before. Blaze got up to take care of his hygiene so he could go out and find the answers he was seeking.

"Weh yaah guh?" Kenise asked as he was leaving out of the room as she was entering.

"I have to shower. There's a couple of things I want to do before we have the service for Dad."

"Mi wa fi chat tuh yuh fos. Sit," she said, motioning him to sit down. "Yuh fada was sick an try calling tuh tell yuh bout di diagnosis. Akoni, I'm nuh blaming yuh fi wah happen, mi wish yuh cud ave talk tuh him before any of this transpired." Dropping her head, looking at the floor, Kenise tried shaking away her pain, it didn't work.

"Mi don't tink Duke had a heart attack. Maven did tell everyone him dead afta him received di call bout Akiel; dat wasn't chu. Duke did nuh breathing wen mi guh tuh wake him. Sumting else happen tuh him."

Listening to his mother, his hunch was on point because he knew his father didn't up and have a heart attack, especially not from hearing that someone died. Hell, many people close to him had died and it didn't faze him at all. Maven was the key to learning what really happened, and Blaze was going to get that information sooner rather than later. For the meantime, he was going out into the village to see what he could find out from the locals. Someone would start talking for the right price, and he was willing to pay whatever.

"Don't worry, Ma. I'm going to get to the bottom of all this shit. Excuse my language. When are the services taking place?" he asked, not really wanting to know the date of seeing his father for the last time.

"Di day afta tomorrow."

"Bet. I'm going to take a shower, then I'm stepping out for a while. I love you, Ma." Getting up, Blaze walked toward the door before stopping with the sound of his mother's voice.

"Mi love yuh too, son. Be careful out there. Yuh luggage inna yuh room."

Nodding his head, Blaze left the room and walked to the other side of the mansion to the east wing. The entire side was designated for him, and it was another world for him. No one was allowed in his space and when he reached his destination, Blaze realized that shit held true even after he was gone off to New York. Gathering everything he would need to freshen up, he laid out an outfit and headed to the bathroom. It took him twenty minutes to get himself together. When he emerged from the stairway, all eyes were on him. Maven was off in the corner whispering with another nigga Blaze didn't recognize.

Something was fishy with the nigga, and Blaze didn't like him and he didn't even know his name. Duke had a few muthafuckas that worked for him from the States and with Blaze knowing how cutthroat niggas could be, he added the stranger to his list of suspects without hesitation. Maven kept his eyes on Blaze's every move. The way Duke's son walked with confidence, was the same way his father had. The shit was intimidating as fuck.

With a white T-shirt, denim jeans, fresh all-white Nikes, and his red and black locs flowing down his back, Blaze wasn't worried about nan nigga mean mugging him on the low. He peeped every move being made as if he had vision in the back of his head. It was something he had to learn hustlin' in the streets of Brooklyn.

"Who the fuck is *that* swole muthafucka?"

"Ask me who the fuck I am!" Blazed retorted. "As a matter of fact, who the fuck are you?"

The minute Leo heard the unknown man speak, he knew he wasn't from Kingston. He knew right away the nigga was from somewhere in New York. Blaze never broke eye contact and neither did Leo. The two stared each other down without saying a word. That was, until Blaze stepped into Leo's space and asked the question once more.

"Nothing to say now, nigga? I asked you a question. Who the fuck are you?"

"Last time I checked, this was Duke's crib. Everybody in this muthafucka knows who I am. I guess you the outsider, *nigga*. It don't matter if you know me or not. I'm not here for yo' ass. I'm here to pay my respects to a man that was like a father to me."

Hearing that shit had Blaze hot, taking in another nigga who wasn't his blood refer to his father as his. Under no circumstances was a cocky muthafucka going to act as if he was more important than he was. Laughing lowly while wiping his hand across his nose, Blaze reached out and yoked Leo off his feet.

"Mi di man round here now dat mi fada gone." Blaze's thick Jamaican accent came out full throttle as he sneered in Leo's face. "He only had one son, and that's me! Don't ever make the mistake of telling another soul he was *like* a father to you."

Blaze tossed Leo to the side like he weighed little to nothing and stared down at his fallen body. Leo jumped up with his tool in hand, aiming it directly at the man he now knew as Duke's son. The information didn't mean shit to him after the violation he had just committed. Blaze's eyes turned charcoal black as his nose flared, looking down the barrel of the gun.

"You better use that muthafucka and make it count, bitch," Blaze sneered.

At that moment, Kenise entered the room and walked in the middle of the two men. She looked from Blaze to Leo, taking in the sights menacingly. Leo lowered his gun and tucked it away out of respect for the woman that stood before him.

"Both of yuh should be ashamed. Dis a nuh di time fi dis. Akoni, dis a Leo. Leo dis a mi son, Akoni."

Instead of replying to the introduction his mother gave, Blaze scoffed in Leo's direction. "The name is Blaze to you, nigga. Remember that shit, because I owe you one," he said as he left the estate.

Hopping in his father's Mercedes Benz coupe, Blaze went straight to Akiel's home to see if he could find some type of clue the police may have overlooked. He and his cousin didn't see eye to eye on many things, but that didn't have shit to do with the fact that somebody took his fuckin' life. Not only was Akiel killed, but he was brutally assassinated. That shit was on the scale of a police officer in the States killing an unarmed black man. Blaze didn't like the shit when they did it, and he definitely didn't like the fact it happened to his blood.

Blaze parked the car in front of his cousin's house and the first thing he saw was a pool of blood in the walkway. All the muthafuckas hanging around his father's house could've at least come over to clean the bloodstains off the ground. There was police tape scattered around as if the place was condemned. Duke paid cash money for Akiel's crib and this was how the family thought of it.

Getting out of the car, Blaze walked up to the door and punched in the code to gain entry. Duke used the same code for everything, and only the immediate family and Maven knew how to access those things. Going straight for the cleaning supplies, he filled a bucket, added bleach, and grabbed a scrub brush. Before even attempting to clean up the blood, Blaze went to find some clothes to put on so he wouldn't destroy the fit he wore.

As he walked into Akiel's bedroom, he got an eerie feeling being there alone. Going into the closet, he found a pair of grey sweatpants and a black T-shirt that he changed into immediately before switching out his white Nikes for a pair of black New Balance shoes. With the feeling he had, he went deeper in the closet and located a Glock 42 and secured it in the pocket of the pants before heading for the door, Blaze grabbed the bucket and brush then set out to clean his cousin's blood from the pavement.

Scrubbing on his knees like his life depended on it, Blaze worked up a sweat until he felt a presence behind him. Turning slowly, he came face to face with a teenager that was no older than seventeen. Rising to his full height, leaving the brush on the ground, Blaze waited for the youngin to speak.

"He was a good man," he said, staring at the blood and water mixture. "Him didn't deserve wah happened tuh him. Mi see everything an kno who did it." A tear slid down the boy's face and it saddened Blaze to see him hurt the way he was. "It was Kadofi an fi him team. Dem shot him up and peeled away. You cya find dem inna di village. Dem always hanging out. Here a waah picha." The boy handed an image over to Blaze and stepped back as he studied Kadofi's face.

"Thank you. What's your name?" Blaze asked.

Shaking his head no, the boy backpedaled slowly. "Mi nuh wa any bady tuh kno mi tell. Mi sorry," he said, then took off running down the road.

"You a dead muthafucka. Soon as the sun goes down, I'll be looking for yo' ass." Blaze folded the picture into a small square and tucked it into the pockets of the sweats he wore before going back to cleaning what was left of his cousin's blood.

Chapter 10

Back at the estate, Leo was fuming because Blaze put hands on him. He would've shot his ass had Kenise not stepped between them. Leo's trigger finger was itching so bad that the thought of sending Duke's son to meet him at the gates of heaven made his dick hard. What really pissed Leo off was the fact of Maven standing there like a scared prostitute standing on the corner for the first time when the nigga approached them.

As soon as Blaze left the premises, Leo left the house towards his car. Maven was on his heels, trying to figure out where he was going. It wasn't Maven's business, but Leo needed to get away from the environment around him before he ended up killing anybody who had something to say about what took place. From the looks of things, nobody in the family gave a fuck about Duke's estranged son. If anything, they were afraid of the nigga, and Leo didn't understand why.

"Where are you going?"

"Look, Maven, I'm here for one reason, and that's to get my muthafuckin' money, then ride out. Leaving this place is best for me because when that nigga comes back and I'm here, I'm liable to blow his fuckin' head off his shoulders. Speaking about that fuck boy, why the fuck you cram up in his presence?"

Maven stood as if he had to think long and hard for an answer to the simple question. Being in the game and scared to be out there alone was a road to destruction in Leo's eyes. Maven didn't have a backbone when it came to running shit. No wonder Duke opted to give his ass cash instead of the crown.

"Take yo' pussy ass back in the crib," Leo said, pushing past Maven. "I gotta go clear my head. I'll see you in the morning at the service. Don't call me for shit. If anything jumps off, take care of that shit, punk."

Leo got in the rental and drove out of the long driveway. Whenever he was stressed, the only thing that could calm him down was pussy. Avita didn't know he was back in Kingston, but she was about to find out. As Leo drove through the streets of Kingston, thoughts of Icy filled his mind and he reached for his phone to call her. However, he shook that shit right out his head. He hadn't bothered to call her in weeks, so he figured he might as well let her get all the shit off her chest whenever he popped up.

Any other nigga in Leo's position would probably call the wedding off instead of stringing a woman along. Not him, because Icy was the woman he loved, but Avita was the mother of his one and only child that he had love for. In his mind, there was no reason to choose when both women would never cross paths. Leo had the best of both worlds, and he planned to ride it out long as he could.

When he pulled up to the house he had built for Avita, there was an unknown car parked beside hers. Leo's first thought was that she had another nigga inside with his baby. Without grabbing his bag, he jumped out of the car, slamming the door behind him. Leo doubled back because he had left his whip running without thinking. Taking the steps two at a time, he felt for his heat, and with keys in hand, inserted the key into the lock. Easing the door open, he closed it quietly and tiptoed further into the house. Hearing voices coming from the sunroom, Leo stood outside the door to allow his heart rate to go back to normal.

"Amancia, I know this is hard for you to take in. Duke and Akiel were like family to you for years," Avita said in her thick accent. "They are in a much better place than this hell hole we live in. I know you miss him, cousin."

"You just don't know how much," she sobbed. Leo sneezed and couldn't muffle the sound. "What was that?"

"I don't know," Avita said, eyeing the doorway.

Leo made his presence known and Avita's face went from scared to happy in a matter of seconds. "Baby, when did you get here?" she asked, jumping to her feet.

"I was just walking through looking for you," he lied.

"You didn't tell me you were coming back."

"You're right. I didn't know Duke was going to die on me either," he said, hunching his shoulders. "I can't believe the shit that happened, man." Leo ran his hand down his face as if he was distraught. Avita wrapped her arms around his waist while rubbing his back.

Clearing her throat, Amancia made her presence known even though Leo saw her the minute he walked into the room. She was just as beautiful as Avita. He was mesmerized by Amancia's beauty to the point he forgot he was wrapped in Avita's arms. Looking down at the mother of his child, Leo kissed her on the forehead, grabbing her hand. They sat on the sofa while Amancia followed their every move while sitting on the loveseat.

"So, you are?" she asked curiously.

Before he could answer her question, the voice of his favorite girl filled his ears. "Mommy, can I...Daddy!" Amoy dismissed whatever she was about to asked and ran full speed toward her father. He scooped her up into his arms as she rained kisses all over his face. "You came back!"

"Of course, I did. Daddy has some business to take care of for a couple days. But I promise I'll be back soon."

"You here now, and that makes me happy. Can I play with my iPad? That's what I was coming to ask Mommy."

Avita nodded her head yes and Leo whispered in his daughter's ear before sitting her down on the floor. Amoy skipped out of the sunroom and things became kind of awkward as Amancia stared at him in disdain. Leo didn't know what her problem was, but he was soon to find out. Avita bit into her bottom lip as she avoided eye contact with her cousin.

"So, you are Amoy's father, huh? Enlighten me on something. Why is it so important for my cousin to keep your identity a secret?"

Leo laughed lowly as he picked a piece of lint from his shirt. "I'm not a secret. Just because you don't know who the fuck I am doesn't mean I'm hiding. I see my daughter as often as I can and take damn good care of her whether I'm here or not," he said, leaning back on the sofa.

"Amoy is three and this is the first time I've ever seen you. Why is that?"

"Who the fuck are you that knowing me on a personal level is so major? Avita and Amoy know me, and that's all that matters.

Your family disowned her long ago. I am her family now. Her welfare wasn't important when she was left out here to fend for herself, was it? I'm the nigga that picked up the pieces. If it wasn't for me, there's no telling where she would be. Any more questions?"

Amancia stood to her feet and grabbed her purse. The man sitting across from her was rude and she wasn't going to entertain him by going back and forth. She was disappointed with her cousin because she only sat back looking like a damn fool. There was a reason no one knew anything about the man that popped in and out of her life whenever he felt fit. He proved her point by throwing Avita's family in the mix instead of answering a simple question flat out.

True enough, what Avita's father did to her was wrong. She didn't have to tell someone who didn't understand the tradition of their religion what went on. Unless they were from their tribe, they would never understand. Amancia herself was upset because her arranged marriage didn't happen the way her parents planned. It was the reason she was so hurt by the news of Duke's untimely death. Even though his son left instead of marrying her, Duke still looked out for her. Amancia's situation was similar but different from Avita's because she was set to marry a man that was the same age as her. Avita was pressured to marry a wealthy older man that was damn near the same age as her father.

Amancia was against the man Avita chose because from his accent, the way he dressed, and his demeanor, he was for sure from the States. Being thousands of miles apart, there's no way her cousin was the only woman in his life. If she was going to share a man, she should've gone ahead and married the man she was arranged to be with. At least she wouldn't have been left alone majority of the time raising a child.

Amancia stormed out of the house and Leo got up to follow behind her. He stopped her from going down the steps by grabbing hold of her arm gently. She snatched away and turned to face him in rage.

"Wah yuh wa?"

"Look, we got off on the wrong foot here. I don't know why you are so upset. You asked a stream of questions and I answered them. What's the problem now?" Leo asked.

"You are the problem! If you truly loved my cousin, you would get her away from here. It doesn't matter how much money you dish out to care for her and Amoy. That little girl needs both parents in her life full-time. What's stopping you from taking her away from here? Knowing everything she's been through, why leave her and go back to your life in the States?" When Leo didn't respond, Amancia continued her rant.

"I know why; you don't have to tell me. You have the best of both worlds and Avita being here helps you keep both of your faces intact. You may be able to pull the wool over her eyes, but I see through your little charade. You won't be able to live your double life too much longer though. God don't like ugly, and he's not too fond of handsome either. Avita can only be stupid for so long."

With that, Amancia walked away from Leo and down the stairs to her car. Leo watched her for a few seconds and went back into the house as a car eased down the street slowly. Fumbling with her keys, Amancia was madder than a pitbull in a dog fight. The window on the passenger side lowered as I guy studied her moves.

"Amancia?"

Looking up after opening the door of her car, Amancia squinted to see who was calling her name. She threw her purse on to the passenger seat and stood up straight. When the door of the vehicle opened and a dark-skinned man stepped out in an all-black jogging suit, she tried her best to identify him and drew a blank. As he got closer, the first thing she noticed was his beard and luscious lips. Once he was standing before her, she followed his eyes and her breath caught in her throat.

"Akoni, is that you?" Her voice shook with every word that fell from her mouth.

"How you doing?"

"Oh my God, what happened to your accent? It's gone. I'm doing fine."

"It's still hidden in there somewhere. You're looking good, ma."

"I'm sorry about your father and Akiel," Amancia said, ignoring the compliment he shot her way.

"Thanks. Shit is fucked up, but I'm dealing with it."

"You sound and look like you were born in the States. Let me find out you forgot where you came from," she smirked.

"Never that. The Jamaican blood still running through my veins. That can't ever be taken away from me. Who was that nigga you were talking to on the porch?"

"Nobody," she laughed. "That's Avita's baby daddy."

"Isn't his name Leo?"

"I don't know his name. All I know about him is, he comes in and out of my cousin's life at will. When I asked him why he hadn't taken her away from here, he didn't have an honest answer for me. I don't like him, and I don't even know him. There's something about him, and it's not good. Avita is blindsided by whatever he tells her. I truly believe she is the other half of his double life. But, if she likes it, I love it."

"Do me a favor when you get Avita alone. Ask as many questions as possible about his ass and report back to me. Where's your phone?" She leaned into the car and came back out with her device. Taking it from her hand, Blaze saved his number into her contacts and texted himself before handing it back to her.

"Make sure you tell your man we're good friends. I'd hate to have to blow off his top for playing with me on some childish shit."

"You don't have to worry about that. I've been single for years, and it won't change anytime soon. Your woman may be the one ready to jump off a bridge if I call and she answers."

Blaze licked his lips as he thought about the years of pent-up frustrations Amancia had bottle up inside of her. The last time he ever touched her was when they were teenagers. She could've been his woman or even his wife by now had their parents not tried to force them to marry years prior. Blaze wouldn't mind settling between the thick thighs that held his attention before he headed back to the States. He was long overdue for a good sex session.

"Well, I have some business to attend to. Be easy, ma. Hopefully, I'll get to see you before I leave in a few days."

"Yeah, maybe. We'll see. Be good, Akoni, and don't get in any trouble while you're here. You aren't the same young man that left Kingston at eighteen. Today, you have the eyes of a killer and I know you are out in these streets trying to find out what happened to Akiel. Be careful because it's not the same out here."

"You're right. I am going to find out what happened, and I don't give a fuck about these muthafuckas in Kingston. Everybody involved is gonna meet the same fate as my cousin because Blaze is in town, and I'm about to play the role of the Grim Reaper."

Blaze kissed Amancia on the cheek, tweaked her chin and walked away. Getting in his father's car, he turned the music up, blasting "Throw Ya Gunz" by Onyx as he peeled away.

***

Blaze had been cruising around, seeing how much things had changed around the villages throughout the years since he left Kingston. The structure of houses was pretty much the same, but the atmosphere was totally different. Whereas when he was younger, the drive to work was instilled in the younger generation, it seemed at the time, the youngsters didn't have the same drive. Many were standing around smoking, drinking, and just bullshitting without a care. The older generation was still taking care of the babies, cooking huge pots of food so the entire family and some of the neighbors could eat.

The image of Kadofi was embedded in Blaze's mind as he drove aimlessly around. The sun was setting and he could hear mother's calling for their kids to come inside for the night. The catcalls were music to his ears because it brought him that much closer to his mission. Flaming up the wood he had pre-rolled, Blaze inhaled the smoke and held it in his lungs. As he rolled by a market, he spotted who he assumed was Kadofi and pulled over. He sat finishing his blunt with the window down as he listened to the happenings around him.

"Mi jus mek mi mark wid did one. Mi wi move up inna di rankings fi sure."

"No doubt. Kadofi send fire through fi him ass."

The mention of the nigga's name, along with confirmation that he and his boys were bragging openly about what he had done, had Blaze on ten. The weed flowing through his system didn't make matters any better for the youngin. Kadofi looked young, but not young enough not to know what he did was wrong. Thinking about how he was about to come for his target, Blaze smiled when he saw one of the cats serve ganja to a passerby.

"Hey, cum yah," Blaze shouted after turning down the radio. Knowing Kadofi as the leader of the group was going to be the one to approach, he laughed when his assumptions were correct.

"Wah yuh wa?" Kadofi asked with his hand on his hip.

"Whoa, mi looking fi sum ganja. Lots of ganja." Looking around nervously, Kadofi brought his attention back to Blaze sizing him up for a minute.

"Mi get ganja. Ow much?"

"A poun," Blaze said, throwing a huge weight amount at him. Doing that, he knew Kadofi would have to leave the premises to get what was needed.

"Follow mi."

Kadofi went back to his crew and spoke lowly. They looked toward Blaze, nodding their heads as Kadofi and another guy jumped in a whip. Honking his horn, Kadofi pulled off with Blaze right behind him. He checked the clip in the gun he had taken from Akiel's place. Blaze was locked and loaded. The shacks that they passed were rundown and shabby. Seeing what the environment was like in the neighborhood he frequented regularly growing up had the wheels turning in Blaze's head to do something financially.

Kadofi slowed down before coming to a complete stop. Motioning Blaze to get out of his vehicle, he stood in wait at the rear of his ride. After he tucked his tool in his pants, Blaze exited and walked up to the youngin while scoping out the place. There was no one out and that kind of worried Blaze, but he didn't show his discomfort.

"Waah dis?"

"Mi yaad. Di ganja inside," Kadofi said, motioning him inside.

Blaze shook his head no, crossing his arms over his chest. "Nah, Mi naah guh inna there. Bring it tuh mi. Duh mi luk stupid tuh yuh?"

Throwing his hands in the air, Kadofi and his boy walked to the house without closing the door behind them. Blaze looked around before following them into the shack. He could hear the two shuffling around in the back along with the conversation they were having. Blaze freed his Glock as he tiptoed to where they were. He could see them weigh the ganja on a scale, preparing for the sale they were about to complete. Little did they know, that shit was not going to happen.

"Get against the muthafuckin' wall," Blaze said, coming into the area with his gun aimed at Kadofi. When they didn't move, he shot a warning above his head. "Now!" Thankfully, he had grabbed the silencer so nobody would alert the authorities for the sounds of gunshots.

"Tek every ting. Just nuh kill mi!" Kadofi cried out.

"Did you give Akiel the opportunity to live, nigga?" At the mention of Akiel's name, Kadofi's eyes expanded three times their size. "I don't want the ganja; I was coming for you. Who sent you to kill my cousin?"

"Mi nuh kill anyone."

"Wrong answer, bwoy!" Blaze barked.

Since Kadofi wanted to play on his top about the information he was seeking, Blaze grabbed his partner and put the gun to his head. "Tell me what I want to know or this muthafucka is dead. Who the fuck put the hit on my cousin?"

"Mi nuh kno."

Blaze stared Kadofi in the eyes as he pushed his partner away from him, shooting him in the back of the head. The body fell face first onto the floor and Blaze quickly trained his Glock on Kadofi. He was petrified to the point of pissing on himself. The scene before him wasn't of any relevance since his main concern was finding out who ordered the hit.

"Did that jar yo' memory? You already know the question; now I'm waiting for the answer. You got to the count of three to start talking before I send yo' ass to hell."

"Okay, hear mi out. A olda guy offa mi five thousand dollars tuh kill him. Mi nuh kno fi him name." Blaze didn't believe that shit for a minute and sent a bullet through Kadofi's kneecap. He crumbled to the floor using the wall as leverage while cradling his wound.

"Aaaarrghhhh!" Kadofi was sweating as if he was in a sauna. The pain that was inflicted caused his veins to protrude from his temples stretching across his forehead.

"Now, one more time. Who. The. Fuck. Called. The. Hit?"

"Olda man! Salt an peppa-colored hair. Him use fi be wid Duke all di time. Di tat pan fi him arm says Loyalty."

The pain that shot into Blaze's chest from what he'd heard was almost unbearable. His mother's words resonated in his mind causing a tear to fall from Blaze's eye. He couldn't believe Maven had a hand in his cousin's murder and was possibly the reason his father was no longer breathing. Before he allowed his emotions to take over, he put his attention back on Kadofi. Youngblood pleading for his life fell on deaf ears.

"Please nuh kill mi! Mi ave sons tuh live fi!"

Blaze lowered his hand then snapped his arm upward while pulling the trigger. A single shot went into Kadofi's chest. His fingers dug into the hole as blood seeped from his mouth. Blaze shook his head and sent the remaining two bullets into each of his eyes.

"Fuck dem kids, muthafucka!"

Chapter 11

Leo was singing a happy tune in the shower while Avita waited patiently for him in the bedroom. She made sure Amoy was fed and in bed because it was Mommy and Daddy time in her mind. All the years she and Leo had been together, Avita had never thought about answering his phone until that night. The phone had been vibrating for the past five minutes back-to-back with the same name on the display. Icy. Not wanting to be the nosy girlfriend, she sat in wait of Leo coming out of the bathroom. When the phone rang again, enough was enough and she snatched it up from the nightstand.

"Hello?"

Back in Chicago, Icy was flabbergasted when she heard the voice on the other end of the line. There was no way in hell Leo was stupid enough to allow another woman to answer his phone when she hadn't heard from him in weeks. The long pause was out of the norm for her because Icy usually was very vocal when it came to speaking her mind. In that instance, she was stuck. Everything Kia said during their girl's outing was rendered true. Icy was indeed blinded by the love Leo showed publicly and he was fucking her over in private.

"Ummmm, hello?" Avita repeated.

"I gotta have the wrong number." Icy found her voice to say before hanging up.

Avita didn't believe what the woman said one bit. She could hear the abashment in her voice. There was definitely a connection between her and Leo. What it was would never be known because obviously, Miss Icy wasn't woman enough to say what she was really thinking.

Leo wasn't being truthful, and Avita was fuming and didn't appreciate him keeping things from her. He'd always assured her there wasn't another woman in his life other than her and Amoy. She believed him until that moment. Avita never questioned anything Leo told her and she didn't have an ounce of doubt when it came to the love he professed for her.

"Maybe I'm overreacting. It could've actually been a wrong number," Avita mumbled, placing the phone back where she found it.

She got comfortable on the bed while flipping through the HBO Max app to find something to watch while waiting for Leo to return. Bringing up the phone call was something she didn't want to do because it would interfere with the night she wanted to have before her man left to go back to the States. Avita didn't know when he would show up again to make love to her in the way only he could.

Icy, on the other hand, sat staring at Leo's number on her recent call list and knew damn well she hadn't dialed the wrong number. The wrong bitch just answered the ain't shit-ass nigga's phone. While she contemplated hitting the button to cuss his ass out, Icy's phone rang in her hand from an unknown number.

"I know this bitch is not hitting me up," she said, frowning.

One thing for sure and two for certain, Icy wasn't about to go back and forth with a random-ass female, especially not on account of Leo's decisions. Instead of answering, Icy declined the call and stood to her feet. Without explanation, Icy started packing to get far away from the home she had shared with his cheating ass for years. She wasn't trying to get into any altercations about his fidelities because she was sure the lies were going to be well thought out by the time he contacted her. If she actually needed Leo, she would hear him out, but that wasn't the case. Icy had her own money, and Leo Miller could kiss her ass if he thought she was going to sit back and accept anything less than she deserved.

As she tossed items into her luggage, thoughts of the many trips he took came to mind, causing her to wonder how many times he used that shit to lay up with the next woman. Icy threw her toiletries on top of her clothes and went to find a few pairs of shoes to put in another bag. She had never left Leo when she was angry, but this time, Icy didn't give two fucks. There wasn't going to be a wedding in December if she had anything to do with it. Signing up for a lifetime of cheating wasn't in her plans. Icy refused to settle just to be miserable in the end.

Zipping the small bag, Icy grabbed the luggage and rolled it out of the bedroom. She walked down the stairs and placed her items by the door before going back upstairs to throw on something comfortable. As she placed her feet into her Coach slides, her phone rang from the same unknown number. Icy ignored the sound and let it ring out, then grabbed her keys , purse, and phone before heading out the door. Taking the luggage to her car, she slammed the trunk and hit the unlock button on her key fob.

Her phone rang for the second time in five minutes and Icy was ready to give the caller a piece of her mind. She slid her thumb across the bar and sat in the driver's seat and pushed the button to start her car. The call connected to the Bluetooth and finally, Icy was ready to act up. She didn't attempt to mask her anger.

"What do you want?" she snapped as she put the gear in reverse.

"That's not the way a woman as beautiful as yourself should answer the phone. Whatever the cause of the frown that I'm sure is upon your face, get rid of it, because it's a problem."

Icy took her foot off the gas forgetting she was in the middle of traffic as the familiar accent filled her ear canal. There was no mistaking the voice belonged to the sexy Jamaican she met days prior, but her mind screamed, how? She remembered vividly walking away from him when he suggested they get to know one another better.

"Who—who is this?" she stammered.

"My Icy. I'm sure you have already figured out who I am. That's why you are over there sounding like you need speech therapy. What has you so upset, Love?"

"Akoni, how did you get my number?" Icy asked as she drove toward her mother's home.

"That's not of importance. I have my ways. Now, back to what has you down in the dumps. Come on, talk to me, Love."

Icy shook her head as she made a quick lane change and took off for the expressway. She didn't feel like explaining what was going on in her relationship. When it came to Staci, Leo could do no wrong, and her mother would swear up and down Icy was thinking too much into her allegations, which in turn was an argument that was bound to happen. Since she loved her mother more than life itself, Icy planned to keep her business to herself long as she possibly could. In the meantime, she figured it wouldn't hurt anything to have a conversation with the man on the other end of her phone.

"I'm having relationship issues. Nothing I can't handle though," Icy responded nonchalantly. "Let's get back to how you were able to contact me."

"That's not important. When I saw you a few days ago, your name was engaged. I know damn well that nigga didn't fumble on the play already. He's playing the position of tight-end, making room for a real nigga to come through for the touchdown. I'm liking where this shit is headed already."

Akoni laughed wickedly, causing Icy to laugh along with him. She knew she shouldn't be entertaining his foolishness, but she needed that laughed more than he knew. Leo messed up in the worst way, and it was time for Icy to have a little fun, just as he had been doing for probably years.

"You know you wrong for that," Icy said, still chuckling. "Are you going to tell me how you obtained my number, Akoni?"

"Nah, if I tell you, then I would have to kill you. I need my source for future endeavors," Akoni said proudly. "It sounds like you're driving. How much longer before you arrive at your destination?"

"I am driving, actually. A destination hasn't come to mind as of yet. My mother's house was an option, but I don't want to explain what's really going on in my life at the moment. So I think I'm going to cruise around until I decide."

"Icy, on some real shit, Love. I don't know where your financial situation lies, but you do realize gas is high as hell, right? Driving around aimlessly is not a good choice, especially in Chicago. Is your guy at home?"

"Nah, he's not. He's away on business supposedly. Why are you asking? You trying to see me?" Icy flirted without trying and didn't realize she had done it.

"Believe me, if I was in Chicago, I would definitely take you up on that. But seriously, I think you should go home, Love."

"That's not happening," Icy said, rolling up to the W hotel. "I will take my chances at a hotel until I find a place of my own." Icy got out after turning on her hazard lights and made her way into the hotel. She held the phone to her ear as she neared the front counter.

"Welcome to the W Lakeshore. How may I help you tonight, ma'am?" the clerk asked.

"Do you have a suite available?"

Tapping away on the computer, the clerk chewed on her bottom lip as she searched through the database to see if they had what Icy wanted. She had never stayed at the W hotel, but always wanted to go just to get away. The time had presented itself and she was going to enjoy every minute while clearing her head.

"You are in luck. We had a cancellation for tonight. If you want it, it's all yours," she said, smiling from ear to ear. "How long are you planning to stay with us?"

"A month. If I need more time, I will let you all know in advance."

The woman's eyes bulged out of her head "Well, ummm, the price of that particular room is three hundred forty-nine dollars *a night.*"

Icy didn't like the way the woman quoted the price of the suite. She felt as if she was being judged by the color of her skin, and that shit burned her soul. Opening her mouth to spaz out on the woman, Icy could hear the muffled sound coming from her phone. Realizing she still had Akoni on the line. she put the device to her ear while mugging the woman in front of her.

"I'm sorry. I forgot I had you on the phone. Give me a minute to take care of this business."

"My Icy, I heard what she said. Just get the room and leave it alone."

"Yeah, okay. Hold on," she said setting the phone face down on the counter. Holding her head down for a few minutes as she counted to ten, Icy took a deep breath and smiled. "I didn't ask how much the room costs. I believe I asked if there was a room available. When you confirmed what I needed to know, the next statement to come out of your mouth should've been, I need your form of payment and identification. Don't ever assume something subliminally because you will always make an ass out of yourself. Now, here is my card and my license. Do your job because trying to figure out my finances isn't part of your job description."

The woman nervously picked the items up from the counter. She kept glancing at Icy over her glasses as her face reddened with every second that ticked away. Icy picked up her phone to continue her conversation with Akoni.

"I'm back."

"You handled that very well. Even though you chopped her ass down a few notches."

"She is lucky you gave me a small pep talk because I was about to read her ass to filth. Bitch called herself judging a book by its cover. So what I have on leggings, a tank top, and slides? That doesn't equate what's in my damn bank account."

"Calm down; it's over. How about you tell me why you are staying in a hotel for a month or longer? First, tell me if you are going to be straight after footing that big-ass bill."

"I will be alright after all of this and I don't want to talk about the why, okay?"

Icy glanced at the woman, wondering what was taking her so long to book the suite. When she was about to question it, the clerk glanced up with a fake smile while holding the room key and Icy's items in her hand. Retrieving the receipt, she placed it down with a pen and Icy automatically read over it to make sure everything was correct.

"I thought you said the suite was three hundred forty-nine dollars a night," Icy said, confused with what she saw on the receipt.

"It is, but I was wrong for my actions and giving you my employee discount plus the rate of our VIP members, that dropped the price drastically. It's my way of apologizing, and I would like to verbally say I'm so sorry for what I've done. If you need anything, please don't hesitate to call me personally," the woman said with tears in her eyes. "I've also given you a discount code on food and drinks. Enjoy your stay at the W Lakeshore."

Icy read over the business card, learning the woman's name was Sofie. She scribbled her signature on the line and pushed the receipt back to her. Leaning on the counter, Icy looked the woman in her eyes before she spoke.

"Sofie, I appreciate what you have done, but you have to understand that every black person isn't the same. This world is fucked up and we all need to learn that society is trying to divide us all as a people. Don't allow the color of one's skin to determine how you treat someone. I'm glad you acknowledge your wrongdoing and I appreciate that so much. Get to know a person before placing judgement."

"I know, and again, I apologize for insulting you."

"Enjoy the rest of your night."

Icy made her way outside and hopped back into her vehicle. She used the keycard to enter the garage of the hotel and found a parking spot close enough to the elevator. After pushing the button to shut off the engine, she got out and retrieved her bags from the backseat before pushing the key fob to secure her car.

Grabbing the handle to her luggage and slinging her bag over her shoulder, Icy made her way to the elevator. She had a suite on the twenty-first floor and couldn't wait to lie down and get some sleep. When the elevator doors opened, her phone rang in her hand. She looked down and saw the unfamiliar number and smiled.

"I'm so sorry, again. I forgot you were on the line. What is with you, Akoni? You are being pretty persistent when it comes to me. Why?"

"I love how you gave me the watered-down version of what I asked, but me being the man I am, I'm pretty straightforward. I was strolling in the store minding my business before I literally bumped into the most beautiful sista I'd ever laid eyes on. My heart thumped in my chest in a way that I knew I had to have her. So, to answer your question, I want you. With me, Love, you won't have to worry about what I'm doing in these streets. You wouldn't be running away from home to live a month in an expensive-ass hotel because I would be there to massage your entire body and soul. You need a man that makes you cry from pleasure, not pain. In due time, I'm going to show you better than I can tell you because as of today, Love, you are rightfully mine."

Icy dropped the room key as she tried to insert it into the door of her suite. Akoni was talking smooth as hell and the shit sounded real good too. Being with Leo for years taught her not to fall for everything a man said to her. She didn't acknowledge his words. Instead, she went into the suite and headed straight for the bedroom.

"You have nothing to say?" he asked.

"Nope. Word play means nothing to me. With the man I'm currently with, it seems as if he wasn't a man of his word either. You gon' have to step out like Missouri, and show me. All this talking is going in one ear and out the other. I'm cool on that thing called dating for a while. Maybe it's just not for me. Anyway, tell me about yourself, Akoni. How long have you lived in Chicago?"

"Interesting of you to ask. I don't reside in Chicago. I was there on business for a few months."

"When you say *was*, does that mean you are no longer here?" Icy asked.

"I'm not in Chicago at the moment, but business is still running as if I was standing on site. I'm back home for a couple days. My father died, and I had to be here for my mother through this trying time. We're burying him in the morning and I wasn't ready. Talking to you kind of prepared me to say my final goodbyes."

Icy wasn't sure how she factored in on his preparation, but she was going to let him have that. Hearing about the passing of his father brought her back to the day she was in the same position. That was the hardest thing she'd ever had to endure in her eighteen years of living. Icy had lost her protector and best friend. She felt the warm tears on her cheeks and realized she was silently crying. Sniffing, Icy walked into the bathroom and blew her nose.

"You okay over there?" Akoni asked.

"Yes. I was thinking about my daddy. Someone killed him when I was eighteen, so I know what you're going through right now. He's in a better place. I know that's not going to make his passing hurt any less, but your father will still be there to guide you through life."

"Thank you so much for your words of encouragement. To be honest, there's nothing anyone can say that will detect how my day is going to be tomorrow. I'm going to let you get settled and if it's alright with you, I'll give you a call tomorrow night sometime. Don't let that nigga convince you to go back. Remember, I'm your man now."

They both laughed at what he said and abided their goodbyes. Icy started putting her clothes away so she could walk through the suite to see how she would be living for the next thirty days. She was tired as hell, but sleep was now the last thing on her mind. Icy had a lot to think about, and she wanted to make sure she was making the right choice to walk away from the only man that loved her for the past five years.

Chapter 12

Sitting at her computer, diligently working on an order for an author, Julz was really into what she was doing. She had been sitting for the past three hours and didn't have any intentions of stopping anytime soon. Designing was her passion and once she was zoned in, that was it. Orders had been coming in on her website like clockwork, so she had been busy the last couple of days.

"I gotta take a break," Julz said, snatching her glasses off her face.

Walking into the kitchen, she opened the refrigerator and took out turkey, cheese, lettuce, and tomato to make a sandwich. She had been working, not noticing that she had missed dinner. It was too late for her to even attempt to cook a real meal. As she warmed her meat in a skillet, her business phone started ringing in the living room. Julz ignored it because it was well after eight and her business hours were from nine to five. Assembling her sandwich, she put a handful of Lays wavy chips on the plate and grabbed a bottle of strawberry peach Mike's Hard Lemonade from the fridge. Making her way back to her office, her business phone rang again. Letting out a deep sigh, she picked the phone up and slide her thumb across the bar.

"Thank you for choosing Julz Creations. My business hours—"

"Don't matter to me. Aye, I need you to come up with a design for my basketball squad as well as T-shirts. I left the details on your website, but you haven't hit me back yet."

The deep baritone of the man on the other end of the phone sent a shiver across Julz's clit. She shook that shit off because the way he had spoken to her had her ready to go off on his ass. The professionalism went straight out the window. There was no way she was about to let him slide with the way he came for her.

"Like I was trying to tell you, my business hours are from nine to five. If you filled out the form on my website, I will get to it when I get to it. Calling my phone throwing your weight around won't make me move any faster for you. I'm quite sure there's more orders in the queue before yours. And another thing, that's not the way you call a business. Now, have a nice night, and I will contact you if I have any questions about your order."

Julz hung up on the man and picked up her sandwich taking a huge bite. "Who the fuck he thought he was?" she muttered. "I should go on the site and delete his muthafuckin' order talking to me like that. As a matter of fact, that's exactly what I'm going to do."

She took her food, sat at her desk, and went to her website. Julz didn't even know the dude's name but she went down the list looking for whatever said something about basketball. When she found the order, she clicked on it and read the content of the order. As she read silently, Julz tallied up the dollar amount in her head as she comprehended everything the man wanted. Deleting the order was a thing of the past and she knew right away she was going to contact the caller first thing in the morning. There was too much money to be made to turn down the sale. It was the one that could put her into another level of business, one she hadn't had the privilege to tackle until that moment.

Noticing the client left his email, Julz decided to send him a message to meet up the next day. Once the email was sent, she was too excited to work anymore. The project she was working on could be finished bright and early in the morning. Powering off her computer and straightening her desk, Julz took her half-eaten food to the kitchen and washed her plate. She went into her bedroom and climbed in the bed to watch tv until she fell asleep.

Final Destination had her attention when her phone rang. Julz glanced at the screen and noticed Leo calling. Without thinking, she answered on the second ring because something had to be wrong with Icy.

"Leo, what's wrong with my sister?" Julz asked, muting the television.

"You tell me. I haven't been able to get her on the phone all day. I've called her several times and it goes straight to voicemail."

Julz thought about the last time she had spoken to Icy and the only day that came to mind was when they went out to lunch. She was busy the last couple days and didn't think to check in because business sometimes kept the two away from one another. Getting the phone call had her heart hammering in her chest wondering where Icy was.

"She's not at the house?"

"I don't fuckin' know! I'm still in Kingston," Leo barked. "Find out where she is and call me back. Tonight, Julie!"

"It's Julz to you, son of a bitch. If you wouldn't go a week at a time before you call checking on her, maybe you wouldn't have to call all over the city for her. Get the fuck off my phone." Julz ended the call with Leo and immediately called her sister friend. Icy answered on the first ring.

"Hey, Julz," she said sleepily.

"Icy, are you okay? Leo just called looking for you like you're missing or some shit."

"I'm fine, and fuck Leo. There won't be a wedding, Julz."

Swinging her legs out of the bed, Julz couldn't believe what she was hearing. Icy was excited about the wedding from the moment Leo proposed. Something happened to change her mind so abruptly. While Julz sat wondering, Icy's voice brought her back to the conversation.

"I called his phone earlier and a woman answered. Julz, I couldn't even question her to see what the fuck was really going on. Leo had to be very comfortable with her ass to even leave his phone unattended. He doesn't have a right to talk with me right now. He still hasn't called to say hello, and it's been damn near three weeks."

"Leo said he called and he kept getting the voicemail."

"He's a damn lie." Icy chuckled. "The nigga was trying to see if you knew anything about the bitch answering his phone. It's the reason I wasn't going to tell you what took place until tomorrow. I've already left the house. Are you going to be available tomorrow? I want to go get the rest of my clothes in case he's heading back."

"I may have an appointment, but I don't know what time. I'm going to call my client in the morning and set a date. You don't have to worry about Leo, at least not right away. He's still in Kingston."

"Of course, he is. Stupid muthafucka. I'm done, Julz. That phone called saved me a lot of heartache and pain. What's done in the dark always comes to light. I received my sign and I'm going to move accordingly."

"Are you at Mama Staci's? I'll come over with you."

"No, I'm not. Please don't tell her anything. This stays between you and I. People would just speculate and talk behind my back if they knew what was going on. I just want to be alone for a minute."

"You don't have to worry. Your secret is safe with me. I'll call Leo back and let him know I didn't get an answer either."

"Fuck him! If he gave a damn, he would be home already. Leo is right where he wants to be, and it's not with me. I'll call you tomorrow. I'm going back to sleep."

"Okay. I love you sis," Julz said sadly.

"I love you too. Cheer up. Soon as I get out of this funk, we are going to party and celebrate my new life as a single woman."

Icy ended the call and Julz sat staring at the screensaver on the front of her phone. Leo didn't have a clue that he'd let the old Icy out to play. Deception was something she didn't tolerate very well, and he was about to find out firsthand how painful dry ice really was.

***

Julz didn't sleep well after talking to Icy the night before. She was up bright and early making calls to clients making sure she called Bryan, who she now knew as the aggressive, pushy one who called after hours. Only because he really needed Julz's help is the reason he bypassed how she had spoken to him on the phone. They agreed to meet at Prime & Provisions Steakhouse downtown. Julz decided on that place because of the location. She was going to swing by and pick up Icy, since her friend told her where she was staying.

After taking care of her hygiene, Julz threw on a pair of Fabletic leggings and a hoodie to match, then stepped into her all-white Air

Force Ones. She also packed a bag for her business lunch with Bryan before heading out for the day. It was pretty nippy outside and it was officially fall in Chicago. Hitting the key fob on her purple Audi A3, Julz turned the music up as the car warmed up a little bit. She had parked in front of her building instead of the designated spot she paid for in the underground garage. Julz picked up her phone to call Icy after turning the heat on high and pushing the button to activate the seat warmer.

"Hey, sis. What's up?"

"I'm on my way. We can go get your things from the house, then chill in your room back at the hotel until it's time for my business lunch."

"Okay, I'll be ready by the time you get here. I bet you're still sitting in that damn car because you didn't park in the garage and didn't think to use the remote starter I have to remind you of having." Icy laughed because she knew what she said was correct.

Julz couldn't argue at all. She just sucked her teeth and rolled her eyes. "Whatever. I'm pulling off now, smart ass."

It took Julz twenty minutes to pull up in front of the W hotel. She called ahead so Icy would be waiting at the entrance. Her friend didn't disappoint. The two hugged before Julz drove away from the curb blending into traffic heading for the south suburbs. She bent corners through the downtown streets beating traffic to get on the expressway. Then Julz put the pedal to the medal, doing over the speed limit toward their destination. Breaking the silence, Julz glanced over at Icy and didn't like the sadness she saw in her eyes.

"I thought about this the entire ride to the hotel. Why don't you know what's going on? It's not like you not to go off on a bitch behind Leo's ass."

Icy chuckled while shaking her head. "That's absolutely true. I'm not subjecting myself to that bullshit anymore. Leo wants to throw away a diamond for rocks; mo' power to him. His ass about to be running around the city crying every day when his niggas see me on the arm of somebody else."

Julz's mouth hung to her chest in surprise. Icy had never talked so calmly but aggressively about leaving Leo for the fuck shit he'd been caught up in. Usually, Icy would find the chick and throw hands like Mohammed Ali wherever she saw her. Now, she was over his cheating ass, and Julz was smiling like a proud mama because Icy was finally saying enough was enough.

"Who the hell you going to be with to make him jealous, Icy?" Julz asked.

"Correction. I'm not trying to make Leo Jealous. Icy Winters is about to do her in the same manner he has done for years. If that shit makes him jealous, that's on him." Icy rolled her eyes with plenty of attitude. "To answer your question. Remember that sexy-ass Jamaican who was crushing hard the other day?" Julz nodded her head yes. "He called last night."

Icy had a devious grin on her face, causing Julz to see a different side of her. For some reason, Julz could feel the darkness inside the car when it came to Icy. It was like she was transforming right before her eyes. Nothing good was going to come from the act of deception on Leo's part. Julz would pray that her friend would come back from whatever she was about to do.

"I wasn't aware you had given him your number."

"To be honest, I have no clue how he obtained my number. When I asked, he said it wasn't important." Icy smiled. "But it really doesn't matter because he made the first move and I'm feeling a little frisky. It's been a minute since the fuck nigga touched me, so I may give his cookies to the monster that's ready to eat."

Julz laughed as they gave one another high five. "You won't be the only one getting your groove back. I'm going to luck up and find me a play thing too. My kitty hasn't been petted in so long I'm virginized all over again."

"I'm not mad atcha. The couple weeks for me feels like a lifetime."

Icy's voice trailed off as Julz drove into her driveway. The mood went from joyous to glum in the matter of seconds. Icy jumped out of the vehicle immediately. Julz followed after shutting the car off. By the time she stepped into the front door, Julz saw the back of Icy's shirt turning the corner at the top of the staircase.

Making sure to secure the premises, Julz skipped the steps two at a time and found Icy throwing mounds of clothing on the bed.

"Damn, you serious."

"You thought I was bullshittin'? I'm done this time, Julz. Go in the closet and throw my shoes in a tote. Be careful with them."

Thirty minutes later, Julz's car was filled to compacity and that wasn't even half of Icy's belongings. They left whatever was left and headed back to the hotel. Leo had called Julz's phone damn near fifteen times, but hadn't attempted to reach out to the one that mattered.

"Give me your phone." Icy wanted to wait until they were settled in the car before asking Julz for her device.

"Just let him find out you're gone when he comes back," Julz pleaded.

"Give me the fuckin' phone!" Icy sneered through clenched teeth.

Julz reluctantly handed over the phone without taking her eyes off the road. She knew Icy wasn't going to hold back on what she had to say, and it was only going to make Leo come for her in the worst way possible. Icy went to the call log, hitting the icon for one of the many missed calls from Leo, and activated the speaker. Leo answered as if he was sitting in wait for Julz to return his call.

"I've been calling you like you're my bitch and you still didn't answer! Why the fuck you didn't call me back last night like I told you, Julz? Where the fuck is Icy, bitch?"

Icy was heated because Leo was in rare form calling her sister out of her. She remained silent to see how far he would actually go with the shit talking. Leo was breathing into the phone like a dragon before he started another tirade.

"Answer me, you white bitch!"

Icy laughed wickedly as Julz's face turned pale as paper listening to Leo's choice of words. "Does it really matter where I am, Leonard? While you've been blowing up the next muthafucka's phone, you could've hit me up yourself. Why haven't you, Leo? I can tell yo' pussy ass why. You know I've found out about the bitch you have hidden away wherever the fuck you are. The cat is out the bag now. You—"

"Muthafucka, are you gon' let me explain?" Leo yelled, cutting Icy off.

"Ain't shit to explain. You fuckin' the bitch, right? Yes or no." Icy waited for him to respond, but Leo didn't say a word. "My point exactly. You wanna play? Let the games begin. Punk ass ain't man enough to stand on yo' shit but want to puff yo' fuckin' chest out at a female that has nothing to do with what the fuck is going on," Icy paused and Leo still didn't utter a word. "I'm done with this so-called engagement."

"Icy, you wouldn't make it across the street without me. Stop playing with yo'self. I'll be home tomorrow and we can talk about it then, okay?"

Icy chuckled. "That's cute. I've been with you five years, Leo. You think I've just been spending your money all this time? You stupid as fuck if you think I didn't prepare for something like this. I've never lived in the slums. My daddy made sure of it. I won't head in that direction after you either. Believe that."

"Icy—"

Leo was interrupted by a female's voice which held a heavy Jamaican accent. "Mi no yuh nuh out here arguing wid anotha uh-man?"

Icy held the device closer to her ear so she could hear better. It seemed as if Leo muted the phone because the line became extremely quiet. She looked at the screen a few minutes later and Leo had hung up. Laughing uncontrollably at his cowardice, Icy placed Julz's phone in the cupholder, in deep thought. Icy sat back in the seat and out of the blue starting singing, "Niggas ain't shit but hoes and tricks."

***

With the help of the bellboy, Julz and Icy emptied the car in a timely manner. Ordering room service, the two of them ate and watched TV until it was time for Julz to start getting ready for her business meeting. Icy was sitting in the middle of the bed when Julz appeared in the doorway.

"Damn, bitch! What type of meeting are you attending? You look like you're going on a date." Icy gave Julz the side eye.

"Stop playing with me. This is strictly business. With the amount of product this client wants, I had to keep it professional."

"Professional my butt, Julz. You have on a form-fitting suit that shows all of your assets. Your boobs are going to meet the man at the door and your ass won't be too far behind." Icy fell over, holding her stomach. She sat up and snapped a picture for safe keeping.

"What the hell you taking pictures for?" Julz asked.

"So whenever you tell me you're feeling this nigga, I'll have the before it all happened shot," she cackled.

"The jokes gonna be on you because I never mix business with pleasure."

Julz pulled on her black lambskin leather coat with fur around the collar. The temperature had dropped drastically since earlier that day and she came prepared for Mother Nature herself. "Do you want me to come back, or are you good?"

"I'll be fine. You just be careful and don't do anything I wouldn't do."

"Girl, you ain't doing shit anyway," Julz snickered. "I'm going to conduct business. Nothing more, nothing less. These fools out here crazy nowadays."

"You ain't never lied. Pay attention to the red flags, sis. You know your pussy tighter than an earring hole. Keep that thang in the panties."

"Yes, Mother. I'll call you later. I gotta run."

"Okay," Icy called out as Julz raced out of the suite.

As soon as she stepped outside the hotel's revolving doors, the hawk clawed at her face. Julz used the doors to block the coldness while waiting for valet to bring her vehicle around. When she spotted her car, Julz didn't move until the attendant got out. Basically, running to the driver door, she jumped in and handed him a tip through the window,

The restaurant was less than ten minutes away, but the downtown traffic was congested, causing her to arrive ten minutes later than expected. Finding a parking spot, Julz paid the meter and rushed inside. Giving her name to the hostess, she was led to a table in the back.

"Sorry I'm late. Traffic was horrible," Julz explained as she neared the table.

The man stood from his seat and she had to strain her neck upward to see his face. He had to be about 6'4 inches tall and he was fine as hell. The shirt he wore hugged the muscles in his arms tightly in a sexy way. His legs were bowed and the lump of coal that sat in the front of his jeans left nothing for her to imagine.

Julz wasn't the only one allowing her eyes to do the talking. Her client was sizing her up as well. Licking his lips while his eyes roamed over her frame, he muttered "damn" under his breath. The owner of Julz Creations didn't appear the way he'd envisioned. He pictured a beautiful sista from the sound of her voice over the phone. The way she put him in his place made his dick jump in his pants. In reality, she was a beautiful snow bunny with thickness on overload. Her body was sick, and he thought of many ways he could have his way with her. The thought of dating outside of his race never crossed his mind, but the woman standing before him was about to change his outlook on all that shit.

"It's aight. I haven't been waiting long," he finally said. "I'm Bryan, by the way, and you are?"

"I'm Julie. Nice to meet you, Bryan." Julz blushed, shaking his hand.

She was glad the conversation from the previous day didn't cause Bryan to judge her. Both of them took their seats after Bryan pulled her chair out. The waitress took no time coming over to take their orders. Julz order a salad and a strawberry margarita because she really wasn't hungry after the lunch she and Icy had earlier. Bryan, on the other hand, ordered lobster tails, ribeye steak, a loaded potato, a side of asparagus, and a shot of bourbon on the rocks. Once the waitress walked off to put their order in, Julz got down to business.

"Did you bring a rough draft of what you had in mind for the design?"

"Actually, I did. Check it, I thought about having two designs. Can you handle that?"

"Let me see what you have, then you can explain your vision, and we can go from there. I brought my laptop along so we can work to get it together now instead of sending drafts back and forth. I have nothing but time. I take pride in my craft, putting my all in every aspect of my profession."

"That's what I'm talking about. Let's get this shit rollin' then. Your ambition is through the roof. I checked out your website and social media pages. You raw with yo' shit, shawty."

The professionalism went out the window as Bryan started to get comfortable. Julz noticed the change in his demeanor and had to squeeze her legs together to stop the heartbeat in her kitty. Bryan was someone who could get the yoni if he made the move. Julz knew she had him at hello, but he had her from the minute he turned around. For the time being, she would concentrate on the project. After they agreed on the design, she would see if he was trying to design a new lining for her love cave.

Over an hour and a half later, Julz had drawn up a design that Bryan loved. He wanted a design for his logo as well as the team shirt. Julz implemented both in one design and it was going to be used for the T-shirts as well. Bryan initially wanted twenty shirts for his team, but after Julz did what she did best, he ordered a total of one hundred T-shirts. Bryan was sure everybody was going to want one once they saw his boys sporting the brand.

"Damn, I gotta shout you out on my page. You are a beast at what you do, shawty. Thank you for calling me even after I was an asshole yesterday. I apologize for my actions, for real."

"It's all good. Don't let that shit happen again. The results would be different as hell and I don't give a fuck about the dollar amount. All money ain't good money." Julz sipped from her margarita as Bryan received a call.

"I gotta take this, ma. Excuse me," he said, connecting the call. "What up?"

Julz tried her best not to listen to his end of the call. She pulled out her phone, scrolling through her social media. Responding to some comments under one of her designs, Bryan's voice caught her attention.

"This bitch want me to peel her shit back. I don't play these types of games. Hold on to Jamiah. I'm on my way. Thanks, brah."

Bryan ended the call with fire in his eyes. If he was a cartoon, character smoke would've been coming from his ears. As he threw back the bourbon, Julz glanced up from her phone and Bryan was staring right at her. She sat up straight as if she didn't hear shit he had said.

"I'm sorry about that. I have something to take care of. Is there anything else we need to discuss about the design and what I need?" Bryan asked casually.

"Nope. I will have those shirts ready for you in about a week and a half. I work alone and it takes a little longer. I have a few orders in front of you, but you will have your items within that time frame."

"I'm going to hit you up sometime tomorrow. It has nothing to do with business though." He smirked. "Would that be cool?"

Julz nodded her head as her cheeks grew hot under his friendly stare. It was softer than the expression he possessed a few minutes prior. She basically melted under his spell and Julz wasn't green to what Bryan wanted to talk about. She was going to embrace that shit and get at least one good roll in the hay out of his ass.

"Aight, bet. I'm sorry to eat and run."

Throwing a couple hundred-dollar bills on the table, Bryan leaned over, kissed Julz on the cheek before walking away. She sat at the table working on the design before getting up to leave. She remembered that she had only paid the meter for two hours, the last thing Julz needed was a ticket from the meter maids that loved to get money for the city of Chicago.

Chapter 13

Blaze walked around the holes where his father and cousin's body laid resting. The groundkeepers were waiting patiently for him to give them the okay to start throwing the dirt over the caskets. They knew not to attempt it because of the reaction they had received minutes prior. With a blunt in one hand and a fifth of Jamaican rum in the other, the tears flowed freely down his face.

Even though Blaze had killed the person responsible for Akiel's death, it didn't stop the hurt in his heart. He still had unfinished business to handle. Maven was going to feel his wrath, but Blaze was going to let him believe he got away with the bullshit he pulled a tad bit longer. At the moment, he wanted to make sure his mother was okay and get back to Chicago to steal that nigga Leo's girl right under his nose.

Taking a swig from the bottle, Blaze kneeled down over his father's grave while taking a deep puff from his wood. Thinking about the years he didn't come home to chop it up with his father was eating Blaze up. Yeah, getting away to find the woman worthy enough to marry was something he had to do. But missing out on years of not being there to laugh, drink, and kick it with his father had Blaze looking down at the box that held the shell of the man he loved even when he was mad at him.

Memories flooded his mental as he heard his father scold him, laugh while doing light chores together, and the last argument they had before Blaze took flight. The tears dropped down into the hole, causing Blaze to cry out loudly. The groundkeepers walked away to allow Blaze to grieve in private. The family had left over an hour prior, so he was the only one left at the site.

"I should've come back to spend time with you. I know it wasn't your time to go, and I'm sorry. I can promise you one thing; every muthafucka involved is going to pay. They took something from me that can't be replaced, and I'm out for blood. Old man, I love you, and I'm gon' make you proud. I got justice for Akiel, but that shit didn't hit the spot. The justice for the two of you will be victory for all of us. Until we meet again."

Blaze stood to his feet, poured what was left in the bottle down the hole, and took one more toke from the weed before walking away. He got into the Mercedes and pulled off with "The Ruler's Back" blasting through the speakers. Heading to his father's estate, Blaze really wanted to go to the airport and take flight, but he couldn't just leave his mother without loving on her. Rapping to the track, he smiled for the first time that day. Murder was on Blaze's mind. He was strategizing as he drove with Jay in his ear. His phone rang interrupting his session. He saw "Mada" on the display, answering quickly.

"Yuh okay, Mada?" he asked with concern in his voice.

"Mi calling tuh check pan yuh, Akoni. Lef dat cemetery an cum tuh mi."

"Mi coming now. Mi wi si yuh soon."

Ending the call, the music started playing again as the air hit Blaze in the face. Icy came to mind, and he couldn't wait to see her again. He didn't know what her dude did to her. It didn't matter, because he was going to show her how a real man was supposed to treat a Queen. Her nigga was going to be a thing of the past once he got his hands on her. Blaze was a philanthropist when it came to the woman he wanted in his life. He knew the blueprint and it was going to be far and beyond anything Icy had ever experienced in her life.

Pulling into his father's estate, his energy darkened upon seeing Leo and Maven in what appeared to be a heated discussion on the side of the house. He wished he was a bee in the bush they stood next to. Whatever they were talking about couldn't be good because Leo had his hand in Maven's face.

Given that Maven was a suspect in his father's death, it only pointed fingers at Leo's bitch ass too. They had to be in cahoots together because that was not the first time Blaze caught them whispering to one another. The time would come when he would get all the information needed to end the mystery once and for all.

Blaze parked a few feet away from where Leo and Maven stood. Leo went to his vehicle and pulled out without even a glimpse in

Blaze's direction. He cut the engine and got out of the whip as Maven walked forward in his direction. Taking a deep breath, Blaze exited the car and headed for the house.

"Akoni, I'm so sorry about what happened to Akiel and you losing Duke on the same day." Blaze stopped in his tracks with Maven's words. Grinding his teeth, he stood with his back to him. His jaw flexed with every syllable Maven spoke. "I'll be here for you any way you may need me. Duke will forever live within you, nephew. I love you."

Blaze nodded his head and stepped into his father's house. Maven stood staring at the man he'd practically help raise from a boy to a man. He felt bad because he was the reason Akoni was sad, and he regretted following through with Leo's plan. Duke was his best friend, more like a brother, and he betrayed him the worst way behind a greedy muthafucka. Maven hoped like hell Akoni never found out he had a hand in his father's demise because if he was anything like his father, Maven knew he was a dead man walking. Not knowing where Akoni's mind was after seeing his father for the last time, Maven decided to stay at his hideaway house until he left Kingston.

Inside the estate, Blaze went looking for his mother. Finding her in the bedroom she shared with his father sitting in the chaise by the window. Kenise turned to her only son with a forced smile.

"Ma, you don't have to pretend you're alright. I know this is hard for you, and it's okay to cry," Blaze said, sitting on the edge of the chaise, grabbing her hand in his. "Duke is still here with you. I can feel him. I'm going to stay as long as you need me. You don't need to be alone."

"Nuh worry bout mi. Mi need yuh tuh call yuh fada attorney. Him ave sum information mi wa yuh tuh hear from him. Guh home tonight, Akoni."

Blaze looked at his mother as if she was crazy. There was no way he was leaving her in Kingston alone with Maven and Leo lurking around after what they had done. Lord forbids if something happened to her. Kingston would be no more and he wouldn't be able to live another day on earth without his mother.

"I'm not leaving you here. You have your own suspicions of Maven and I won't leave you open to his bullshit." Blaze seethed with anger.

"Maven nah harm mi. Truss wah mi tell yuh. Eff yuh stay him ago bi nervous. Mi wa him fi get comfortable again. Wah di attorney tell yuh will mek it easia fi yuh tuh cum up wid a plan."

"Ma, I'm not feeling this at all. What if something happens while I'm back in the States? I'm not chancing it. I'm staying."

"No, yuh guh. Mi wi call every day. Mi ago bi safe. I ave security. Yuh wi cum back wen di time right."

Kenise got up and went to a picture hanging over the bed, moving it to the side. There was a safe behind it. Entering the code, she opened the door and pulled out an envelope that she handed to Blaze. He opened it slowly and read the contents before him. Blaze was stunned by the document he held. There was no way Duke was dumb enough to give Maven damn near one hundred million and Leo over fifty million. He wasn't worried about what was left to himself. The will stated it was supposed to be settled directly after Duke was dead and buried.

"Do either one of them know about this shit?" Blaze asked.

"Leo nuh, mi nuh sure bout Maven. Di papas yuh ave inna yuh hands did neva given tuh di attorney tuh change di will. Him wud haffi explain tings furtha. Mi luh yuh, son." Kenise walked over to her son and hugged him around the waist.

"I love you too, Ma. Protect yourself at all costs and don't forget to call me. I will call you as soon as I touch down."

Blaze had a bad feeling about leaving his mother. She wanted him out of Kingston, and he didn't know exactly why. After calling the pilot to get the jet fueled, Blaze had two hours before he had to head out for the airport. Grabbing his bag that he failed to unpack when he arrived, he went into his father's study and sat in the chair. Blaze opened the drawers one by one and when he attempted to open the bottom drawer, it wouldn't budge. Scanning the desk for a key, Blaze came up blank, so he started feeling underneath the desk until his hand touched something hard. He slid what he found to be a magnetic box into his hand and opened it. Inside was a small key.

146

"What are you hiding, Duke?" Blaze mumbled.

Praying the key was for the locked drawer, he inserted it and lo and behold, it turned. Blaze got up to close and lock the door to the study before sitting down to go through the contents he'd found. There were manilla envelopes of every worker Duke had on his roster. Blaze was happy to see that his father was very much hands-on when it came to his finances and how much he paid out to his team. Blaze had access to all of his father's accounts and could see who else had access. Beside his mother, Maven was on every one of the accounts. Blaze made note to keep an eye on any money going out from that day forth.

As he shuffled through more of the documents, Blaze happened upon a folder with the name Leonard Miller printed on top. Placing the envelope on the desk, he rubbed his hands together as he got excited about what he would find between the pages. Blaze reached across the folder and grabbed the elephant his father kept full of ganja and lifted the wooden box lid and found the rolling papers. Even though he preferred a fat blunt, what he had would do. After taking a long puff, he held the smoke in long as he could before releasing it through his nose. Flipping the folder open, he began to read.

Leonard "Leo" Miller

Born: July 15, 1988 in Chicago, Illinois to Solange Kelly and Larry Miller

Children: Amoy Miller (Avita Farquharson)

Net worth: three million

Address: 19512 Kevin Ln. Mokena, IL 60448

Spouse: Icy Winters (fiancée)

Blaze sat back and grinned from ear to ear. What a coincidence it was to find out the woman he was smitten with was connected to the muthafucka he was eventually going to send to his maker. The information not only made him happy; it had the wheels rolling in his head conjuring up the stage of his plan. He had to see Icy as soon as he touched down because Blaze wanted to know everything regarding her walking away from her man.

Putting the file in his bag, Blaze picked up another and that one contained the information on a Zander Miller. The plot had thickened because Leo had a relative in the business and he would have to look into his ass too. Adding that file to his bag as well, Blaze thumbed through until he found the file he was looking for. Maven Whyte.

There wasn't anything in the file which indicated Maven was against Duke in any way. Blaze read further, finding out Maven served on the Jamaican Defense Force for twenty years and started working with Duke soon after. He was Duke's right-hand man and specialized in sharp shooting and performing undetected deaths. His specialty was usage of cyanide. That line had Blaze's eyebrows furrowing because the drug could go undetected unless it was something the medical examiner was looking for specifically. Knowing Maven was in the home when his father died told him all he needed to know as he shut the file and added it to his bag.

Blaze was about to close the drawer when a file with medical records caught his eye. He snatched it up and thumb through the pages as he read the diagnosis his father had received from his doctor. Tears welled in Blaze's eyes because even though his father was only given six months to live from his cancer, a couple of bitch-made niggas took him away before his time. They would pay for that shit.

Locking the drawer back the way he found it, Blaze took the key and his bag and went to search for his mother once more. He found her sitting in the same spot he'd left her and handed her the magnetic box. Kenise looked at him in confusion as Blaze sat on the edge of the bed.

"Listen to me, Ma. This is the key to Duke's desk in his study. Put it in the safe and you know nothing about it. I took a couple files from that drawer and will look over them thoroughly when I get back to the States. I need access to Duke's accounts. Go to the bank and make it happen. I will call you later for the information and I need you to tell me about movement of money between now and the time you give me access."

Kenise nodded in agreement.

"Did Duke take any medication at any time the night of his death?" Blaze asked.

"Him tek a pill by mout every day call temozolomide. Mi give him dosage early afternoon an him guh tuh rest a hour lata."

"Where is that medicine now? Kenise walked around the bed and handed Blaze the prescription bottle. Adding that to his bag as well, he kissed his mother on the forehead while hugging her to his chest. "Be careful, Ma. Make sure you're never alone with Maven. As a matter of fact, I'm going to tell him he needs to stay somewhere else until I return. Don't worry, I would make it believable; you need time to yourself. I love you, and I'm going to go now."

"I luh yuh too, Akoni." Kenise smiled as he turned to leave. "Wait! Mi wan yuh tuh meet di security before yuh lef."

Blaze followed his mother out of the bedroom and down the stairs. There were about six guys standing throughout the lower level of the estate and all of them turned with hands on their weapons as the mother and son descended the steps. Realizing it was Kenise, they relaxed?

"Mrs. Ottey, how are you doing?" one of the guards asked in a Jamaican accent.

"Mi fine. Dis a mi son, Akoni. Mi wa him tuh si fi himself mi inna gud hands.

"Kenise will be well protected. I give you my word on that. I'm Bembe. I've been around protecting your mother for about three years now. I never let her out my sight. Now that Duke is gone, I feel I need to protect her even more. About Maven—"

"He is not allowed on the premises at his time. Until I find out what happened to my cousin, no one, not even family, is allowed in this house with my mother. When she goes out, she should be surrounded at all times. At this point, she is precious cargo, and if anything happens to her, you all will die by my hands. Are we clear?" Blaze looked around at all the men and they all nodded their heads in understanding.

"I need one of you to get in touch with a locksmith and change all the locks around the entire estate. Install a topnotch security system and send me the app and codes so I can view the live footage from my devices. Even though y'all will have eyes on my mother, I want to have eyes on all of you. No disrespect, but this has to be done because I trust no one until I feel comfortable doing so. I want all the food in this house thrown out. One of you take my mother shopping to buy everything she needs to restock. Like I said, I don't trust anything or anyone. Pull out your phones." Doing as they were told; Blaze recited his number for all of them to store in their devices.

"Call me at any time if there's anything y'all feel I need to know. I want you all to make sure my mother is as comfortable as she can be. There are no limitations to what she can do. Allow her to live her life without feeling as if she's a prisoner. Am I understood?"

Bembe spoke up as he stood tall. "I admire you as a man, Akoni. I would do the same for my mother, if she was still with me. I promise I'm going to hold down Mrs. Kenise as if she was my mother. Much respect to you, brother," Bembe said, shaking Blaze's hand.

Dishing out orders, Bembe took charge and everything was put in motion as Blaze stood watching. He turned to Kenise, grabbed her hands and prayed silently before kissing her cheek. Expressing how much he loved her one last time, Blaze left his mother in the hands of the men he surely knew would keep her safe. He got into the vehicle that waited to take him to the airport and placed a much-needed phone call.

"Nephew, how you holding up?" Maven asked.

"I'm good. Check this out. Until I find out what happened to Akiel, I don't want anyone in the home with my mother. She has guards and I'm having alterations done to the estate. Don't go over there until I tell you it's alright to do so. You won't have access. Don't think too much into what I'm doing because I have to protect my mother from afar because I won't be in Kingston. In fact, I'm leaving as we speak. Keep your phone on because I will be reaching out whenever I find out who killed my cousin."

"No, I understand. If there's anything I can do, just let me know and I'm on it."

Maven was nervous and glad Blaze couldn't see his facial expression. If he could, Blaze would've known the person he was looking for was closer than he thought. Knowing Duke's son was doing his own investigation scared the shit out of Maven. If he was anything like his father, it wouldn't be long before he found the details of everything that took place. Maven had to tread lightly because his life's end was slowly approaching.

Meesha

Chapter 14

Zan was excited about the news he'd just received. Stepping out of his car as he prepared to see his lawyer about the documents Sam sent over, Zan adjusted his tie before walking into Smith and Son's Inc. Jerry called and wanted him to sign the papers pronto before Sam decided to change his mind. Going up to the fifteenth floor of the high rise building on Clark Street, Zan exited the elevator and all eyes turned in his direction. The receptionist was all smiles as he neared her desk.

"Good morning, Zander. It's good to see you. Jerry is waiting in his office."

"Good morning, Hannah, and thank you," he said, accepting the cup of coffee she had ready for him.

Hannah had high hopes of Zan leaving his wife and giving her the time of day to at least smell the scent of his balls. Luck wasn't on her side because he was always pleasant, but that was as far as their communication had gone. That didn't stop her from admiring the man from afar though. In her heart, she knew one day he would be hers.

Zan took a sip of the mocha java and knocked on Jerry's door before letting himself in. Jerry looked up from the mounds of papers on his desk without greeting Zan. Jerry had been on Zan's team for about five years and they treated each other like brothers. Taking a seat across from his friend, Zan kept drinking his morning wake up until Jerry decided he was ready to conduct business.

Finally talking to his brother, Zan found out Leo was coming back to the city the next day, which didn't excite him because he was over the bullshit. Boom had reached out to Zan about the whole Slick fiasco and learned two of their traps had been riddled with bullets, causing them to close down shop for a week. When he addressed Leo about it, he shrugged it off as if it was nothing. The whole dilemma was crazy because Zan was around at the time of Rico's murder and could be in the line of fire. All he could do was watch his back at every turn and protect himself out in the streets.

"Earth to Zander," Jerry said, waving his hand in Zan's face.

"Man, gon' head with that Zander shit," he said, placing his cup on the corner of the desk. "What do you have for me?"

"Well, Samuel Jackson has to be in quite a bind. The documentation he sent over clearly states the property he has is on the brink of foreclosure."

"I'm aware of that," Zan said, shrugging his shoulder. "He explained that to me already. What's new?"

"What Sam failed to mention was the fact that the bank isn't accepting any monetary payments on his behalf. Which means, whatever is paid won't go towards the payments he owes. I suggest you allow me to contact the bank on your behalf and pay the asking price for the building and it would then belong to you and not Samuel Jackson. Your friend is a lost cause, and there's nothing you can do for him without bringing yourself down in the process. You would benefit the most going into this business plan alone without him being involved at all."

Zan was pissed that Sam may have known this from the jump, but thought he would just sign off on the shit without getting someone to look over the documents. What Sam tried to do was bamboozle Zan and he didn't like it one bit. Originally, they talked about a thirty-seventy split, but now that he learned he was only out for his money, Zan was prepared to do exactly what he threatened and take a hundred percent of the profits.

"Do that shit, Jay. He thought he had a sucka. I was willing to bring him in and we would build together. Now the muthafucka gon' lose every fuckin' thing he was crying about when he sought me out. I don't deal with that snake shit. What Sam didn't do was his homework. I'm not the same nerdy nigga he went to school with. I'm actually a little bit smarter with a lot more street cred. He better hope I don't shoot his ass in the process with his bitch ass."

"Calm down. There is nothing he can do on the account of him basically losing the building for nonpayment. You would legally own the dispensary, Zan."

"I know that. What I was talking about is the street side to all of this. Sam isn't going to take this come-up sitting down. While he's thinking he pulled one over on me, he actually fucked himself in the process. He's going to come guns blazing behind this."

"We're not worried about that. Do what you have to do and I will do my part by keeping your involvement out of the police database. Problem solved."

Zan sat back as Jerry worked his magic on the computer. He called the bank inquiring about the property and the information was sent to him within minutes. Once all the paperwork was signed and sent back to the bank, Zan did a wire transfer and was the sole owner of Z Smokes dispensary. With the connections Jerry had, the transaction went smoothly. Zan wouldn't be able to open his operation for a couple of months, but he was ready to get started.

Leaving out of the building, Zan jumped in his whip and decided to go see Stack to talk to him about working with him at the dispensary. Out of all of Leo's workers, Stack was the one he could trust the most. Zan was going to need someone to work alongside him on his new endeavor. Beside the dispensary, Zan had two car washes, a laundromat, and a fast-food joint he owned. He was thinking about opening a strip club, but didn't want to deal with the drama that came along with that line of work.

Driving to the southside Zan thought about calling Sam, but didn't want to take that leap at the time. He jumped off the expressway at 87th Street and turned right before stopping at Harold's to buy six wings with fries and extra mild sauce. The wait was well worth the food he had in his hands, and Zan couldn't wait to get back to his ride to fuck the chicken up. He put the food in the passenger seat as he started the engine before grabbing a piece of the meat.

Oblivious to the car that was trailing behind him, Zan continued enjoying his chicken while cruising through every light he approached. Any other time, he would've been stuck at a red light at each intersection. God must've been on his side because the occupants of the other car were waiting for Zan to stand still.

Black sat on the passenger side of the old school Chevy with his .44 Magnum sitting in his lap. He was ready to put a couple of slugs in the nigga driving a few cars in front of him. When Slick gave the order to go after whoever was close to that nigga Leo, he and his boys had been searching high and low for them. It was just their luck when they saw Zan walk out of the Harold's Chicken Shack. Black was itching to wet some shit up.

"Man, let's get that muthafucka now!" Black yelled, hitting the dashboard.

"Calm yo' ass down, nigga. Don't you see all these cars surrounding his shit? We gon' wait until his ass pull over. Long as he's in our sights, we got him."

"Fuck that shit. He might be going where other muthafuckas at and we could be outgunned. You thought about that?" Black shot back.

"Let me see if I can get over," Demon said, hitting his turn signal. "Man, see, there's kids in that car right there!"

"I'm not aiming for *that* car! I should've drove! Yo' ass out here trying to kill a muthafucka with a conscience and shit. Me, on the other hand, would've had the job done while handling the wheel. Yo' ass a lost fuckin' cause." Black was mad as hell until he saw Zan turn onto a residential street.

Demon went a block over and cut through an alley. They peeped their target sitting in his ride firing up as they parked and got out. A woman and another nigga came out of the crib. Black had it in his mind that all of them were going to die that day. Pulling the ski masks over their faces, both Demon and Black jogged across the street with their guns aimed.

The female saw them first and upped a gun of her own and fired off shots quick as hell. She hit Demon in the head and missed Black by inches as he dove into a bush. Firing at Zan's whip he didn't know if he hit the target or not. Black was cursing himself out for not blasting while running. He fucked up and was in a bind because bullets where now hitting the side of the house he was hiding beside. Looking around, he noticed a window in the basement opened and he jumped right through it.

Finding his way out the back of the house, an alarm sounded, causing Black to run high speed to the car he and Demon had abandoned. Black jumped in the driver seat and peeled out of the neighborhood. Zan, on the other hand, got hit in the shoulder but it was only a flesh wound. Somebody called the police and Stack took the guns to put them in the stash spot in his basement. When he returned, officers had the street blocked off with red crime scene tape and two detectives were questioning Zan and Kia.

The way she handled her tool turned Stack on to another level. He knew she was a woman of the streets, but he didn't know she was doing shit like that. Kia was far different from Icy and he was glad to have her on his team. No doubt about it, Kia took care of business and had saved Zan's life. Stack walked up just as the cops started their line of questioning.

"What happened out here?"

"I don't know. I hit the ground soon as I heard the first shot ring out," Kia lied with a straight face and Stack laughed on the inside.

"Who were the people shooting at and what color was the car?" the other detective asked.

"What the fuck did I just say? I was out here watering my grass and my cousin pulled up. I was walking to his car when they started shooting. I fell to the ground and didn't know my cousin was shot until the gunfire stopped. There were two cars involved, but they all peeled away after dude over there fell face first on the pavement."

The detectives look at one another not believing the story that was told. They looked at Zan as an EMT checked his wound and patched him up. Observing his clothing, he didn't appear to have any street affiliation, but in their line of work, looks could be deceiving.

"What was your involvement in this, Mr…"

"Zander. My name is Zander Kelly," Zan said, using his mother's last name. "I had nothing to do with whatever happened out here. I just came from seeing my lawyer and came to pay my cousin a visit. Shots rang out and I ducked inside my vehicle, but I guess I wasn't low enough because a bullet shattered my passenger window and I got hit in the shoulder. I was lucky as hell."

"Why did you have to see your lawyer? You fighting a case or something?" the detective asked.

Zan looked at the pig as if he had two heads. "Why would you assume I'm fighting a case? Every black man walking the street isn't a criminal. Since you all in my business, I just bought the dispensary on Canal and Van Buren."

"How did you get the money to do that? Drugs? Gun distribution? Come on, you can tell me." The detective smirked.

Zan looked at the detective with detestation. All professionalism went out the window when the cop tried to defame his character. Without answering, Zan went into his inside pocket and produced a business card. It listed all of his businesses and the contact information to reach him. Zan had legally added Kelly to his name when he turned twenty-one and he was glad he had because that was the last name his businesses were in.

"Oh, we have us a true entrepreneur in front of us, huh? Well, keep your phone on because we may need you to answer more questions further into this investigation."

Zan scoffed, "I won't be able to help you because I didn't see shit. I told you, my head was under my steering wheel."

The officer's walked away and joined the officers that were surrounding the deceased body. They had yet to cover him up, but they had removed the ski mask, giving Zan, Kia, and Stack a clear view of who Kia had shot. They walked to the porch and sat on the stairs as they watched the investigation unfold before them.

"That's Demon. The nigga runs with Rico's brother Slick. This was a hit, Zan," Stack said low enough for only the three of them to hear. "I knew that shit was going to come back to bite us. Them niggas can't get to Leo and now they are coming for anybody close to him. I'm tired of this shit, and most of the others on the team are too. Leo has been missing in action for almost a month and we've been holding shit down. What the fuck he got going on?"

"That's something y'all gotta ask him. I don't know if he outright said anything, but I walked away from this shit for this very reason. Now that I'm out, I've caught my first bullet, and that shit hurt like hell." Zan laughed. "Seriously, I'm going all the way legit, Stack. I'm opening a dispensary and want you to come work with me."

"Fuck all that right now," Kia cut in. "If these niggas came for you, they may try to get at my muthafuckin' cousin. Leo's bitch ass ain't around to protect her. We need to let her know what's going on." Kia's phone rang in her hand and low and behold it was Icy. Kia answered quickly. "Cuz, where you at?" she asked without saying hello.

"Hello to you too, Kia. I'm sitting back chilling. Why. what's up?"

"I need you to get away from the house for a couple of days. Leo is hot and I don't want you to get caught up in his bullshit."

"That's why I was calling. I left Leo's ass. Some bitch answered his phone and he didn't have much to say about it. Then I heard the female in the background and he hung up the phone. I'm done with that shit man."

"Well, where are you staying?" Kia asked with concern. "You could've come to my house, Icy."

"Nah, I'm good. Your spot is going to be the first place he checks whenever he decides to show his face. I'm at the W hotel on Lakeshore. Keep that between us. I don't want anyone outside of you and Julz to know where I'm laying my head. Even though I told Leo I was done, he doesn't know I packed my shit."

"Fuck him, cuz. Zan just got shot. He good though so don't panic. Some niggas looking for Leo and it seems they are going after whoever is affiliated with him."

"Where's Zan?" Icy asked.

"He's right here." Kia handed Zan the phone and he walked away to talk to Icy.

"Ice, what's going on with you, sis?"

"Zan, don't act like nothing is wrong. Are you okay for real?" Icy asked with tears in her eyes.

"I'm straight, Ice. I'm more worried about you. Shit is getting real in these streets. There's a bounty on my brother's head and they came for me in the process. I'm about to come get you so I'll know you're safe."

"I'm good, bro. I've already left the house because I'm not deal-ing with your brother and his cheating ways anymore. Did you know he had a bitch in Jamaica?"

"Nah, to be truthful with you, I had suspicions because every time we're there, he is missing for long periods of time. Leo never told me about any female so I don't know who it could be. I'm for-ever telling him he needs to do right by you before he loses you. I guess he didn't listen. Ice, you have to do what's best for you. I won't love you any less if you leave his ass for good."

"Thanks, because I'm done. Look, tell Kia to call me later be-cause I have to answer this call. I love you, bro."

Icy hung up before he could tell her he loved him too, but Zan would let her have that. Giving Kia back her phone, he sat back down, thinking about everything that unfolded. Taking his phone from his pocket, Zan dialed Leo's number and waited until he an-swered. When the phone connected, he was shocked.

"Hello. Who is this?" the little girl asked sweetly.

"This is Zan. Who is this?"

"My name is Amoy. I'm three and my Mommy and Daddy is in the room praying."

Zan was confused because Leo was not a nigga that prayed to anybody's God. "How do you know they're praying?" he asked cu-riously.

"Cause Mommy always screams 'Oh God' when they have the door closed."

Zan laughed because he couldn't believe a three-year-old was disclosing the information to him. She didn't know what her parents were actually doing, but he did. Leo needed his ass whooped be-cause he had Icy sitting back waiting for him and he had a whole child nobody knew about. He was going to carry that secret to his grave.

"What's up, Zan?" Leo asked as if he didn't just take the phone out of his daughter's hand.

"So, you were never going to inform me that I had a niece? You foul, dawg."

"Man, you called for a reason and my daughter wasn't it. What can I do for you?"

"You need to get back to the States. Slick is out for blood and he almost capitalized off that shit with me. I was shot, and I thank the same God you and yo' girl was just praising for saving my life," Zan said sarcastically.

"I'll be back sometime tomorrow. I told you, there was no way out of this business. Now you want my protection."

"Nigga, I don't need shit from you. I want you to come back so they can shoot the muthafucka responsible for the shit you did. I can hold my own out here, but you just let me know you ain't shit and will never be shit. Punk muthafucka!"

Zan disconnected the call and rose to his feet. He turned to Stack. "You better think long and hard about what I proposed to you. Leo don't give a fuck about y'all. If he could say fuck me, imagine what he'd do to you. I'm out because when I see that nigga, I'm beating his ass."

Zan walked off and got in his ride. He didn't give a fuck that the police didn't give him permission to leave. All he wanted to do was get home to his wife and child. Zan could hear Cherelle pissing a fit about him being shot before he even got close to his home. Leo was never going to be allowed to step foot in their space again.

Meesha

Chapter 15

Icy had been relaxing and learning how to be on her own without Leo. She went to visit her mother to make sure she was good. Icy told her mother about the other woman because it was weighing on her heavily since she never held secrets from Staci. Her mother understood why Icy left and told her she would understand if she went back. Staci knew how it was to love a man and live with his infidelities. She went through the exact same thing with Birdman, and that was the life of dealing with a man who lived his life in the streets.

Though she heard her mother out, Icy wasn't going back and she was going to stand on her decision. When she left, there was no turning back for forgiveness. Akoni had been keeping her company for most of the week via telephone. Icy was waiting for the food she ordered from room service while trying to find a movie to indulge in for the night. Here phone rang and she smiled widely when she noticed who was calling.

"Hellooooo," she sang into the phone.

"Hello to you to, Ms. Icy. You sound happy this evening. Who has you over there in this joyous state?" Akoni asked.

"I guess seeing your call did something to me."

"Damn, that makes me wonder what your reaction would be if I was at your door."

"If you weren't in Jamaica, you could find out."

There was a light knock on the door causing Icy to temporarily stop her and Akoni flirting. She walked to the door because she couldn't wait to eat. Pulling it open, she jumped back in shock when she saw Akoni standing on the other side with a bouquet of blue roses and a small Tiffany's bag.

"What are you doing here?" she asked into the device.

"Hang up the phone and invite me in, Ice."

The way Akoni said Ice was different from how Zan said it. She moved to the side, allowing him to enter as she checked him out from head to feet. He was dressed down in a black long-sleeved Nike shirt, a pair of grey sweatpants, with black AirMax 270 on his feet. His locs flowed freely over the backpack he had on his back and it was sexy as hell to Icy. He turned around, and her heart skipped a beat because his beard turned her own every time she saw it.

"Why are you still standing there, beautiful? Come give me a hug or something." He smiled, showing off his perfectly white teeth. "You were the one that said if I wasn't in Jamaica I could find out. Now that I'm here, you acting all shy and shit."

Icy couldn't stop herself from blushing as she walked across the room where he was standing. As she went to walk into his out-stretched arms, there was another knock on the door. Doing an about-face, Icy went to get what she knew for sure was her food. Allowing the attendant to push the cart inside, she thanked her and handed the attendant the tip she had waiting on the table by the door. Icy lifted the lid on the food and Akoni watched her every move.

"I'm still waiting on my hug. You can eat after the fact."

Icy melted in his arms as she breathed in his scent. She moved back a bit as Akoni held on to her hands. "What's that cologne you're wearing?"

"It's called Savoir Faire Soul Café. It's a black owned business by the same name. You like it?"

"I do. It smells really good on you," Icy responded, looking up at him with her bottom lip between her teeth. "Are you hungry?"

"No, love, I'm good." Akoni gave the flowers to Icy along with the bag he held. "Sit down and enjoy the gifts I've provided. I'll bring your dinner to you."

Icy smirked as she watched him walk into the bathroom to wash his hands. She smelled the flowers and placed them on the table on the side of the sofa. Peering in the bag, Icy removed the jewelry box and held it in her hands for a bit. Opening the box, Icy gasped at the diamond tennis bracelet that glistened against the black lining. There was a heart pendant with a handcrafted engravement which read "My Icy" on one side and a snowflake on the other.

The bracelet was beautiful, but Icy knew it was expensive. She heard the door to the bathroom open and placed the gift on the coffee table. Akoni looked at the bracelet and smiled at her. He reached over and removed the bracelet and motioned for her to hold out her wrist.

"There are no strings attached. I saw something that was just as beautiful as the woman I decided to shower with something nice. Call it an early Christmas gift," he said with a wink.

"Thank you. I love it," Icy said, admiring the piece on her wrist.

Akoni moved the cart closer to the sofa she was sitting on and removed all the lids from the plates. Icy was hungry as hell when she placed the order, but at that moment, she didn't think she could eat anything with the man standing before her in the same room. Akoni put one of the lobster tails on the plate with a little bit of seafood mac and cheese, broccoli, and a slice of garlic bread. There was enough food for three people. Icy didn't realize VIP had portions of that magnitude in high-end hotels. Akoni handed her the plate along with a napkin before going to the kitchen and returning with a bottle of cranberry juice she had bought earlier in the week.

As she picked at her food, Akoni smirked as he watched her because he knew she was hungry as hell. "Girl, you better stop playing and eat that damn food. This may be the first time you're eating in front of me, but it won't be the last."

"I don't want you to judge me though," Icy truthfully said.

"No judgement coming from me, Love. Trust. In the meantime, since you're playing with your food, tell me a little bit about Icy. We've talked, but never got the chance to learn much about each other."

"Well, I believe I told you I was twenty-nine years old. I own three salons—"

"That's nothing new to me, Ms. Winters. I already know you're a businesswoman that is holding down the fort when it comes to your salons. Tell me about Icy. Your likes, dislikes, your upbringing, parents, siblings, that type of shit."

"Well, my favorite color is green. I dislike liars. Either be straight up with me or leave me the fuck alone. I'm an only child. It has been just me and my mother since I as eighteen years old. My best friend Julz and my cousin Kia are the closest I have to siblings.

My father was murdered in front of me eleven years ago." Icy got quiet as she stared down at her plate.

"You don't have to talk about that if you don't want. I get what you're saying."

"No, I think I need to talk about it with you so that you understand me as a person. I miss my daddy so much and the person that killed him was never caught. I've been in a couple relationships in my life, but the relationship I just left was the one I thought would be the last. Oh, how wrong I was. I recently found out he's been cheating for God knows how long. Leo has been in my life for the past five years and I was finally able to get out of the grieving state I was in for years. He was like my savior when it came to letting go of the fact I would never see my father again. I never thought he would betray me the way he has."

Akoni wanted Icy to bring up Leo's name so he could tell her everything he knew about her beloved fiancé. When he got back to his hotel room, Akoni went through the file with a fine-toothed comb, learning a lot of things about the man Icy fell in love with. He wasn't the man he portrayed himself to be and Akoni was going to be the one to tell her the truth about Leo Miller. Sitting quietly, he listened to Icy speak and felt her pain.

"Not to put his business out there, but he did business with a man in Kingston, Jamaica by the name of Duke Ottey. Duke was like a father. Even though I've only met him once, he called often to make sure I was okay. When I found out he died, it did something to me. I hadn't heard from Leo for weeks and I was worried because I knew he was in Kingston at the time of Duke's passing. It was strange for him not to reach out to me, so I called his phone to make sure he was okay. A woman answered the phone and I froze, stating I had the wrong number. That was the day I packed up and moved into this hotel."

Icy had confirmed what Akoni wasn't sure about and that was Leo being in Kingston when his father and cousin died. He ran his hand down his face and faced the beautiful woman sitting beside him. Akoni had to make sure Icy was done with Leo on all levels.

"So, are you done with this cat?" he asked.

"I'm so done with him. I called him from my friend's phone and he didn't deny cheating, but his actions after I heard a woman in the background proved what I already knew. So, yes, there's no going back to him."

"Not even if I ask you to do so for me?" Akoni asked.

"What do you mean go back for you?" Icy placed her plate on the coffee table as she moved away from him.

Akoni cleared his throat as he prepared to share everything he'd learned in Kingston. "Remember when I told you I was in Jamaica because my father passed away? Aduke Ottey was my father." Icy gasped in surprise as he continued. "I don't want you to think I sought you out purposely, because that wasn't the case. I literally ran into you that day on accident. My father didn't die until days later. While I was back home in Kingston, I somewhat met Leo when I had to put him on his ass. It wasn't until after my father and cousin was buried that I found out Leo was the fiancé you spoke of."

"Wow, this is crazy. Why would you want me to get back with Leo? If I do that, I would have to go through with the wedding."

"Leo had a hand in my family dying that day. He and Maven—"

"I've met Maven! He was the one that called Leo when it was time for him to re-up on his product."

Akoni nodded his head in agreement before he continued what he had to say. "He and Maven got together and conjured up a plan to get rid of my father and Akiel, my cousin, for monetary value. My father had altered his will, leaving both of them with large sums of money. Unbeknownst to either Leo nor Maven, they killed him off before he could finalize the will. My father was murdered for nothing, and both of them will pay for what they have done."

Icy didn't know what to say. The only thing she wanted was to go on with her life without Leo being anywhere in it. She liked Akoni and wanted to get to know him on a whole other level, not with the added drama. There was no way she would be able to build something with him long as Leo had a hand in killing his father.

"How do you know for sure he is the one that killed your father?" Icy questioned.

"I paid a lot of money for the medical examiner back home to work diligently on my father's toxicology report. They found a high dosage of cyanide in his results. When I got back to the States, I went to New York and had his medication tested, and the same drug was found in the pills he was prescribed for the cancer my father had. Maven specializes in the use of cyanide and he and Leo got together and played God with my father's life."

Hearing Akoni talk about what happened to his father pained Icy from within. She already knew what happened to Akiel, and that for a fact was an assassination hit. She never would've believed Leo would kill for money. It wasn't like he was broke. The man had made millions of dollars on the streets of Chicago.

"There's more that I want to share with you. Leo isn't the man he portrays himself to be, Icy. He kept you close because he had to. It wasn't to protect you, sweetheart. Leo was the man that fired the fatal shot that killed Birdman."

"You're lying!" Icy said, jumping up from her place on the sofa. "Leo couldn't have killed my father, Akoni!"

Tears streamed down her face as Akoni reached into his back-pack, pulling out the very folder he took from his father's study. Thumbing through the pages, he pulled out a sheet and handed it over to Icy. Skimming the page Icy cried silently as she read the text message printout.

Leo: Duke, I fucked up. I need to come to Kingston for a few months until shit blow over.

Duke: What the hell did you do?

Leo: I killed a big-time kingpin by the name of Birdman. I've never killed anyone before. You have to help me.

Icy stopped reading and tossed the paper in front of Akoni. She walked to the bedroom and slammed the door. Her cries could be heard from the other side of the door. Akoni stood to go console her, but figured he would give her the time she needed to soak in everything she had learned.

***

Akoni stretched out on the couch after cleaning up the food Icy barely ate and fell asleep. He had a feeling someone was watching him and it caused him to open his eyes. Icy was sitting on the other side of the room with a glass in her hand. Sitting up, Akoni opened his mouth to speak, but closed it when Icy held her hand up stopping him. She had all of the documents spread out on the table in front of her. He never got the opportunity to tell her about Avita and Amoy. If she read through the pages in the folder, she already knew the truth.

"Do you know this woman, Avita?"

"I knew her when we were younger. The woman she is today, no, I don't know her. Amancia, the woman I was arranged to marry, is her cousin. I just recently found that out while in Kingston. The little girl I didn't know about until that day. Amancia was in a heated conversation with Leo when I was passing the house and noticed her. She told me Leo was the father of her cousin's daughter. I knew nothing about your connection to his ass at the time."

"It's okay. You are not at fault for this. Leo is. I'm going to help you with this because I want him to pay for what he did to my father. Our entire relationship was a lie, and I've been sleeping with the enemy for the past five years. My daddy has been rolling over in his grave the entire time because I was stupid enough to fall in love with the man that saved me the night Daron beat my ass. I wouldn't put it past his ass that he set that relationship up too just so he can play captain save a muthafucka. Give me time and I will set things in motion. I don't want him to think getting back with me would be that easy."

"I'm sorry you had to find out this way, Icy. I didn't mean to bring bad news to you and hurt you this way."

"It's not your fault. I respect you for bringing all of this to my attention even if there was a motive behind you doing so. You have every right for wanting revenge and I'm right there with you. I just need time to prepare myself mentally before I go back to that house. On top of that, this nigga has a three-year-old daughter I knew nothing about," Icy chuckled. "What kind of man hides a whole child and make plans to get married so he can make more babies to hide? Bitch-ass muthafucka."

"Come here, Icy," Akoni said, sitting up on the sofa.

She threw back the contents of the glass and made her way to where he sat. Pulling her onto his lap, Akoni hugged her close and ran his fingers through her hair. Icy laid her head in the crook of his neck. The three glasses of wine she'd consumed while Akoni was asleep was taking control of her body.

"Fuck me, Akoni," Icy whispered in his ear as her hand traveled between his legs.

Akoni raised up from the sofa and walked to the bedroom. Pulling the duvet back on the bed, he placed Icy down and covered her up before kicking off his shoes. Taking his shirt off, he exposed his muscles that protruded under the wife beater he wore. Climbing in the bed on top of the covers he cuddled Icy close to his body.

"Get some sleep, Love. You not ready for the love I'm gonna bring into your life soon enough. The time is not now, but it will be worth waiting for.

Akoni closed his eyes and went to sleep to the light snores that came from Icy mere minutes later.

Chapter 16

"I've been calling Icy for the two weeks and she has yet to answer the phone! If any of you niggas see her in these streets, bring her ass straight to me!"

Leo got back to Chicago the day after Amoy answered his phone for Zan. When he arrived home, Icy was nowhere to be found. Her side of the closet was half full and most of her shoes were gone. He knew she had been gone for a good minute because the food in the refrigerator had expired and the fruit in the bowl on the counter was rotten. There were all types of flies and bugs in his home, and the shit pissed him off.

Every time he called her phone, Icy let it ring until the voicemail came on. Leo left so many messages to the point the voice box was full and he couldn't leave anymore. That led him to start texting, which didn't make a difference because Icy didn't respond and left him on read. Truthfully speaking, she was pissing him off for not wanting to address the situation. Leo had gone to Julz's crib; no Icy. He went to Kia's crib and was met with a lot of shit talk from her cousin, but no Icy. When he went to her mother's house, Staci didn't treat him any differently. She offered him food and a little bit of advice. Allow Icy space until she was ready to talk about what was going on between the two of them. Leo wasn't trying to hear none of that. He just wanted to see Icy.

"Man, are you listening?" Stack pounded on the table to get Leo's attention. "What the fuck we gon' do about Slick and nem? They fuckin' with our money with these constant drive-bys. We can't sell shit because they got twelve all around our traps."

"Find them muthafuckas! You sitting in my face talking shit about something that should've been handled while I was taking care of business in Jamaica! What the fuck I'm paying you for?" Leo snapped.

"You can't pay me enough to go out there getting shot at while yo' ass playing the back. This yo' shit, Leo! Since when you leave another muthafucka to do yo' dirty work? You don't even have a plan to get at these niggas."

"If you don't want to go out there and give them a taste of the heat they're bringing to us, then go find a nine to five and get the fuck outta my face. Ain't no pussies in my camp! The shop is closed until we get a handle on this shit with Slick! Get the fuck out!"

Leo didn't need to be in the streets after the lick he had pulled off in Kingston. He truly didn't give a damn what happened to the niggas that couldn't hold shit down in his absence. His streets were dry because they couldn't do a simple job of eliminating the problem. Every other day they were calling him about somebody getting shot, or how the police was hot on the block. A bunch of followers that couldn't stand on their own two feet without him was what he had surrounding him at that point.

After everybody cleared the warehouse, Leo thought long and hard about how he would track down Icy. They were set to marry in a month and a half and he didn't know where the fuck she was. He'd checked the bank statements, and Icy hadn't touched a dime of his money. Leo had never seen any cards in her purse outside of the ones he provided for her. Yeah, she said she saved money, but where the fuck was it? Leo paid all the bills and even set up her business account for Winter Dreamz. Icy couldn't do a mutha-fuckin' thing without Leo's help.

Settling for Desiree's pussy since he couldn't get with Icy, Leo didn't feel as if he got the nut he was seeking. On top of that, being around Desiree put him back at square one with her believing he wanted to be with her. Little did she know, that was one of her dreams that would never come true because she was far from wifey material.

The door to the warehouse opened and Leo snatched his tool off the table. Zan came into sight, and he lowered his piece. He hadn't spoken a word to his brother since the day he questioned Leo about Amoy.

"Why are you here, Zan?" Leo asked as he broke down the weed to stuff into the wood he had on the table.

"I'm trying to figure out what the fuck is going on with you! The way you're moving is kind of like you're on a suicide mission," Zan said with his arms folded over his chest. "You had something to do with that shit in Kingston, didn't you?"

"Why would you think that?" Leo asked as he rolled the blunt with precision.

"Nigga, stop playing dumb! If you didn't have anything to do with it, I'd be surprised, but I know better. You would do anything for Duke, and that includes finding out what happened to him. Not one time did you call and tell me he was dead. I had to find out on the news about him and Akiel. Now I'm gon' ask you again, did you have anything to do with that shit?"

"Nope, now, where is Icy?" Leo lit the tip of the wood, giving Zan a deathly stare.

"I hope she stays far away from your snake ass. Don't say shit else to her, Leo. You have enough bitches to hold you over because you will never find another Icy." Zan turned around to leave when Leo's voice stopped him in his tracks.

"If I find out you're hiding Icy, I'm going to kill you myself, brother."

Zan laughed. "I'll be ready for you too, muthafucka."

He left out the same way he came in and Leo didn't budge from his spot at the table. His phone rang, and Leo didn't know who it could be. Letting the phone ring out, it started right back up before he could place the phone down.

"Yo," Leo said as he puffed on his blunt.

"Leonard Miller, you are a hard man to get in touch with. How you doing?"

"Who the fuck is this?"

"My name is James Monroe. I think it's time for us to meet. It's been long enough, and since I've finally found you after all these years, I believe we are both old enough to come together and share stories."

"I don't know who the fuck you are and we don't have shit to discuss, muthafucka!"

Leo hung up the phone and got up, leaving the warehouse. He locked up and hopped in his whip and revved the engine as he waited for the heat to kick in. His phone chimed with a text. Opening the message, Leo read what it said and looked up in bewilderment, then sent a response before putting the car in gear.

"This shit can't be," he said as he drove toward the expressway.

The caller wanted to meet at Piccolo Mondo in Hyde Park, and Leo was on his way. After the text, Leo knew he and the caller had a lot to talk about. There was no way the shit was possible, but he would find out soon enough how a whole person could drop a bomb so powerful on him the way this person had done.

There weren't any parking spots close to the restaurant, so Leo ended up leaving his car in the UPS store parking lot and walking over. Getting a table in the middle of the establishment, Leo sat facing the door so he could see everyone that entered. After twenty minutes, the person hadn't made his entrance. Leo sent a text letting James know he was there. Five minutes later, his phone rang and he answered on the first ring.

"Yeah, what's up?"

"We have a problem, Leo. I believe Blaze is on to us." Maven spoke fast with nervousness.

"There's no way anybody knows what took place, Maven. You just paranoid. Get a stiff drink and take your ass to sleep. We pulled off the perfect murder, and we're about to get paid for it. Duke is a thing of the past, and we are the new it boys. Trust me, we're safe, and can take this shit to the grave."

"I don't know, man. Blaze had all the locks changed on the doors and I haven't been contacted about the will reading. It's been two weeks since Duke died. The will should've been read soon as he was declared dead. Something ain't right, Leo."

"Shit like this takes time. We have to sit tight. We can make it without a hundred million for a while longer. Go to sleep, Maven. I'll talk to you later. I'm in the middle of handling something right now."

Maven hung up without saying goodbye, and that didn't sit well with Leo. A scared man in the predicament they were in was bound to run his mouth like a bitch. Maven better keep his lips closed because he would be dead before he gave up any information.

James heard every word Leo spoke of because he was sitting in the booth directly behind him with his back turned to the door with a sly grin on his face. He would no longer live paycheck to paycheck with the information he was sitting on. Leo was loaded, and he wanted what he was owed. The life he lived while Leo and Zan lived lavishly was a thing of the past.

Getting up to leave the restaurant, James made sure his face wasn't seen as he made his way out. As he got further down the street, he pulled his phone out and sent a text to Leo.

312-555-7841: I want one hundred fifty thousand dollars or I'm going to send this to the Chicago Police and the Jamaican authorities. LOL

James inserted the recording of Leo's conversation into the text pressing send as he walked down the street rapping, "It's All About the Benjamins".

***

Leo was pissed that someone had the audacity to call themselves blackmailing him. He called James numerous times to no avail. The shit didn't sit well with Leo because he wanted to know why he had gone from talking to drastically throwing a dollar amount at him. Leo knew it was his mistake for talking out loud about what he'd done without checking to see how close the next person was to hear his conversation. Beating himself up all the way to his house, Leo was trying to figure out what he would do to about the situation.

He wasn't home a good twenty minutes before his phone was ringing off the hook. Ignoring the first three calls, Leo finally snatched the device from the nightstand to see what the hell was going on. It was Boom calling like his ass was on fire.

"Boom, what's the emergency, nigga?"

"I'm down at the strip club and Slick just came in. Get here and settle this shit once and for all."

Boom ended the call and Leo's first mind was to call and tell him to handle it himself. Leo thought about how Slick had been terrorizing his business and Zan getting shot and sprang into action. He threw on a black hoodie and a pair of black Timbs before grabbing his phone and keys running out of the house. When he got outside, Leo headed for his whip, but something came to mind as he looked at the Mercedes truck he had bought Icy for her birthday the year before. Going back in the house, he swapped keys and left right back out.

Backing the car out of the driveway, he connected his phone to the Bluetooth and made a phone call. As he waited for the person to answer, he rushed to the expressway. It was mid-October and there was light snowfall, but it wasn't anything Leo couldn't handle. A soft voice filled the interior of the vehicle and Leo smiled.

"What, Leo?" Desiree asked dryly.

"Baby, I need you to take a ride with me. I'm on my way. Wear all black and make sure your hair is covered."

"I'm not getting involved with your bullshit tonight, Leo."

"You better be ready when I get there! Make sure you bring the toy I bought you too. We have work to do."

"I'm not going!" Desiree snapped.

"Oh, you going! If you don't have your ass downstairs waiting on me, you will be right outside with the snow freezing yo' ass off. It will take one hit of a button to cut your muthafuckin' ass off completely. Don't play with me, bitch. I'm on my way."

Traffic was light, making it easy for Leo to get from his home in Mokena to the southside of the city. He wasn't worried about Slick leaving the club before he made it there because pussy was every man's weakness, which got them caught up every time. It took an additional thirty minutes to arrive downtown and park in front of Desiree's building. Her goofy ass came out with a frown on her face. Leo didn't give a damn how mad she was. If she loved him the way she claimed, she would have no problem pulling this off with him.

"Where are we going, Leo?" Desiree asked as she slammed the door of the truck.

"Respect my shit and get all that attitude out ya throat. Sit back and enjoy the ride. You about to catch yo' first body. As a matter of fact, you drive," Leo said, getting out of the truck.

"I'm not driving yo' bitch's shit! What the fuck I look like?"

"A muthafucka that's about to get fucked up for telling me what you not gon' do. Say something else and watch me beat yo' ass out here," Leo sneered. "Now get the fuck out and drive!"

Desiree got out of the truck and Leo pushed her in the back almost causing her to fall. She had to use the side of the truck for leverage, but knew not to say another word. Adjusting the seat, Desiree put the truck in drive. She didn't know where they were going, so when she stopped at the stop sign at the end of the block, Desiree turned to Leo, waiting for him to tell her which way to go.

"We're going to Pussy Katz."

Making a right turn, she headed for the to the strip club which wasn't too far from her condo. The ride was quiet as hell. Desiree couldn't stomach the eerie silence another minute, so she turned on the radio. The snow was starting to come down faster, making her activate the windshield wipers. Desiree hating driving in the snow and the man sitting next to her knew that. As much as she wanted to leave Leo alone, it was too late to get a large sum of money out of him. That alone put her in a compromising position because he was right. If she didn't do as he asked, Desiree would be bouncing from shelter to shelter.

Leo looked over at Desiree shaking his head. In his mind, she was a lost cause and she held no value to his life. She was nothing more than a fill-in for him. Leo knew he was wrong for what he was about to do, but life wasn't always fair in the world of love and war. Since Icy wanted to play games, he had plans to make her sit and think about how miserable she had made his life in a matter of weeks. All she had to do was respond to him when he called or texted. Instead, she wanted to act like he never mattered to her. Somebody should've told her not to play with the big bad wolf because she was liable to get chewed up and spit out in the process.

Turning in to the parking lot of the strip club, Leo directed Desiree to park a short distance from the entrance. Leo sat tapping on his phone without making an attempt to get out. They sat for a few minutes before she decided to address the reason they were there.

"Are we just going to sit here?" she asked.

"Wait until I tell you what the fuck to do. Just keep the car running and make sure yo' piece is set to go."

Doing as she was told, Desiree checked the custom nine-millimeter and made sure the extra clip was in the pocket of her hoodie. Running her thumb over the side she hummed along with "B.S." as she rocked from side to side. Leo frowned at her and wanted to slap the shit out of her ass. The song came on at the wrong time because it had him in his feelings because Desiree started singing the track with her whole heart.

"Don't let that song get yo' teeth knocked down yo' throat."

Desiree chuckled as she watched the door of the club. Leo got a text and he looked up after responding to the message.

"Look for a nigga in a white coat and black pants. He gon' be with a bitch. Soon as you see him, jump out and blast his ass just like we practiced at the range. Let's see if my money was worth the lessons."

"What about the female?" Desiree's voice shook with every syllable that came out of her mouth.

"Leave no witnesses."

The moment the words left Leo's lips, the unknown nigga made his exit and Desiree threw the hood over her head, concealing her face. She jumped out of the truck and let her bitch ride. Leo was sitting like a proud father as he watched her lay down the target. His dick got hard when he saw her reload and empty another clip before running back to the truck. Desiree peeled away from the scene like she was Cleo from the *Set It Off* movie. One down and who knows how many more to go.

Chapter 17

Icy had laid low for the entire month of October while she tried her best to camouflage the hate she held in her heart for Leo. Knowing he was behind the death of her father was a hard pill to swallow, but she knew she had to let it go for the time being. She had to act out the façade she had in place so it was believable to everyone that would be in attendance at the wedding. The only person who would know the truth was Akoni.

Since it wasn't safe for her to be out and about in Chicago with him, Akoni arranged for the two of them to spend three weeks in the Bahamas. The sexual tension was thick between them. If she had anything to do with what went down, they would've fucked every day they were away. Like the night she asked him to fuck her, Akoni held his own and didn't allow sex to interfere with the real reason he took her on the trip. He wanted Icy to relax and have fun before she had to put on the charade of a lifetime.

Icy was pampered and treated like a Queen every minute of the day. She and Akoni enjoyed the sights, excursions, and good food. Now, she was back in Chicago, and he went to Jamaica to check on his mother. The first thing Icy did when she returned to the hotel was call her managers to check on her salons. Once she found out business was still booming, she called Julz and Kia to chill with her. The day had arrived to let them know she was going to give Leo another chance. She knew they would be against it, but going back was her choice.

While she waited for Julz to show up, Icy took the time to finally call Leo. Her hands shook uncontrollably and she had to pause for a second. Taking deep breaths, she tried again. *He killed your father, Icy. Fuck that nigga. Blow his muthafuckin' head off*, a voice in her head yelled. Icy was on the verge of crying, but she sucked that shit up and ignored the devil that was trying to get her to deter away from the plan that was already set in place. Pressing on Leo's name, he answered right away.

"Icy, baby. Where are you? I've been going crazy over here. I haven't been able to eat, sleep, or nothing."

Icy knew Leo's ass was lying through his teeth. She swallowed the laugh that tried making its way out of her mouth. *Slice his ass into tiny pieces!* Icy shook the thought away and cleared her throat.

"Hey, Leo. I hear what you're saying. Please allow me to speak in entirety, then I will hear you out. Deal?"

"Go 'head, baby, I'm listening," Leo said calmly.

"Okay. I had to take time to myself because for years, it's been all about you. My loyalty speaks for itself, and there's no denying I've been all about you the entire time through. I'm not about to sit here and throw everything you have done in your face, but you know well as I do that you have not given me the same loyalty in return."

"I—"

"Aht, aht! It's not your turn, Leo," Icy said, cutting him off. "I've forgiven you and turned a blind eye on many occasions to your bullshit in order for the love we supposedly had for one another to work. You played on the fact of me loving you with my all while you gave me bits and pieces of love with a lot of materialistic shit. You should've known I couldn't be bought from the beginning, Leo. I've never needed you, baby. All I asked you for was love and you half did that and I stuck it out. Why? Because I loved you." Icy paused as anger pushed its way to the forefront of her tongue.

"See, this last bitch cut deeper than others because you hid her well. That only means she meant something to you, Leo. Why not just tell me you didn't want me and go on with your life with her? Instead, you fucked, sucked, and expressed your love for me. So much that you went out your way and bought a ring, asking me to be Mrs. Icy Miller. How the fuck does that work, Leo? You expected me to stick around after you were comfortable with the bitch answering your phone and you showing up damn near a month later.

That shit didn't feel good when I did it, right? You were sitting wondering where did you go wrong? Why would she leave when she knows how much I love her? Didn't I love her enough for her to stay with me and only me? Lying in bed at night crying because your peace wasn't lying next to you to hold you close. Scared out of your mind that something horrible happened and that's the reason you hadn't heard from the one that made your heart beat.

Well, guess what Leo? I don't know about you, but that's exactly how I felt every day you were missing in action as you laid up with the next bitch. Why? That's all I want to know. I'm giving you one chance to lay everything out on the table or I'm gone forever."

Leo didn't even know where to begin after the way Icy laid everything out for him. To be honest, the hurt in her voice had him feeling like shit. He owed her the truth, and he didn't think she could handle what really took place in the last few years.

"I'm going to tell you the truth. Yes, I've been involved with a woman in Kingston. I met her on one of my business trips four years ago. We had a one nightstand and I ended up getting her pregnant. I was wrong and I know this is hurting you to the core, Icy. I should've told you about my daughter a long time ago, but I didn't want you to leave. Believe it or not, I love the fuck outta you, man. Other than my daughter, I have no dealings with her mother."

Icy was seething on the inside as she listened to Leo give half the truth, even though she could put the missing places where they belonged in his story. She sat silently as he thought long and hard about what he was going to allow to come out of his mouth next.

"I love my daughter and I didn't want to have to choose between you and her. That's something no man would ever want to be in position to do, so I opted to keep her a secret and provide for her from afar. When I was in Kingston, Duke died and Akiel was killed. You know how I felt about that man. He was the closest thing to a father to me and to you too. I was fucked up behind that shit and shut everybody out until after his funeral."

Muting the phone, Icy had to cackle after hearing that shit. Leo was a compulsive liar that could sell ice to an Eskimo if need be. She unmuted the phone when she realized he had stopped talking.

"If you knew Duke was there for me and I loved him as if he was my own father, why wasn't I the first person you reached out to when he died? I had to find out about his death on the news and when I called to make sure you were okay, I was ignored."

"My mind was all over the place, Icy. I was also helping Duke's wife and his son make the arrangements. They needed all hands on deck and I did what needed to be done to put Duke away properly."

His lies were getting better each time he added to his story. The hole Leo was digging was growing deeper by the minute, and it was hard for Icy to keep the truth to herself. A headache was coming on, so Icy knew she had to end the conversation sooner rather than later.

"Look, the shit was bogus as hell on every level. I love you, Leo, and I'm not the type of female that's going to make a child pay for the actions of their parent. You would have to explain a lot to your daughter and I will be there any way I can to help you support her. The mother, not so much, because I have to take your word about things being over between y'all. You have no more chances, Leo. If you fuck up this time, you're going to have to kill me because I'm going to leave and never return. I'll be back at the house soon. Be ready to act like you want to be my damn husband."

"I promise, I got you."

"Don't make promises you're not willing to keep. Action speaks louder than words. I'll talk to you later."

Icy ended the call just as several knocks came through the door. She let Julz and Kia in and they sat down, wondering what Icy had to talk to them about. Icy grabbed a glass and the bottle of wine and got comfortable to hear them ridicule her on going back to Leo.

"What's up, cuz?" Kia asked as she pulled her coat off.

Icy took a huge gulp of the wine and set her glass on the table. She looked at both Kia and Julz trying to figure out how to say what she was about to do. Icy knew there was no way other than just speaking her truth.

"I'm going back to Leo," she blurted out.

"Wait, what?" Julz asked as she reared her head back. "You're going back to his shiesty ass after everything he has done? Why?"

"Yeah, why the fuck would you do that? There's plenty of dick out here, and what about Akoni? I think he is the better choice for you."

"I don't care how y'all feel about my decision. I'm going back to my man, and that's it. I figured I would tell y'all myself before either of you saw me back all lovey dovey with him. Leo is all I know. Akoni is a good man. To be honest, I'm ready to be married and I don't have time to go through the motions of a new relationship. Just be happy for me, y'all."

"Icy, I think you're making a big mistake but this is your life and I can't tell you how to live it. I'll be there anyway I can. I'm not going to lie though, I'm never going to kick it with that nigga like all is good," Kia said, shaking her head.

"I'm with Kia. I don't know if I can pretend to like Leo after this. I'll see you when you're not with him. I have a month to practice my happy face before this bootlegged-ass wedding. After that, it's going to be see ya when I see ya."

Julz stood to leave and Icy cried silently. They had never been at odds until that moment. Icy wanted to tell them the real reason she was going back. She just didn't want anything to get in the way of what she had in place. Kia was grilling her hard and had yet to speak her mind. Icy waited, and the words never left her cousin's mouth. Standing to her feet, Kia hugged Icy, telling her she loved her and left just as Julz had. Icy was left alone with her treacherous thoughts as she started packing all her belongings to leave the hotel for good. It was going to be the longest month of her life, and she wasn't ready to live a lie.

***

It took Icy three days to move back to the house she shared with Leo. Things were very awkward for her in the beginning. Icy couldn't sleep comfortably next to him because she had real bad nightmares about him smothering her. Leo even tried to cook dinner and Icy refused to eat, believing he would poison her. Every time he hugged her from behind unexpectedly, she would jump and have to play it off as if she wasn't actually afraid. Deep inside, Icy missed the comfortability with Akoni and wished she could be in his arms instead.

"Babe, what do you have planned for the day?" Icy cringed upon hearing Leo call her babe. "I thought maybe we could go get massages together. You have been really tense since coming back home.

"That sounds good to me. What time are we scheduled to go?" Icy called out from the bathroom.

"We have to be there at two. That gives us a little bit to have some us time."

Icy could hear the excitement in Leo's voice and she knew he was going to end up being in his feelings because she didn't have any intentions of having sex with him. Fiancé or not, Icy wasn't feeling being intimate with him. She knew eventually, the day would present itself when she would have to give in to his advances. Icy chose not to respond to what he said and continued to pull the shirt over her head.

Exiting the bathroom, Icy stopped in the doorway as her eyes landed on Leo lying in the middle of the bed stroking his member. She sat on the edge of the bed and he grinned at her. The way he licked his lips turned her stomach. Icy could only see the image of Leo fucking another woman and it only angered her.

"Come top me off, babe."

"Top you off? You have never talked to me like that. Don't start now. I'm gon' need you to focus on the woman standing in front of you," Icy said calmly as she sat on the edge of the bed.

"Why you want to do this? I'm trying to get us back to where we used to be and you blockin' it at every turn!" Leo was getting mad because rejection was not something he was used to, especially not from Icy.

"I'm sorry, okay? You have to give me time, Leo."

"How much time do you need? We will be getting married soon and you treating a nigga like I got a damn STI or some shit. I went to the doctor like you asked and I still can't get no pussy!"

"Is that all you want from me? Why can't we just spend time together and gradually ease back into the sexual prospect of this relationship? Remember, you are the reason—nevermind."

184

Icy stood and started taking her clothes off. She smiled as she stepped out of her leggings and joined Leo in the bed. Lying on her back, Leo wasted no time finding his place between her thighs. Blowing on her pearl, he nibbled before running his tongue along her folds. Leo used his forefinger and thumb to hold her lower lips apart before going in for the kill. Before Icy would become instantly wet, but not that time. She was drier than the Sahara Desert. Leo's mustache was hurting her down there and it caused Icy to push his head back.

"What's wrong?" he asked, looking up.

"Nothing. Keep going."

Icy had to do something to make her kitty come to life or Leo would get pissed all over again because she wasn't reacting to him sexually. Closing her eyes, she envisioned Akoni and her kitty became instantly soaked. Icy pinched her nipples through her shit and imagined the lips that were pleasing her belonged to the sexy dread head that she really wanted to make her cum. The suction was taking her over the edge. Grabbing the back of Leo's head, she rotated her hips, feeding him pussy vigorously.

"Fuck. Mm-hmm. Right there," Icy moaned.

Leo was taking his time to please his woman and the moans she let out had his dick hard as hell. He couldn't wait to slide deep into her love cave. Icy's sugar walls was what he'd been craving since he came back to the States. The way her clit swelled in his mouth let him know the sweet nectar was about to bless his tastebuds. When he stuck his middle finger into her kitty, her muscles clamped on it and he knew she hadn't been with another nigga.

"Oh, shit A...Aaahhhhh!" Icy barely caught herself from screaming out Akoni's name as she squirted down Leo's throat. The slip-up could've been deadly for her had she acted out her fantasy in real life.

Leo came up wiping the cum from his chin as he used the excess onto his harden member. Getting on her knees, Icy turned away from him and arched her back as he slid in. That position gave her the ability to fantasize more about Akoni giving her that big-ass log he had between his legs. Smacking her on the ass, Leo was truly fucking up the mood with all of his sex talk. At one point she loved that shit, but she wanted him to shut the fuck and get his nut so he could get the hell away from her.

"I miss this pussy. Shit still the best I've ever had." Rolling her eyes hard, Icy squeezed her muscles with all her might to cut the session short. She'd had enough of Leo's lies and just wanted it to be over.

"Don't do that, baby. You gon' make me cum and I'm not ready," Leo groaned.

You better get ready, nigga, 'cause your time is up. Icy continued to suck his dick with her yoni. Leo was dripping sweat on her back and she felt dirtier than a shitty piece of tissue. Growling in her ear, he finally let his babies sail toward her uterus. Icy was glad she followed her first mind and started her birth control before going to the Bahamas. Leo's ass was not going to impregnate her if she had anything to do with it.

"That shit was so good, Icy. Give me a minute and we can go another round. I can't get enough of you."

Leo looked down and Icy was snoring lightly. He started laughing as he got out of the bed to get a towel to clean her up. After wiping his love juice from between her legs, Leo covered Icy with the blanket and went to take a nice hot shower. The moment the shower came on, Icy opened her eyes because she had dodged that bullet. There was no way she could pretend someone else was in their bedroom a second time.

Chapter 18

Maven sat in his car outside of Duke's estate, building up the courage to ring the doorbell. He hadn't heard anything about the reading of the will and he felt that Kenise was holding out on valuable information. He had many questions and she better be able to provide him with the answers or she was for sure going to join her husband in death. Checking his hip to make sure his gun was where he placed it before leaving his home, Maven cut the engine and got out of his vehicle. Walking up the steps, he rang the doorbell with a mug on his face. The door opened seconds later, and Maven felt the urge to take a shit.

"What brings you to my mother's doorstep, Maven?" Blaze asked.

"I—I—I need to speak to Kenise about a private matter," Maven stammered.

"Nah, there's no private talks going on around here. I know everything that's going on that concerns my mother. Now talk, before we have major problems."

"I just wanted to know how she was doing. Since you changed the locks, I haven't been able to check on her."

"Well, that's all you had to say, Unc. You out here looking real suspect and shit. Come in," Blaze said, opening the door wider to allow him access to the home.

Blaze noticed Maven had come to sit in front of the house for the past three days without getting out of his car from the camera monitors. He laughed, knowing one day he would get the nerve to come to the door. When he saw him that day, he sent his mother to the guest house because he didn't want her to have any parts of what was going to happen to her husband's long-time friend.

Maven looked around the quiet foyer as he followed Blaze further into the home. Every time he saw Kenise, she was surrounded by security and they wouldn't let too many people in her space. As they passed the kitchen, Maven strained his neck to see if anyone was there. Blaze looked back and chuckled.

"Ma isn't here, Unc. She went out to get some oxtails for dinner. You can come downstairs with me. She should be back soon.

Blaze had been busy turning the lower half of the estate into a torture chamber, but Maven didn't need to know that. He was quite sure Maven thought it was still a family room. Taking his time picking out every trinket known to man, Blaze couldn't wait to test every last one of them out on human flesh. As they got closer to the door, Maven had a change of heart and turned back to leave.

"Unc, where you going?"

"Uh, I need to go get something from the car," he replied as his eyes shifted in the sockets.

"Why the hell you so nervous? You practically lived in this house. It's the same spot you used to hang with Duke to watch the games and shit. I promise, his spirit is only in the bedroom these days." Blaze laughed, trying to lighten the mood. "For real, there's nothing to worry about. I miss the old dude too."

"You right. Come on, nephew. What you got going on down there?" Maven asked.

"Shit, I was just shooting a little pool. You been good though?" Blaze opened the door and moved to the side so Maven could go down first.

"Pool? What you know about that, youngin?" Maven chuckled.

"I know how to sink the eight ball in the corner pocket, then guess what? Game over, muthafucka!"

Blaze pushed Maven down the remainder of the stairs and walked slowly to the bottom. The carpet saved his ass from getting hurt too much. As Maven scrambled for his waist, Blaze skipped the last two steps, landing right on Maven's left arm. Howling out in pain, Maven turned on his side as Blaze bent down and snatched the Glock from his waistband and released the clip.

"Nigga, you thought you were going to get away with what the fuck you did to my muthafuckin' family? You should've known better, bitch!" Blaze was so mad he was foaming at the mouth. He held onto the collar of Maven's shirt and dragged him across the floor.

"My father literally gave you the shirt off his back and you stabbed him in the muthafucka while he was down! Weren't you ever taught not to bite the hand that fed yo' ass? My father did that and more for yo' snake ass and you let a pussy-ass nigga talk you into turning on the one man that was there for you through all yo' fucked-up struggles." Punching Maven in the top of his head. "Stand the fuck up!"

"I would never bring harm to Duke. That was my brother, nephew. I loved him too much to do anything like that; I swear to God! Please, Akoni," Maven pled loudly as he struggled to stand upright.

"Akoni isn't in this bitch. You about to feel the wrath of Blaze," he leered. "Your malicious ways about to have you beggin' for your life, but that shit won't work tonight."

"Hear me out, Akoni!" Maven cried.

"I'm listening." Blaze stood in front of Maven with his harms folded over his chest.

"It was Leo's plan. He was angry because Duke handed everything over to Akiel. Leo didn't like the fact that he was looked over as next in line. With Duke out of the way, Leo was set to gain a fortune and he wanted it. I had nothing to do with any of it. That's why he was in Kingston as long as he was."

"You see, Maven, I lost even more respect for you with that bullshit. Own up to your part in this shit! Tell me what the fuck *you* did."

"I didn't do shit! It was all Leo!"

Blaze bit his bottom lip as he restrained from breaking Maven's neck with one punch. "I'm going to let you in on a little secret." Blaze gaze at Maven with fire in his eyes. "I killed Kadofi," he said, seething with rage. "I found out you called the hit months ago! Why do you think I protected my mother?"

Maven's eyes expanded three times their size upon hearing what Blaze knew.

"Since you won't tell me, I'll run what I know to you then you confirm the accuracy, 'kay?"

Maven nodded his head because at that point he figured he'd lied enough and the truth may just get him a second chance at life.

"Leo's bitch ass was mad because he didn't get to run my father's empire. He threw a tantrum and conjured up a plan to get rid of both Akiel and Duke *after* you told him about what you *thought* was in the will." Blaze smiled as he licked his lips. "Oh, you didn't know? You muthafuckas killed my father for nothing because y'all ain't getting shit!" Blaze screamed, punching Maven in the face causing the chair to fall back.

Blaze pulled Maven and the chair upright as Maven spit out the blood that filled his mouth. "Back to what I was saying. You found some lil tough punks to ride down on my cousin and had him assassinated. While that was taking place, yo' goofy ass was here at the estate lacing my father's medication with high dosages of cyanide. My mother, as a wife, gives her husband, my father, his cancer medicine and he falls asleep, never waking up because of yo' pussy ass! You killed two birds with one stone, and for what? Nothing, nigga!"

Jumping to his feet, Blaze ran blows over ever part of Maven's body. Maven didn't know which way to block any of the hits. His face was swelling with every punch that was thrown. He even felt a few of his ribs crack in the process, making it hard for him to breathe.

"Call that muthafucka! I want you to let him know the stupid shit y'all did has just cost you your life and his ass next!"

"You broke my ribs and my arm," Maven cried out.

"That's the least of your worries. Now call him!" Maven fished his phone out of his pants pocket and hit Leo's name on the screen. "Put it on speaker, bitch," Blaze snarled.

"What up, Mav?" Leo's voice filled the room.

"He knows what happened."

"Who the fuck is he? What you talking 'bout?"

"Blaze knows what we did and he's going to kill me, then he's coming for you," Maven cried.

"That nigga right there, ain't he? I knew you was gon' snitch wit' yo' weak ass. Whatever happens to you is on you because I told you to keep ya mouth closed. For you, bitch-ass nigga," Leo said, referring to Blaze, "come find me." Leo ended the call, leaving Maven to fend for himself.

Maven dropped the phone and laid back on the floor in defeat. The muthafucka that he was in cahoots with had turned his back on him in the worst way possible. Blaze, on the other hand, was getting a kick out of the shit. Maven was a stupid muthafucka that gave up the life Duke provided for him to end up dying in the process himself.

After getting himself together, Blaze lifted Maven off the floor by his arm and hugged him tightly. "I think you should choose your partner's wisely next time. Killing you ain't worth my troubles, Unc. Plus, I'm not really a killer and don't want your death on my conscience. I'm not my father, Maven," Blaze said, walking him toward the side door that led outside. "I'm gonna let you go, but you ain't walking through my mother's house leaking blood all over shit. Thank my father for this, because he just saved you from above."

As they walked outside, Maven noticed Blaze had installed a small pond. It was beautiful, and under different circumstances, he would've loved to sit and enjoy the scene before him. Walking along the path around the pond, Blaze started speaking again.

"I see you are admiring my handiwork, huh?" Blaze said as he pulled a blunt from his pocket before setting fire to the tip.

"Yeah. You did good, nephew," Maven said, wincing as he held his ribcage.

"Good, because it's all yours now," Blaze said, slicing Maven's arm before pushing him into the pond.

Within seconds, Maven's blood was smelled by the hundreds of piranhas that hadn't eaten in a month. The species tore into Maven's flesh while he screamed in agony. Blaze sat in a lounge chair, kicked his feet up, and smoked while he enjoyed the show.

Meesha

Chapter 19

The day before the wedding

"Sorry about that," Leo said as he took a seat at his desk. "That was the news I was waiting on."

"Talk to me, nigga, I need my bread," James barked from the chair he was sitting in.

"You know, I don't usually let a muthafucka strong-arm me into doing shit. With the information you have put on my heart, I'm gon' let that shit slide this time," Leo replied. "You gotta do something for me in return though. It's nothing that would put you in a jam, I promise. I need you to be on standby for my wedding tomorrow. One of my groomsmen may not be able to make it and if that happens, my soon-to-be wife would be upset. Can you do that?"

James looked at Leo like he was crazy for asking him something like that. He'd come into his life out of thin air, blackmailed him for a hundred and fifty racks, and now Leo wanted him to be part of his wedding party. The shit didn't sound right to him.

"What the fuck you on, nigga?" James asked.

"Nothing, man. I just need you to do this for me."

Leo pushed a button on his phone that caused the sound of a text being sent to his phone. Sliding the phone across the desk, James picked it up and smiled. There was a message on Leo's phone stating one hundred million was just deposited in his account.

"Your hundred-fifty will be available soon as we go to the bank and open an account for you. We can stop by the tuxedo shop and get your fit and shoes so you can be ready for tomorrow. And you need a haircut, nigga. I got a position for you too after all this because I like the way you move. There's money out here for all of us."

James was green to Leo's grimy ways. Knowing he would have a steady income was music to his ears and he was ready to jump in feet first. Going over how much the money would help was running nonstop in his head. James would be able to leave the shared home he was staying in and buy a new car, not to mention find an apartment of his own.

"I'll do it. I'm ready to whatever it takes to get back on."

Leo did everything he told James he would do. He even put him up in a hotel for a week and gave him a few dollars until the money cleared in his new account. To James, all Leo had done was legit, but one had to know Leonard Miller in order to know they had been bamboozled. The only thing that was true about anything Leo had done for James was the garment bag he took to his room for the wedding. It was going to be a little too late by the time James caught on to the trap that had been put in place.

Arriving home to an empty house, Leo thought about all that had happened in the past three months. He was glad things turned out the way it did with Icy, but Desiree was giving him the blues. Even with the wedding taking place the next day, she still tried her best to convince Leo not to go through with the ceremony. He knew she would stand by his side regardless and didn't pay her any attention.

Leo had been trying to get in touch with Maven since the day he called, to no avail. That only told Leo that he was dead. Plans to go back to Jamaica to get what was owed to him was on the top of his list after he and Icy returned from their honeymoon in Aruba. Kenise was coming off that money or he would kill her ass and take it. Blaze scared all of them niggas in Kingston, but he didn't rattle shit in Leo. Maven couldn't have told him much of anything because it had been a month and he hadn't brought no smoke.

As Leo sat thinking about his moves, his phone rang in his pocket. He was shocked to see Zan calling his line. He hadn't heard from his brother since the day he came to the warehouse. No matter what happened, Zan would always be there for his brother.

"What's up, stranger? I thought you counted me out of yo' life."

"Leo, you are still my brother and I will be still be there to stand by your side at the wedding. I'm glad you made things right with Ice, and please do right by her this time."

"Stay in your place, little brother. I still owe you for walking out on me. Icy ain't going anywhere and I'm still gon' have my bitches. Now what do you want?" Leo asked irritably.

"You not gon' learn until something drastic happens to yo' ass. You have too many enemies to act like you're invisible, Leo. I was calling to let you know that muthafuckas are out to kill you."

"I'm not hard to find. Stop worrying about small shit and just be at the venue on time. I got shit to do."

Hanging up on his brother, Leo sat with a feeling that something bad was going to happen to him at his wedding. He wasn't a bitch by far and was going to marry the woman of his dreams with his head held high and his Glock by his side. He had nothing but time on his hands because Icy was spending the night at the hotel. She was worried about that superstitious shit of the bride and groom seeing one another before the wedding being bad luck. Leo, on the other hand, was going out to hit Desiree one more time for the road. At least until he came back from his honeymoon.

Heading up the stairs to take care of his hygiene, Leo took a shower and threw on a pair of black joggers, black hoodie, and a pair of J's. There was no reason to get geared up to lay down to watch his dick disappear like magic in and out of Desiree's mouth. After gathering his garment bag, accessory tote, and shoes, Leo grabbed his keys and phone before leaving the house. He was closing the trunk when an unmarked Crown Vic blocked his car in the driveway.

"Here they go with this bullshit," Leo huffed, turning around.

Two plain-clothed cops got out of the vehicle, heading toward him. Cynthia Scott stared at Leo with pure disgust. She held plenty of animosity in her heart for him because of the way he played her before she became detective. Cynthia was in love with Leo and he turned his back in a flash. She made a vow to get back at him, and her day had finally presented itself. Leo had no idea Cynthia was in the academy when they were dealing with one another. Never knowing what he did for a living, Cynthia's nipples hardened like Grand Canyon mountains with the thought of getting major payback for the shit he put her through.

"Well, well, well. If it's not the infamous Leo Miller. Where are you running off to so fast? I know you're not leaving town."

Leo smirked because he knew they were on a whole other level with the bullshit. Cynthia was still beautiful as ever with her thick thighs, voluptuous ass, and that monkey that stood firm between her legs. The slacks she wore couldn't hide the camel toe he came to love back in the day. Cynthia knew the thoughts that were going through Leo's mind because their sexual encounters were flying through hers.

"Cyn, how you doing, baby girl? You of all people know I don't run from shit. To answer your question, I'm quite sure since you're at my crib, you know I'm getting married tomorrow."

Cynthia's mouth gaped open until she realized she was wearing her feelings on her sleeve. "It's Detective Scott to you. Don't talk to me as if you know me personally."

"But I do. That's why you low-key mad about finding out I'm getting married." Leo turned to Cynthia's partner. "Shawty trying to act as if I don't know her. She has a pussy that would hold on to yo' shit like a pair of vice grips. The muscles in her jaws stronger than a Hoover vac and would have a muthafucka droppin' babies down her throat prematurely. Brah, you should ask her to test that shit out. Best blowjob of yo' life comes from Cyn. I just found better."

There were a few minutes of silence between the detectives, but Leo was laughing his ass off. Walking to around to the driver side of his whip, he placed his hand on the handle with his eyes trained on Cynthia.

"Move ya shit so I can roll out. Y'all have taken up enough of my time already."

"We're watching you, Leo. Your empire is going down, and you will spend countless years in prison," Detective Boyd snidely stated.

"My empire is legit. I pay taxes on that shit and have the paperwork to prove it. There's nothing illegal about owning several condominiums and making good money off of it too. Other than that, you don't have nothing on me that would have me sitting for any period of time. Yo' scare tactic won't work with me."

"There's plenty of proof of your drug involvement, Mr. Miller. You and your brother Zander Miller are the ringleaders."

Leo didn't flinch at the mention of drugs. He wasn't worried about getting caught on that because his hands were clean as a whistle. Now, if they were talking about murder, they would see him sweating bullets. His coy demeanor was starting to piss Detective Boyd off.

"I guess you need to be interrogating Zan about that then, You're in the wrong nigga's face. Unless you have proof of *me* selling anything other than real estate, you barking up the wrong tree. Now again, what else do y'all want to speculate about? I got shit to do."

Cynthia snarled in Leo's direction and she was hotter than a habanero pepper standing in the freezing cold of Chicago. Leo's cockiness on top of how he blatantly disrespected her had Cynthia on another level. She was prepared to knock him right off the high horse he was riding on.

"Who's speculating? You, your brother, and your bitch are going down." Leo frowned at Cynthia's mention of Icy. He knew for a fact she had nothing to do with his operation.

"Icy Winters is in the middle of your bullshit, Leo. I know all about her being the daughter of Jerome 'Birdman' Winters. You thought she would be safe? I'm coming for your ass for old and new, muthafucka!" she gritted.

"Stay the fuck away from Icy, Cyn! That's a subject you don't want to touch on. If one hair is out of place on account of you, I'm coming for yo' head, bitch!" Leo opened the door of his Range Rover placing one foot on the ledge, Cynthia's voice paused his movements because she always needed to have the last word.

"Is that a threat?"

"Nawl. It's a muthafuckin' promise. Take it however you want, but you heard what the fuck I said. Get the fuck off my property. Now!"

Sitting inside the vehicle, Leo slammed the door and pushed the button bringing the engine to life. Cynthia got into the Crown Vic on the passenger side while her partner occupied the driver's seat. The car inch forward just enough for Leo to back out and speed away in the opposite direction. Inside, the two detectives sat quietly before Detective Boyd broke the silence.

"You never mentioned knowing Mr. Miller on a personal level. What the hell were you thinking and what type of inside information do you know?"

"Ron, my encounters with Leo were years ago. I don't give a damn about him today. He is scum and he's going down!" Cynthia shot back.

"This personal shit between you and him can jeopardize the investigation. You do know that, right? It's time you fill me in on what you know so I won't be blindsided when the shit hits the fan. I'm not going down for your vindictive way of bringing this down, Scott."

"When I arrest Leo's ass, it will be justified. He's going to pay for everything he has ever done."

"I have a bad feeling about this," Boyd mumbled as he shook his head, driving off down the street.

***

With the pigs breathing down his neck, Leo wanted to double back and go home. The feeling of something happening to him was at an all-time high at that point. Seeing Cynthia suited up with a badge caught him by surprise. When he met her, she was going to school by day and taking his dick at night. The relationship they had was pure sexual; nothing more. Icy had suspicions of him cheating and he almost got caught up. After that encounter, he ended things with Cynthia. She didn't take the news well and tried to make his life a living hell, causing him to change his number and get lost in the city where they lived.

Leo wasn't hard to find, but Cynthia didn't know a lot about his way of living. He never thought much about her because she up and disappeared after a while. Now she was back and out for blood. If she had anything to bring him down, there was no doubt she would do whatever it took to make the charges stick.

Gathering his things from the car, Leo made his way upstairs and stood in the hall, thinking about how his life had turned out in such a short period of time. The door to Desiree's condo opened and she stood in a pair of boy shorts, watching Leo as he zoned out not even noticing her. She waited to see just how long it took for him to glance up while he stood in the hall.

Leo lifted his head and stared directly at Desiree, but still didn't put forth the effort to go in. Shaking her head, she cursed him out silently before going back inside. Leo knew she was about to be extra and thought about leaving without getting his dick wet. He wasn't trying to argue the night away about shit that wasn't going to change. He grabbed everything from the floor and used his key to gain entry since Desiree locked the door being her pretty self.

"You saw me standing out there. Why lock the door?" Leo asked, stepping into the kitchen where Desiree was slamming dishes around.

"Why are you even here?" she scoffed, looking over her shoulder. Eyeing the items in his hands, Desiree cackled and turned back to what she was doing. "For a muthafucka that's getting married tomorrow, you shole about to start that shit off on the wrong foot."

"I didn't come here for all that, Des. All you should be worried about is me being in your presence. It shouldn't matter what I have going on after today. How many times do I have to tell you that we're never gon' be on the outs? Des, you are just as important to me as Icy. Marriage is just a legal document binding me and Icy together. What we have is fairly different, Des. We don't need anything to bind us together other than the love we share for each other."

Leo's speech was a crock of shit entering Desiree's ears. It only pissed her off more than she already was. She hated the fact that he was holding on to her basically because he knew he could. Desiree was beating herself up for every time she went out buying extravagant shit instead of saving.

The thought of quitting school based on a man saying he would always take care of her strangled her internally. Everything Desiree had done for Leo wasn't worth the bare minimum of so-called love he dished out to her. She didn't know her worth making it very easy for Leo to continue manipulating her to believe he was all she needed.

"Bullshit!" Desiree screamed over the sound of shattering glass from the plate she slammed into the sink. "I've been involved in this love triangle too long. Being in the face of the woman whose man sucks on my pussy every chance he gets before returning home to kiss her goodnight has become tiring. I've done so much for you and it's never enough. I've even killed for your ass, and that's more than the bitch you're about to say I do to has ever done. Fuck you and fuck ya bitch too! Get the hell out of my house, Leo!"

Leo placed his bags on the nearest chair with a sly grin. His eyes never left Desiree as he crossed his arms over his chest. Leo stood with his legs spread apart licking his lips. Desiree's words resonated in his mind and he didn't believe anything she said.

"So, you ready to ride out, Des?"

Desiree's lips quivered and her eyes filled to the brim before she blinked which caused the tears to cascade down her face. Not really wanting to admit what she was thinking, Desiree stayed quiet. Her heart was breaking right before him and he didn't seem to care one bit.

"Answer me," he calmly said, breaking the silence. "You were on a roll for a minute. Stand on yo' shit, Des. If you ready to walk, let that shit be known. It's obvious you sick and tired of playing yo' position. I won't fight you to stay if that's not what you really want to do." Waiting for her to speak up, Leo stood with his head tilted to the side. When Desiree continued to cry, he leaned against the counter, clearing his throat.

"We can settle this shit right now. I'll drop twenty bands in your account so you can sail into the sunset and be happy. But, when it runs out, don't bring yo' ass back when the shit run out. Ain't no more where that came from."

Desiree bawled openly wiping the tears away but they flooded faster than she could control them. "I don't want your money, Leo. I want you! Please don't marry her," Desiree cried. "I would do whatever it takes just please don't do this to me."

Leo walked over and pulled her into his arms. "Don't cry. I'm gon' make sure you're straight. I owe you that much." Leo ran his hands through her hair as she cried with her face buried in his chest. "You deserve a man that's going to love you and only you. I'm not that man, Des. My heart is with Icy."

"That's not enough!" She wailed grabbing a fistful of his shirt. "Don't leave me. Tell me what you want from me!"

Desiree held onto him for dear life. Leo hated the fact that she loved him the way she did. He was shining the light on her and she still didn't see where he was coming from, but he couldn't make her understand. Being the nothing-ass nigga he was, Leo lifted her onto the counter sliding her shorts to the side. He licked her folds slowly before going in for the kill. After Leo detonated the bomb in her center, Desiree became lightheaded from the oral massage he was delivering. She was going to do whatever the fuck Leo wanted her to do once he was finished putting her in a euphoric coma. Desiree had no idea what was in store for her. She should've walked away when he gave her the chance. Now she better be ready, because she asked for every muthafuckin' thing that was destined to come her way.

Meesha

Chapter 20

Wedding Day

"There's nothing out here, bae," Icy said, pulling the coat tighter around her neck."

"Be patient," he said, shifting his feet.

Leo looked around at the crowd of people and nodded his head. A big truck made its way down the street, and Icy was curious as it got closer to where they stood. The driver got out and went to the back of the truck with his partner. Leo placed his hands over her eyes, preventing Icy from seeing anything until he was ready for her to do so. Icy could hear the whispers and she wanted to see too. The sound of something being lowered had her excited.

"Baby, you know I love you and will give you anything your heart desires. Today is the day I present you with this." Leo's voice was a tad bit higher than usual, but the excitement she felt had her canceling it out.

Leo lowered his hands and Icy screamed as she jumped up and down. Leo had bought her the Porsche Cayenne coupe that she had her eye on for the longest time. Icy even had a name picked out for it. Midnight, because the car was midnight black from the exterior to the interior. He'd given her a brand-new home as an engagement present and Icy loved that house, even though there wasn't any genuine love within the walls.

"Thank you, baby!" Icy screamed, more so about the car than Leo presenting it to her.

Leo pulled her towards the car and handed over the keys. Icy opened the door and that baby was fully loaded! She loved every aspect of the vehicle, and all she could think about was cruising the streets of Chicago in her new whip. Sitting in the driver's seat, Leo leaned down and kissed Icy tenderly and stood tall with his chest out, then hit the pavement with a thud.

"Leo!" Icy cried out.

Jumping out of the car, Icy got down on her knees as she cradled his head in her lap. Leo's blood was soaking through her coat as his brain matter oozed into the palm of Icy's hand. She was shocked as hell to see Leo lying there struggling to breathe. The first thing that came to mind was Blaze. He wanted her to go through with the plan of going back to Leo so he could kill him.

"I need a fuckin' ambulance, now!" Zan screamed into his phone as he kneeled down beside Icy. "Leo, open your eyes! Stay with me, bro."

Zan had pulled off his coat and placed it under Leo's head. He used his vest to apply pressure to the gunshot wound in the back of his head. Zan knew there was no way his brother was going to live after being shot. The way his eyes kept disappearing in their sockets, it was only a matter of time before they closed permanently. Sirens were heard in the distance, causing Zan to go through Leo's pockets. As he searched, he realized Leo didn't have anything on him.

"Did Leo give you any of his shit to hold, Ice?"

She shook her head no. "Make sure you get his gun off his hip, Zan. You can put it in the new car for now," she said as she looked down at Leo. The ambulance pulled up and the EMTs jumped out with a stretcher.

"He don't have a gun," Zan said as the paramedics got closer. The paramedics were asking question after question before Leo was lifted onto the stretcher and rushed away to the ambulance.

"What hospital?" Icy yelled out to one of the workers.

"Northwestern," the female responded before jumping into the passenger side of the ambulance.

Watching the ambulance race down the street with sirens blaring, Icy stared silently at the blood all over her coat and hands. She didn't feel anything about Leo being shot. The thought of Leo not having any identification on him and the gun she knew he had on his hip throughout the day that wasn't there either was puzzling. *What the hell is going on?* she wondered.

"Come on, Ice. We have to get to the hospital." Zan grabbed her by her shoulders shaking her a little bit.

"I'm going to drive the car and meet you there. I have to get my mama first."

"She's by the door with Julz and Kia. This shit is fucked up. I'm out, man. I'll see you in a minute."

Zan ran to his car and jumped in. Once Cherelle was safely inside, he pulled off without waiting for her to close the door completely. Staci ran over to Icy with tears streaming down her face. Icy hadn't dropped one tear. She was hurt because Leo was possibly dead, but he brought that shit on himself.

"I'm so sorry, Icy. Leo is going to be okay. Come on so we can go see about him."

"Ma, Leo was damn near dead before they picked him up. He's gone. I can feel it."

"He can't be gone!" Desiree cried out of nowhere. "I just told him I loved him last night!"

Hearing Desiree confirm what she already knew brought the rage Icy was holding inside out full force. She lunged at Desiree, but was held back by Stack and Pip. Laughing uncontrollably, Icy didn't put up a fight because it wasn't worth it.

"You can tell him again when you see his ass. I never thought of you as a snake-ass bitch, Desiree. I hope you didn't think smiling in my face was going to lead you to taking my place. Leo didn't love you; he loved the pussy you dished out to his ass at his beck and call. This is not the time for me to beat yo' ass, so I'm gon' let you make it."

"I may not have been able to take your place, but I know I had a spot in his heart. I mattered!"

"Whatever, bitch. When you see me, you better get out of dodge. Leo is not a factor in what I have in store for your ass. I owe you a round for the disrespectful shit you had going on behind my back. Karma is a bitch and baby, I'm wintertime cold from this day forward."

Icy walked to the brand-new car and got in. Waiting for her mother, Julz, and Kia to join her, Icy brought the vehicle to life. Seeing Leo hit the pavement took her back to the day her father was gunned down. A lonely tear fell from her eye and she smiled. *That was for you, Daddy*, Icy said to herself as the doors opened.

***

Icy pulled into the parking lot of the hospital and got out as she popped the trunk. She chucked her coat inside and slammed the trunk shut. Walking briskly into the emergency room entrance, the waiting area was packed and everyone was surrounding Zan as he cried like a baby. Seeing him in that manner told her that Leo didn't make it. Pushing her way through the crowd, Icy got down on her knees in front of Zan and held him tight.

"I'm so sorry, Zan."

"He's gone, Ice. My fuckin' brother is gone!" he wept. "We were going through shit, but I didn't ever want him to die! I gotta find that nigga that popped up at the venue. He did this shit!"

Icy couldn't open her mouth to agree or disagree with Zan because she knew Blaze was responsible for Leo's demise.

"I had to give them all of his information because he didn't have anything on him to identify him. They told me to wait until they got him cleaned up and then they would let me back to see him. I can't do this by myself, Ice."

The doors to the back opened and a doctor stepped out looking around the room. "The family of Leonard Miller?" Zan stood abruptly and stepped out into the open before going to stand in front of the doctor. Icy followed close behind to hear what was being said. "You can go back now. I'm sorry for your loss."

"Thank you. This is his wife and she's going to accompany me back there," Zan said somberly.

The doctor looked down at Icy's wedding dress with a look of sorrow. It hurt his heart that the woman standing before him was only able to enjoy her new husband for a few hours. He couldn't imagine what she was going through at the time.

"That's fine. I would say congratulations, but that wouldn't be appropriate due to the circumstances. I'm so sorry."

Being led to the elevators after the awkward moment from the doctor, Icy's mind was not on what was going on around her. She was thinking about the moment she would be able to talk to Akoni. Icy wasn't mad about what he had done. She was more pissed about not being informed about his plans. Leo was bound to die, but she didn't expect for him to be shot in the head in front of all of their family and friends.

Icy didn't recall the moment she stepped onto the elevator until the doors opened and they were escorted to a floor that was eerily quiet. Walking down the hall, Icy looked into every room she passed, causing her heart to beat faster than the seconds on a clock. When they stopped at the last door on the right, Zan slumped against the wall with his head in his hands.

"It's going to be okay, Zan. We just have to properly identify him and then we can leave. I'm with you every step of the way."

Zan glanced over at Icy, perplexed. "We were all we had, Ice. That nigga left me here by myself!" he exclaimed, punching the wall. "Shit been rocky, but that was still my muthafuckin' brother and he was taken away from me!"

Drawing him into her arms, Icy held Zan until his weeping subsided. He squared his shoulders and took the first step into the building. Leo was lying on his back with the sheets pulled to his chin. There was a bandage taped to the back of his head and to Icy, he appeared asleep.

"Is this your brother, Mr. Miller?"

Zan whispered yes and walked further into the room. Inspecting Leo's face, Zan didn't see the scar in his eyebrow he got when he fell off the monkey bars at the park when he was ten. There was a mole under his eye that wasn't there hours before. Curious to examine the body further, Zan moved the sheet down to Leo's chest in search of the tattoo the two of them got together years back. It wasn't there.

"Um, Doc, would you excuse us and give us some time alone to say our goodbyes in private?" Zan asked without turning around.

"Sure. Take all the time you need. There's a button on the wall you can push once you all are ready to leave." The doctor left closing the door behind him.

Icy walked over and stared down at her husband's face. Reaching under the sheets to hold Leo's left hand, she stroked the top of it and noticed his nails were dirty as hell. Leo would never have nails of that magnitude and he knew Icy would have a fit if she saw it. That hand belonged to someone that fixed cars for a living and it was disgusting. On top of that, Leo had his hands all over Icy during the wedding and at the reception. His hands didn't look like they were at that moment.

"Zan, something isn't right. Look at his nails."

"His nails? This person is two shades lighter than Leo. He doesn't have the lion tattoo on his chest, and he has a mole under his eye. This is not my brother, Ice."

"How can this be? Leo doesn't have a twin brother...do he?"

"Nah, it's just me and him. My mama didn't have any more kids. I'm have to find out some shit and I need to reach out to some of my nothing-ass family members to figure this shit out. In the meantime, we have to plan a funeral for this person under the guise of him being Leo. This shit crazy."

Zan pushed the button and waited for the doctor to come back into the room. When he appeared, Zan told him he would contact a funeral home to come pick up the body. As they made their way back to the main floor, Icy had more thoughts going through her head and she was nervous as fuck.

"Do you think Leo faked his own death?" she asked.

"I don't know. There was no way Leo knew this shit was gon' happen beforehand. That nigga Blaze did this shit and I need to holla at his ass pronto. He was threatening my brother in the middle of the venue, and now he's dead."

"Or is he?" Icy questioned.

Zan didn't respond as the doors to the elevators opened. The lobby was still crowded when they stepped into the room. Icy went right to her people and her mother hugged her tightly. In the midst of it all, Cynthia Scott and her partner was waiting for the moment

Icy and Zan showed their faces. Pushing their way through with their badges out, the two detectives stopped in front of Zan.

"Zander Miller, you are under arrest for racketeering and drug distribution. Turn around and put your hands behind your back."

Rearing his head back, Zan was pissed instantly. "What the fuck you talking about? I ain't did shit!" he yelled as he was thrown against the wall and cuffed.

"Zan, don't worry, I will contact the lawyer. Calm down," Icy said standing next to him.

"Well, if it's not the Icy Winters. We've been looking for you too," Cynthia smiled.

Icy was puzzled by the cop saying they were looking for her. There was no way in hell they were about to attempt to implicate her into anything Leo or Zan had going on. She knew for a fact everything she did to make money was legit and couldn't be taken from her because she earned every dime she made from her salons. Leo didn't put one cent into her business.

"You are under arrest for the murder of Isaac "Slick" Clark! You have the right to remain silent…"

To Be Continued…
Baby, I'm Wintertime Cold 2
Coming Soon

Follow Me…

Facebook: https://www.facebook.com/mesha.king1
Instagram: https://www.instagram.com/author_meesha/
Twitter: https://twitter.com/AuthorMeesha
Tiktok: https://vm.tiktok.com/TTPdkx6LEW/
Website: www.authormeesha.com

Lock Down Publications and Ca$h Presents assisted
publishing packages.

BASIC PACKAGE $499
Editing
Cover Design
Formatting

UPGRADED PACKAGE $800
Typing
Editing
Cover Design
Formatting

ADVANCE PACKAGE $1,200
Typing
Editing
Cover Design
Formatting
Copyright registration
Proofreading
Upload book to Amazon

LDP SUPREME PACKAGE $1,500
Typing
Editing
Cover Design
Formatting
Copyright registration
Proofreading
Set up Amazon account
Upload book to Amazon
Advertise on LDP Amazon and Facebook page

***Other services available upon request. Additional charges may apply
Lock Down Publications
P.O. Box 944
Stockbridge, GA 30281-9998
Phone # 470 303-9761

Submission Guideline

Submit the first three chapters of your completed manuscript to <u>ldpsubmissions@gmail.com</u>, subject line: Your book's title. The manuscript must be in a .doc file and sent as an attachment. Document should be in Times New Roman, double spaced and in size 12 font. Also, provide your synopsis and full contact information. If sending multiple submissions, they must each be in a separate email.

Have a story but no way to send it electronically? You can still submit to LDP/Ca$h Presents. Send in the first three chapters, written or typed, of your completed manuscript to:

LDP: Submissions Dept
Po Box 944
Stockbridge, Ga 30281

DO NOT send original manuscript. Must be a duplicate.

Provide your synopsis and a cover letter containing your full contact information.

Thanks for considering LDP and Ca$h Presents.

<u>NEW RELEASES</u>

LIFE OF A SAVAGE 4 by ROMELL TUKES

CHI'RAQ GANGSTAS 4 by ROMELL TUKES

TORN BETWEEN A GANGSTER AND A GENTLEMAN
by J-BLUNT & MISS KIM

BABY, I'M WINTERTIME COLD by MEESHA

Coming Soon from Lock Down Publications/Ca$h Presents

BLOOD OF A BOSS **VI**

SHADOWS OF THE GAME II

TRAP BASTARD II

By **Askari**

LOYAL TO THE GAME **IV**

By **T.J. & Jelissa**

TRUE SAVAGE **VIII**

MIDNIGHT CARTEL IV

DOPE BOY MAGIC IV

CITY OF KINGZ III

NIGHTMARE ON SILENT AVE II

THE PLUG OF LIL MEXICO II

CLASSIC CITY II

By **Chris Green**

BLAST FOR ME **III**

A SAVAGE DOPEBOY III

CUTTHROAT MAFIA III

DUFFLE BAG CARTEL VII

HEARTLESS GOON VI

By **Ghost**

A HUSTLER'S DECEIT III

KILL ZONE II

BAE BELONGS TO ME III

TIL DEATH II

By **Aryanna**

KING OF THE TRAP III

By **T.J. Edwards**

GORILLAZ IN THE BAY V

3X KRAZY III

STRAIGHT BEAST MODE III

De'Kari

KINGPIN KILLAZ IV

STREET KINGS III

PAID IN BLOOD III

CARTEL KILLAZ IV

DOPE GODS III

Hood Rich

SINS OF A HUSTLA II

ASAD

RICH $AVAGE III

By Martell Troublesome Bolden

YAYO V

Bred In The Game 2

S. Allen

THE STREETS WILL TALK II

By Yolanda Moore

SON OF A DOPE FIEND III

HEAVEN GOT A GHETTO II

SKI MASK MONEY II

By Renta

LOYALTY AIN'T PROMISED III

By Keith Williams

I'M NOTHING WITHOUT HIS LOVE II

SINS OF A THUG II

TO THE THUG I LOVED BEFORE II

IN A HUSTLER I TRUST II

By Monet Dragun

QUIET MONEY IV

EXTENDED CLIP III

THUG LIFE IV

By **Trai'Quan**

THE STREETS MADE ME IV

By **Larry D. Wright**

IF YOU CROSS ME ONCE II

ANGEL IV

By **Anthony Fields**

THE STREETS WILL NEVER CLOSE IV

By K'ajji

HARD AND RUTHLESS III

KILLA KOUNTY III

By Khufu

MONEY GAME III

By Smoove Dolla

JACK BOYS VS DOPE BOYS IV

A GANGSTA'S QUR'AN V

COKE GIRLZ II

COKE BOYS II

LIFE OF A SAVAGE V

CHI'RAQ GANGSTAS V

By Romell Tukes

MURDA WAS THE CASE III

Elijah R. Freeman

THE STREETS NEVER LET GO III

By Robert Baptiste

AN UNFORESEEN LOVE IV

BABY, I'M WINTERTIME COLD II

By **Meesha**

MONEY MAFIA II

Meesha

By **Jibril Williams**
QUEEN OF THE ZOO III
By **Black Migo**
VICIOUS LOYALTY III
By Kingpen
A GANGSTA'S PAIN III
By J-Blunt
CONFESSIONS OF A JACKBOY III
By Nicholas Lock
GRIMEY WAYS III
By Ray Vinci
KING KILLA II
By Vincent "Vitto" Holloway
BETRAYAL OF A THUG II
By Fre$h
THE MURDER QUEENS III
By Michael Gallon
THE BIRTH OF A GANGSTER III
By Delmont Player
TREAL LOVE II
By Le'Monica Jackson
FOR THE LOVE OF BLOOD II
By Jamel Mitchell
RAN OFF ON DA PLUG II
By Paper Boi Rari
HOOD CONSIGLIERE II
By Keese
PRETTY GIRLS DO NASTY THINGS II
By Nicole Goosby
PROTÉGÉ OF A LEGEND II

By Corey Robinson

IT'S JUST ME AND YOU II

By Ah'Million

BORN IN THE GRAVE II

By Self Made Tay

FOREVER GANGSTA III

By Adrian Dulan

GORILLAZ IN THE TRENCHES II

By SayNoMore

Available Now

RESTRAINING ORDER **I & II**

By **CA$H & Coffee**

LOVE KNOWS NO BOUNDARIES **I II & III**

By **Coffee**

RAISED AS A GOON I, II, III & IV

BRED BY THE SLUMS I, II, III

BLAST FOR ME I & II

ROTTEN TO THE CORE I II III

A BRONX TALE I, II, III

DUFFLE BAG CARTEL I II III IV V VI

HEARTLESS GOON I II III IV V

A SAVAGE DOPEBOY I II

219

DRUG LORDS I II III

CUTTHROAT MAFIA I II

KING OF THE TRENCHES

By **Ghost**

LAY IT DOWN **I & II**

LAST OF A DYING BREED I II

BLOOD STAINS OF A SHOTTA I & II III

By **Jamaica**

LOYAL TO THE GAME I II III

LIFE OF SIN I, II III

By **TJ & Jelissa**

BLOODY COMMAS I & II

SKI MASK CARTEL I II & III

KING OF NEW YORK I II,III IV V

RISE TO POWER I II III

COKE KINGS I II III IV V

BORN HEARTLESS I II III IV

KING OF THE TRAP I II

By **T.J. Edwards**

IF LOVING HIM IS WRONG…I & II

LOVE ME EVEN WHEN IT HURTS I II III

By **Jelissa**

WHEN THE STREETS CLAP BACK I & II III

THE HEART OF A SAVAGE I II III IV

MONEY MAFIA

LOYAL TO THE SOIL I II III

By **Jibril Williams**

A DISTINGUISHED THUG STOLE MY HEART I II & III

LOVE SHOULDN'T HURT I II III IV

RENEGADE BOYS I II III IV

PAID IN KARMA I II III

SAVAGE STORMS I II III

AN UNFORESEEN LOVE I II III

BABY, I'M WINTERTIME COLD

By **Meesha**

A GANGSTER'S CODE I &, II III

A GANGSTER'S SYN I II III

THE SAVAGE LIFE I II III

CHAINED TO THE STREETS I II III

BLOOD ON THE MONEY I II III

A GANGSTA'S PAIN I II

By J-Blunt

PUSH IT TO THE LIMIT

By **Bre' Hayes**

BLOOD OF A BOSS **I, II, III, IV, V**

SHADOWS OF THE GAME

TRAP BASTARD

By **Askari**

THE STREETS BLEED MURDER **I, II & III**

THE HEART OF A GANGSTA I II& III

By **Jerry Jackson**

CUM FOR ME I II III IV V VI VII VIII

An **LDP Erotica Collaboration**

BRIDE OF A HUSTLA **I II & II**

THE FETTI GIRLS **I, II& III**

CORRUPTED BY A GANGSTA I, II III, IV

BLINDED BY HIS LOVE

THE PRICE YOU PAY FOR LOVE I, II ,III

DOPE GIRL MAGIC I II III

By **Destiny Skai**

Meesha

WHEN A GOOD GIRL GOES BAD

By **Adrienne**

THE COST OF LOYALTY I II III

By Kweli

A GANGSTER'S REVENGE **I II III & IV**

THE BOSS MAN'S DAUGHTERS I II III IV V

A SAVAGE LOVE **I & II**

BAE BELONGS TO ME I II

A HUSTLER'S DECEIT I, II, III

WHAT BAD BITCHES DO I, II, III

SOUL OF A MONSTER I II III

KILL ZONE

A DOPE BOY'S QUEEN I II III

TIL DEATH

By **Aryanna**

A KINGPIN'S AMBITON

A KINGPIN'S AMBITION **II**

I MURDER FOR THE DOUGH

By **Ambitious**

TRUE SAVAGE I II III IV V VI VII

DOPE BOY MAGIC I, II, III

MIDNIGHT CARTEL I II III

CITY OF KINGZ I II

NIGHTMARE ON SILENT AVE

THE PLUG OF LIL MEXICO II

CLASSIC CITY

By **Chris Green**

A DOPEBOY'S PRAYER

By **Eddie "Wolf" Lee**

THE KING CARTEL **I, II & III**

222

Baby, I'm Wintertime Cold

By **Frank Gresham**
THESE NIGGAS AIN'T LOYAL **I, II & III**
By **Nikki Tee**
GANGSTA SHYT **I II &III**
By **CATO**
THE ULTIMATE BETRAYAL
By **Phoenix**
BOSS'N UP **I , II & III**
By **Royal Nicole**
I LOVE YOU TO DEATH
By **Destiny J**
I RIDE FOR MY HITTA
I STILL RIDE FOR MY HITTA
By **Misty Holt**
LOVE & CHASIN' PAPER
By **Qay Crockett**
TO DIE IN VAIN
SINS OF A HUSTLA
By **ASAD**
BROOKLYN HUSTLAZ
By **Boogsy Morina**
BROOKLYN ON LOCK I & II
By **Sonovia**
GANGSTA CITY
By **Teddy Duke**
A DRUG KING AND HIS DIAMOND I & II III
A DOPEMAN'S RICHES
HER MAN, MINE'S TOO I, II
CASH MONEY HO'S
THE WIFEY I USED TO BE I II

Meesha

PRETTY GIRLS DO NASTY THINGS
By Nicole Goosby
TRAPHOUSE KING **I II & III**
KINGPIN KILLAZ I II III
STREET KINGS I II
PAID IN BLOOD **I II**
CARTEL KILLAZ I II III
DOPE GODS I II
By **Hood Rich**
LIPSTICK KILLAH **I, II, III**
CRIME OF PASSION I II & III
FRIEND OR FOE I II III
By **Mimi**
STEADY MOBBN' **I, II, III**
THE STREETS STAINED MY SOUL I II III
By **Marcellus Allen**
WHO SHOT YA **I, II, III**
SON OF A DOPE FIEND I II
HEAVEN GOT A GHETTO
SKI MASK MONEY
Renta
GORILLAZ IN THE BAY **I II III IV**
TEARS OF A GANGSTA I II
3X KRAZY I II
STRAIGHT BEAST MODE I II
DE'KARI
TRIGGADALE I II III
MURDAROBER WAS THE CASE I II
Elijah R. Freeman
GOD BLESS THE TRAPPERS I, II, III

Baby, I'm Wintertime Cold

THESE SCANDALOUS STREETS I, II, III
FEAR MY GANGSTA I, II, III IV, V
THESE STREETS DON'T LOVE NOBODY I, II
BURY ME A G I, II, III, IV, V
A GANGSTA'S EMPIRE I, II, III, IV
THE DOPEMAN'S BODYGAURD I II
THE REALEST KILLAZ I II III
THE LAST OF THE OGS I II III
Tranay Adams
THE STREETS ARE CALLING
Duquie Wilson
MARRIED TO A BOSS I II III
By Destiny Skai & Chris Green
KINGZ OF THE GAME I II III IV V VI
Playa Ray
SLAUGHTER GANG I II III
RUTHLESS HEART I II III
By Willie Slaughter
FUK SHYT
By Blakk Diamond
DON'T F#CK WITH MY HEART I II
By Linnea
ADDICTED TO THE DRAMA I II III
IN THE ARM OF HIS BOSS II
By Jamila
YAYO I II III IV
A SHOOTER'S AMBITION I II
BRED IN THE GAME
By S. Allen
TRAP GOD I II III

Meesha

RICH $AVAGE I II

MONEY IN THE GRAVE I II III

By Martell Troublesome Bolden

FOREVER GANGSTA I II

GLOCKS ON SATIN SHEETS I II

By Adrian Dulan

TOE TAGZ I II III IV

LEVELS TO THIS SHYT I II

IT'S JUST ME AND YOU

By Ah'Million

KINGPIN DREAMS I II III

RAN OFF ON DA PLUG

By Paper Boi Rari

CONFESSIONS OF A GANGSTA I II III IV

CONFESSIONS OF A JACKBOY I II

By Nicholas Lock

I'M NOTHING WITHOUT HIS LOVE

SINS OF A THUG

TO THE THUG I LOVED BEFORE

A GANGSTA SAVED XMAS

IN A HUSTLER I TRUST

By Monet Dragun

CAUGHT UP IN THE LIFE I II III

THE STREETS NEVER LET GO I II

By Robert Baptiste

NEW TO THE GAME I II III

MONEY, MURDER & MEMORIES I II III

By **Malik D. Rice**

LIFE OF A SAVAGE I II III IV

A GANGSTA'S QUR'AN I II III IV

226

Baby, I'm Wintertime Cold

MURDA SEASON I II III

GANGLAND CARTEL I II III

CHI'RAQ GANGSTAS I II III IV

KILLERS ON ELM STREET I II III

JACK BOYZ N DA BRONX I II III

A DOPEBOY'S DREAM I II III

JACK BOYS VS DOPE BOYS I II III

COKE GIRLZ

COKE BOYS

By Romell Tukes

LOYALTY AIN'T PROMISED I II

By Keith Williams

QUIET MONEY I II III

THUG LIFE I II III

EXTENDED CLIP I II

A GANGSTA'S PARADISE

By **Trai'Quan**

THE STREETS MADE ME I II III

By **Larry D. Wright**

THE ULTIMATE SACRIFICE I, II, III, IV, V, VI

KHADIFI

IF YOU CROSS ME ONCE

ANGEL I II III

IN THE BLINK OF AN EYE

By **Anthony Fields**

THE LIFE OF A HOOD STAR

By Ca$h & Rashia Wilson

THE STREETS WILL NEVER CLOSE I II III

By K'ajji

CREAM I II III

227

Meesha

THE STREETS WILL TALK

By Yolanda Moore

NIGHTMARES OF A HUSTLA I II III

By King Dream

CONCRETE KILLA I II III

VICIOUS LOYALTY I II

By Kingpen

HARD AND RUTHLESS I II

MOB TOWN 251

THE BILLIONAIRE BENTLEYS I II III

By Von Diesel

GHOST MOB

Stilloan Robinson

MOB TIES I II III IV V VI

SOUL OF A HUSTLER, HEART OF A KILLER

GORILLAZ IN THE TRENCHES

By SayNoMore

BODYMORE MURDERLAND I II III

THE BIRTH OF A GANGSTER I II

By Delmont Player

FOR THE LOVE OF A BOSS

By C. D. Blue

MOBBED UP I II III IV

THE BRICK MAN I II III IV

THE COCAINE PRINCESS I II III IV V

By King Rio

KILLA KOUNTY I II III

By Khufu

MONEY GAME I II

By Smoove Dolla

A GANGSTA'S KARMA I II
By FLAME
KING OF THE TRENCHES I II III
by **GHOST & TRANAY ADAMS**
QUEEN OF THE ZOO I II
By **Black Migo**
GRIMEY WAYS I II
By Ray Vinci
XMAS WITH AN ATL SHOOTER
By Ca$h & Destiny Skai
KING KILLA
By Vincent "Vitto" Holloway
BETRAYAL OF A THUG
By Fre$h
THE MURDER QUEENS I II
By Michael Gallon
TREAL LOVE
By Le'Monica Jackson
FOR THE LOVE OF BLOOD
By Jamel Mitchell
HOOD CONSIGLIERE
By Keese
PROTÉGÉ OF A LEGEND
By Corey Robinson
BORN IN THE GRAVE
By Self Made Tay
MOAN IN MY MOUTH
By XTASY
TORN BETWEEN A GANGSTER AND A GENTLEMAN
By J-BLUNT & Miss Kim

BOOKS BY LDP'S CEO, CA$H

TRUST IN NO MAN

TRUST IN NO MAN 2

TRUST IN NO MAN 3

BONDED BY BLOOD

SHORTY GOT A THUG

THUGS CRY

THUGS CRY 2

THUGS CRY 3

TRUST NO BITCH

TRUST NO BITCH 2

TRUST NO BITCH 3

TIL MY CASKET DROPS

RESTRAINING ORDER

RESTRAINING ORDER 2

IN LOVE WITH A CONVICT

LIFE OF A HOOD STAR

XMAS WITH AN ATL SHOOTER

Baby, I'm Wintertime Cold

CPSIA information can be obtained
at www.ICGtesting.com
Printed in the USA
LVHW020223241122
733905LV00004B/444